ASCENDED

WAR OF THE COVENS

S. YOUNG

ASCENDED

War of the Covens
Book Three

By S. Young
Copyright © 2021 Samantha Young
Previously titled 'Blood Solstice (Tale of Lunarmorte #3)'
Copyright © 2011 Samantha Young

Edited by Jennifer Sommersby Young
Cover Design by Samantha Young
Cover Stock Image by Inara Prusakova

OTHER TITLES

Other titles by S. Young

Hunted (War of the Covens #1)

Destined (War of the Covens #2)

War of Hearts (A True Immortality Novel)

Kiss of Vengeance (A True Immortality Novel)

Kiss of Eternity (A True Immortality Short Story)

Bound by Forever (A True Immortality Novel)

Fear of Fire and Shadow

Other Adult Contemporary Novels by Samantha Young

Play On

As Dust Dances

Black Tangled Heart

Hold On: A Play On Novella

Into the Deep

Out of the Shallows

Hero

Villain: A Hero Novella

One Day: A Valentine Novella

Fight or Flight

Much Ado About You

Outmatched (co-write with Kristen Callihan)

On Dublin Street Series:

On Dublin Street

To all the dream catchers

The secret of happiness is freedom,
and the secret of freedom, courage.
Thucydides

PREFACE

THE WHY AND THE WHEREFORES

Existing in the shadows of our world are supernatural races, children blessed by the ancient Greek gods with unimaginable gifts. At present, they are fighting a two-thousand-year-old war with one another. The Midnight Coven, an alliance of dark magiks, faeries, and daemons born of black magik, believe that vampyres and lykans are lesser supernaturals and a threat to mankind. They are at war with the Daylight Coven, a confederate of light magiks, faeries, vampyres, and lykans who believe in equality of the races.

Into this war nineteen-year-old Caia Ribeiro is born ... a lykan with a heritage unlike any other. A consequence of the manipulation of the gods and fate, Caia is unique—half lykan, half water magik. And to make it even more complicated, her mother was the daughter of the Head of the Midnight Coven—Caia is half Daylight, half Midnight.

Since her visit to the Center, the Daylight's headquarters and training institution, Caia's world has been flipped upside down. Not only is she convinced that many Midnights are good people looking for a way out of the war, but she acted on that conviction by orchestrating the escape of a young

Midnight girl, Laila, from Daylight prison. To make matters worse, Caia discovered that Marita, the Head of the Daylight Coven, was abusing her power by experimenting on lykan children to breed a stronger army, and the one person she wants to complete that experimentation is Caia's best friend, Jaeden, a lykan with telekinetic abilities.

Caia's fear over telling Lucien, her mate, all she'd discovered was unfounded, and Caia has at last a group of loyal supporters, despite Pack Errante's misgivings over her revelations. However, with Marita growing steadily more unstable, imprisoning the Council, evolving the coven into an autocracy, it seems likely that they will need Caia's guidance.

But slithering in the shadows of their conflict is a being with a far bigger part to play than he'd let on. Who is Jaeden's friend, the vampyre Reuben? Why does he seem so chummy with Nikolai, the Regent of the Midnight Coven, when they're supposed to be blood enemies?

And why has their friendly neighborhood vampyre kidnapped Caia?

Caia, the one person they need to rescue the Council and bring the coven back from the brink of disaster.

CHAPTER 1

THE CAGE

*H*e hunkered onto his haunches so they were face-to-face and he winced. "I'm sorry I hit you so hard. I wasn't sure how much strength I'd need to knock you out. However ... you're pretty fragile for a lykan."

A growl rumbled from the pit of Caia's chest and erupted into snarling snaps. She had never wanted to tear at someone the way she wanted to at Reuben.

He studied her with a look akin to sadness. "We don't want you in this cage, Caia. You're only there until we're sure you aren't going to attack Nikolai. We don't want to hurt you."

She guffawed. "Hurt me? I'd worry about myself if I were you."

"Caia, please don't try anything foolish. You've been out for twenty-four hours. You're very weak."

Twenty-four hours? How was that possible?

"Again, apologies for my friend's overzealousness." Nikolai glared at Reuben.

She searched the two desperately for any clue as to why they had her here. She'd been gone a day. Lucien would be going crazy, not to mention Jaeden and Ryder and everybody …

"Jaeden," she snapped at Reuben. "She trusted you."

His face remained expressionless. "I needed her. So I fudged with the truth. She can still trust me."

"Oh yeah, 'cause kidnapping her Alpha's mate is such a trustworthy thing to do."

He nodded, silently telling her he understood her anger. She didn't want his damn understanding.

"Perhaps you will allow me to explain myself?" he queried, regret lacing his words. She broke eye contact and stared pointedly around the cage. "I'm not going anywhere."

Reuben stood. "Nikolai, a chair, perhaps?" Instantly a comfortable armchair appeared behind him and he sank into it while Nikolai stood vigilant at his back. "We need you, Caia … to end the war."

Caia chuckled. Of course he did. And what did he think? That she would blithely follow his orders when she was doing everything in her power to remove herself from Marita's rule? "I have no intention of fighting for the Midnights. Nor the Daylights. That's not my plan."

"It would seem we agree on that much, but your actual plan is crumbling around you as we speak."

She frowned. What the Hades did he know about her plan? "What do you mean?"

"Marita has dissolved the Council and imprisoned them."

How did he know that? Her expression must have asked as much because he shrugged elegantly, crossing one leg over the other and relaxing into his chair. "I have important assets inside the Center."

Her mouth fell open and a riot of butterflies erupted in her belly. She had no idea who she was dealing with, but the fact that he had assets inside the Center … "What do you want from me?"

"I want what you want. I don't want to kill Daylights or Midnights. I just want this war to end … and I've been working on bringing it to a conclusion long before you were born."

"And I'm supposed to believe that?" she sneered, the dull throbbing in her head worsening.

"Of course not. That's why I'm going to go back to the beginning. I'm going to tell you my story, Caia. I'm going to tell you why this war *really* began."

CHAPTER 2

THE ILIADIC TRUTH

Athens, Greece, 461 BC

*H*is heart thudded rapidly behind its thick-boned prison, the pulse in his neck throbbing. He almost smiled at that. If he weren't a vampyre, his parents, Phaedrus and Xanthippe, would consider him an impossibly delicious meal with that vein pulsing them into temptation. Instead they looked up at him in bewilderment, their mouths and chins smeared with the blood and skin of the unconscious man in their arms.

They sat crowded together on one of the pillowed klines in the andrōn where his father held symposia in their home. The man's feet dragged to the floor, the light chiton he wore coming undone from the obvious struggle he'd undergone at the hands of Kirios's parents. Blood stained the fabric and ran in rivulets from the victim's masticated neck to puddle on the mosaic floor. Kirios watched as it spread into the expensive tiling, wondering how they would explain the stain. He frowned. Perhaps his father would say wine had been spilled during one of the vigorous symposia he held to blend in with the men he served with on the Heliaia, the jury of the supreme court of Athens.

"We thought you might like to finish him off?" Xanthippe smiled, a horrifying, gory gargle of the man's lifeblood distorting her voice.

Kirios shook his head in a mixture of anger and despair. His parents were never going to understand. They were so old, two of the first souls to be sent by Hades back from the Underworld to wreak revenge. They had once been so savage, it was a miracle they'd ever fallen in love with one another. But two thousand years of immortal nomadic life seemed to have grown dull for them, and they'd fallen into a companionship of killing, making love, and looting tholos tombs, before growing rich on the growing Mycenaean trade.

Their strange life in Athens began after Hades had stolen Persephone into the Underworld and made her his queen. Outraged, her mother, the goddess Demeter, "blessed" his vampyres with fertility. And living actively (rather than their usual avoidance) through the Greco-Persian Wars with souls easier burdened than before had changed everything for Xanthippe and Phaedrus. There was nothing on earth that could put one more in touch with humanity than war, and Kirios's mother was no longer the flagitious animal she'd once been ... well ... to an extent.

Despite her appetite and nature, she had grown to love her husband and wanted a child. So they went to Athens and insinuated themselves into the middle-class region of the polis to raise their son. But Kirios hadn't been what they were expecting. He had powers of mesmerism and an appetite for blood, but he did not have the soul of a killer.

Looking away from the dark image before him, he remembered his thirteenth year. They had always brought him his blood as a child; now they wanted him to learn to fend for himself ... to execute his first kill. The memory pierced him like a spear. How disgusted he'd been by what they wanted of him. He had no taste *for killing humans, and although he loved his parents, it was becoming clear they were never going to understand that vital fact.*

And the truth was ... looking upon the painful sight of the man dying in his parents' arms, Kirios did not think he could stand by and watch them murder innocents any longer. He was in his eighteenth year now. It was time to—

His jaw dropped as he recognized the dying figure in their arms. "Are you insane?" he hissed. "That's Ephialtes!"

"Be silent," Phaedrus ordered quietly, steel warning in his tone. "Anyone may hear you."

Kirios felt himself paling, as if it were even possible for him to be any paler. "Father, you've killed a statesman of the democratic party. He's Pericles's bloody mentor, for Gaia's sake! Have you gone mad?" Pericles was one of the most influential, popular, wealthiest members of the demos.

Xanthippe shrugged. "We're leaving Athens ... and Ephialtes has always irritated me. I thought it a fitting going-away present to myself."

Kirios shook his head in disbelief. "How are you going to fix this mess before you leave?"

Phaedrus seemed annoyed by his son's question. "The usual ... we'll leave him somewhere and mesmerize someone else to take the blame. Perhaps Pericles."

"You will not," Kirios snapped, inwardly surprised he was standing up to his father.

Phaedrus looked just as shocked. "I beg your pardon?"

"Father, please promise me you will not put the blame on Pericles. You are leaving Athens ... please do not leave it in a complete upheaval by killing one member of the democratic party and turning another into a murderer."

"How dull of you, son."

"I happen to be fond of my city. That is all."

Xanthippe sighed. "Oh, very well. We promise."

"Thank you." He exhaled in relief, running his hands through

his hair in frustration before turning from them. He couldn't bear to look any longer at the mess they'd made of Ephialtes.

"We leave at dusk," Phaedrus informed him.

Gods, he hoped they wouldn't overreact. "I'm not coming with you. I'm leaving too ... but not with you."

At their continued silence, he finally got up the nerve to look at them. Their faces were mirror images of their usual blankness. "I'm not like you," he tried to explain.

Finally, Xanthippe replied, "We know. We ... are trying to understand."

Kirios smiled. It was more than anyone could ask of them. "But you never will. So ... I must leave you both."

Phaedrus growled, "You are more human than vampyre ... I curse Demeter for this."

Even Xanthippe gasped. Kirios frowned. "Father, please don't. I don't wish anything untoward to happen to you."

"You are my son. You should be with me, exhilarating in the kill."

He felt so helpless in the face of his father's despair. So much the disappointment. "I am truly sorry, Father."

"I don't blame you."

There was more emotion in that statement than he'd ever heard from either of his parents since his thirteenth year. A little of the dark heaviness eased from his chest.

"I will leave you both now."

They nodded at him. "Fare thee well, son."

"And you both."

* * *

TYRAS, Miletus, 441 BC

7

THE TALL MAGIK stared at him with an expression of sympathy and understanding.

"I cannot let you have Eneas. I cannot let you commit any act of violence within my home."

Frustration and the need for revenge bubbled beneath Kirios's skin like hot springs in a winter landscape.

Eneas.

He wanted the hunter dead.

"Your parents were murderers, Kirios. Eneas was merely doing the job that was asked of him."

"Under whose authority?"

A look of dead calm and the superiority of one with his power settled over the magik's face. "My own."

Kirios sneered and yet found himself lowering his eyes in submission. Galen, the magik before him, was famous throughout the supernatural world. He had established himself here in Miletus, under a colony called Tyras, situated on the northwest coast of the Black Sea. After Alexander the Great had rescued Miletus from Persian grasp, Galen had "persuaded" Alexander to bestow the colony upon him and his followers. Kirios had heard of this Galen before he tracked Eneas here. His infamy had grown because of his crusade—his crusade to find peace from the human wars and supernatural predators.

And to do so, he had enlisted supernaturals such as the lykanthrope, Eneas, who hunted those who preyed upon the humans. Kirios could not find fault in the crusade. He could find fault, however, in the fact that he'd had no life to speak of for the last twenty years ... for it had been spent hunting Eneas, after discovering the lykan had killed Xanthippe and Phaedrus—the penalty for killing Ephialtes.

Kirios exhaled slowly. "It is a matter of honor. I must exact revenge against those who took that which is mine."

Galen nodded. "And you are an honorable vampyre, Kirios. I know. I have heard of you. You are of the second generation. You feed on the blood of animals. You travel from place to place. You've even been known to rescue humans utilizing your superior power. You ... are not so different from Eneas. In fact, if not for the obvious, I think you would rather like him."

"You will not even let me challenge him?"

Galen shook his head. "I would ask you to stay. Live here with my people, Kirios. Become one of my hunters."

He tried not to let the surprise show on his face. Why on Gaia's earth would Galen want him? He was a nobody. More to the point, he wanted to kill one of Galen's men.

"Why?"

Subtly—so subtle Kirios almost didn't feel it—the irritation and rage beneath his skin waned as Galen spoke of the world he envisioned. He preached that they, as supernaturals with their blessed gifts, should be protecting the humans' fragile existence in gratitude for what the gods had given them. Humans were the children of the gods just as much as they themselves were. All this Kirios had known, had appreciated, but it was only now under this magik's spellbinding presence that he began to see he was just as culpable as those who hunted humans, for he had the power to hunt the hunters, protect the hunted, to give back to the gods ... and he had not been doing so.

* * *

Tyras, 377 BC

"Galen?"

No answer.

"Galen?"

He was catatonic. Kirios glanced anxiously around at the others. His friend, the magik Agamemnon, shook his head.

"What has happened?" Kirios demanded.

"Parthenia is dead."

Kirios stumbled back. Oh Gaia, no. How could Galen bear it?

Eneas.

Kirios rushed from the entrance hall, through the grounds, his speed knocking over ornaments and fripperies as he went. How had these last fourteen years come to this?

After struggling with his anger, he'd finally settled into his life as Galen's man, hunting supernatural predators. It hadn't taken him long to fall easily into the way of life, to make friends into family, for Galen to become like a father. It had taken thirty years to unbend toward Eneas. And now ... now sixty years on, Eneas was like a brother. How could it be possible that he had betrayed Galen, betrayed them all?

In truth, Kirios would say it had all begun fourteen years before when Galen had fallen in love with a human girl, Kleisthenes. They married, had children. She'd been completely aware of who and what they all were, and that their children would have magikal gifts. For the closest of them, they had been comfortable in her presence. There had been others, however, who had a difficult time with Kleisthenes.

Kirios blanched upon remembering his friend, a vampyre, who'd confessed to dreaming of Kleisthenes each night, dreaming of drinking her blood until his obsession was sated. Sadly, he could not be counselled through it, and when he attacked her, it was Kirios who saved her, and Kirios who was chosen to execute his friend.

Soon after, the household of supernaturals dwindled, until only Eneas and Kirios remained among the magiks and faeries. Only a few years after the incident, Galen had come to Kirios in confidence, revealing fears that his wife was having an affair. Kirios could not believe it of Kleisthenes but had promised to investigate Galen's suspicions.

He felt sick as the vision of her lovely figure posed so elegantly in her bedchamber flashed before his eyes, blood soaking the bedcovers, a gaping hole in her chest where her heart had been savagely cut out. They found Kleisthenes murdered the very day after Galen had come to him. The household had been devastated, Kirios also, but he had gladly assumed the task he and Eneas were charged with—to find the culprit and bring him to Galen alive.

For a number of days, the trail had been cold, until one evening Galen's eldest daughter came to Kirios's room with Kleisthenes's journal. Parthenia had claimed she knew who had murdered her mother and urged Kirios to read the pages.

Eneas.

He had been the one carrying on the affair with Kleisthenes ... it was fair to assume he'd been the one to silence her. Kirios made Parthenia promise not to tell anyone until he found Eneas and discovered the truth for himself. This very night, Kirios set out to catch up with him where he was questioning townspeople. But Kirios was dragged back to the house by a messenger with urgent news.

Parthenia.

Hades, Eneas! Kirios crashed into the bedchamber with hopes of finding the journal pieces. He stopped abruptly, instantly sensing his room had been disturbed. That's when he felt the cold press of the blade to his throat and the heat of the lykan at his back.

"Brother," he pleaded in Kirios's ear, "you have to understand."

"Understand what?" Kirios bit out, trembling with rage and desolation. "That you would kill me to cover your crime?"

"I made a mistake, brother. She wasn't even worth it. I can't lose Galen. He's like my father, he is all I have ever known."

"And yet you took what was most precious to him."

Eneas growled, spittle flecking the side of Kirios's face. "She seduced me! It wasn't my fault."

"Ye gods, what has become of you, Eneas, that you would blame a hapless human for your own folly?"

"Hers as well."

11

"Yes. But she is gone and with her, an innocent child by your hand."

Eneas held still, seeming to have stopped breathing altogether. And then ... "This can only end with your death, brother. I am truly sorry."

Before the blade could pierce his skin, Kirios whirled as if a tornado, took the blade from Eneas's hand, and plunged it into his black heart.

Blood soaked Kirios's hands and tears his face.

* * *

SEVEN NIGHTS *later*

HIS PRISON WAS cold and solitary. Like his heart, he snorted. Bitterness threatened to overwhelm Kirios, but he held true. This was not his fault. Who knew Galen was a poisoned dagger, biding its time before plunging its blade into the hearts of those he befriended? The beginning of a war was brewing, and it had only been a few days.

After Kirios sought out Galen with evidence of Eneas's treachery, Galen had gone mad, almost as if he'd been taken over by the gods themselves. What had once been a magik of, yes, mercurial moods, was now a magik of molten violence who held a deep hostility toward lykans and vampyres. He threw Kirios in prison (an act of mercy, ha!) and was already enlisting faeries into espionage, searching for powerful communities of vampyres and lykans that he and his remaining children could destroy.

"Kirios."

He blinked in surprise to see Agamemnon towering over his naked form. "Agamemnon? W-w-what are you doing here?"

The magik's mouth twisted. "Freeing you."

"Why? Galen?"

He shook his head. "He doesn't know I am here. I'm getting you out and then I'm leaving. I want no part in this madman's war." At that he reached out and touched Kirios, his magik flowing over him until he was clothed. Kirios barely had time to nod his thanks before the magik grabbed hold of his hand and the world whirled past them with sickening speed. The sound of crashing water met his ears, the invigorating scent of salty ocean cleansing his dirt-filled nose and waking his numb senses. He blinked. They stood on the dark shore, the sea a black mass before them.

"This is where I leave you, friend." Agamemnon handed him a clay bowl. The liquid was coagulated, but Kirios almost wept with relief.

Blood.

"I don't know how to thank you, my dear friend."

"Just stay alive and out of Galen's path."

And then he was gone.

* * *

Brundisium, 253 AD

IT HAD BEEN MORE than five hundred years, and yet there was a yesteryear familiarity in being held captive by the Galen family. Galen himself was gone now; his children and grandchildren were Kirios's captors. "Stupidity," he murmured weakly under his breath, his head lying against the jutting cold stone of his cell, his neck aching with the awkward angle.

He didn't move, though. He couldn't. He was starving and had been for ... Gaia, how long had he been here? The sound of the shore off Tyras still rang clear in his memory, as if it had only been yesterday he had fled from Galen. Back to a life of a nomad for him. And every time Kirios had heard of Galen's movement growing closer to his location, off he would flee once more.

After centuries of travel, Kirios found a certain peace in Athens *for a time, mesmerizing his way back into citizenship. No one knew or remembered his family or their connection to Ephialtes's murder. Indeed, it was a legend now. A mystery.*

The familiarity of Athens, its bustling metropolis and beautiful women, were a salve to his weary and sorrow-filled soul. However, it was not long before rumblings of Galen's movement grew among the supernatural elements of Athens. His first home was no longer safe.

With a great sadness, Kirios left and traveled to Rome. He hid easily within the city, mesmerizing anyone who challenged him. After a while, though, even Rome was not safe from Galen's madness. It had been a century since Galen had started his campaign, a century of trying to create a furor against vampyres and lykans. But the gods, Artemis in particular, were wrathful in their vengeance upon those who committed atrocities against the vampyres and lykans. Many magiks and faeries were fearful of the consequences of joining Galen. Yet Galen could not be stopped.

Instead, he and three of his most powerful magiks tried to invoke Athena, the goddess of war, into their cause. Kirios smirked at the thought. Athena had not been impressed by their warmongering. Unfortunately, her half-brother, Ares, the god of War, favored Galen. They sacrificed an entire village to Ares, and he bound the three magiks to Galen through what would become known as trace magik. Galen was inextricably connected to the men and to any children they bore.

Eventually, their company grew into a coven, and one of the Romans suggested they call themselves the Medium Nox Noctis —the Midnight—because they believed they were rightfully sending lesser supernaturals to the Underworld, where they would never see daylight again.

Word spread. Their opposition turned to Athena. Enraged at her brother's idiocy, she decided to even the battlefield by granting the same binding trace magik to a magik called Penelope and her second- and third-in-command, lykan and vampyre. They were now a coven unto themselves: the Dies Lux Lucis—the Daylight.

It was not long after those lines were drawn that the unimaginable happened. Kirios groaned in remembrance, the emotional agony as fresh as it had been then. The omnipotent protection of the gods was lost to them, their last weapon in Galen's war. It was the beginning of the second century AD, and it was becoming more and more apparent the gods' power on Earth was waning. A new faith had spread, a belief in one almighty God. Some said his birth had killed their gods and that only those with supernatural children had survived, although trapped on their mountain in the Otherworld and down within the Underworld.

Kirios's grief, like all his brothers and sisters of Gaia, was great ... but he endured and moved forward, traveling the centuries alone in the new world. He found sanctuary for a time in Brittania, but then Emperor Commodus's death created such a crisis, Kirios was forced to return to the Mediterranean. He almost smiled, remembering the heat of the sun on his cold skin, the fragrant sea air, the lightness of his steps where he touched shore. How different the climate of Brittania was. He hadn't realized how much he'd missed home. He snorted. How wrong he had been. He wasn't home. This was an entirely different landscape from the one he remembered.

Galen was dead, defeated in battle against an opposing magik. And with the entrapment of the gods, younger magiks were no longer living eternal lives, although their life span was greater than human and they were still difficult to kill. Galen had been hundreds of years old and his son was his only remaining child. His children and grandchildren carried on his name, bound as the others within the Midnight Coven by the trace magik.

How curious Kirios became as he wandered his home country, encountering members of the Daylight Coven and hiding from Midnight. He thanked the gods each day for being one of the few left within the supernatural world who was not bound by the trace magik. They were at war in truth now. And rather than the trace *being a helpful weapon, Kirios believed it was the unbreakable lock keeping a tight leash on the subsistence of the war.*

Despite his bitterness, his misgivings, Kirios's curiosity got the better of him, and he found himself wanting a glimpse of the Midnight Coven and their impressive organization. They had set themselves up in Brundisium on the southeastern coast of the boot of the Roman Empire ... it was a chief port of embarkation for Greece, an excellent place to lay traps for "lesser" immortals; more than that, they could enlist magiks to their cause.

Kirios shifted slightly and winced at the scrape of stone on his head. A warm, gooey feeling let him know he had cut his head open again. Damn his curiosity. It was why he was here, trapped. He was supposed to consider himself lucky. Galen's son had remembered him and his father's wishes and ordered him to be imprisoned and starved, but not killed. Ye gods, but what was the difference between the two?

How many years had he been here? He was too weak to have even grown into madness. Perhaps madness would have been more entertaining than just sitting here recounting the last few hundred years over and over and over ...

And then there were the stories he heard filtering down from above this hole he was stuck in. With the gods out of reach, the war was growing more aggressive.

* * *

A LOT of bellowing and cursing alerted Kirios to people coming down into the caverns they called a prison.

"I wasn't trying to escape!" a voice cried in outrage. Grunting and shuffling followed, before Kirios watched, wide-eyed, as a young magik was brought toward his cell by two others.

They frowned at one another. "Are we sure we should put him in here with that creature?"

"There are no other cells available. Anyway, look at him. He cannot even move."

"Hmm, fine."

And with that, the magik was thrown into the cell with the force of their powers and bound by the spell that kept Kirios from touching the space between his cell and the exit. Not that he could move.

The magik grunted and watched them warily as they left. He said not a word for what seemed like forever before looking at Kirios with a strange smile on his face.

"I'm sorry it took me so long to see you, my son."

Kirios shook his head, not understanding. Then the magik sighed, his eyes full of sadness. "What a mess they have made of you." He shuffled closer so that he sat by Kirios's side.

"Who are you?" Kirios croaked, proud of himself for remembering how to make his mouth form words.

"Around here, they just call me the Prophet."

He raised an eyebrow in question, and the Prophet grinned.

"I am a seer."

Kirios almost choked. This magik was a Cassandrian?

Cassandrians were prophets, magiks who Athena, wisest of the gods, had favored at birth. There were few of them, and as the war had grown steadily more aggressive, they were fought over fiercely as prizes. Just as the Cassandrians were being killed and fought over, so were the Asclepians—magiks who were descendants of a witch who'd once been healed by Asclepius. His powers of healing and bringing those souls lost to the Underworld back from the dead had worked its way into the magik's blood and passed down through her bloodline, all through Gaia's will.

So rare were Cassandrians and Asclepians, Kirios had never met either before.

"I am a Midnight," the Prophet told him with a bitter twist to his lips. "Unlike you, I was not lucky enough to be born without the trace. You are among a rare few yourself now. And in four hundred

17

years' time, you will be the only supernatural who is not bound to the trace."

Kirios shook his head, confused, unsure of what the Prophet was trying to explain.

"I can manipulate the trace, however. The gods tell me from their mountain that I am the only one who can. I dare not ask why they've blessed me with that gift. I'm just grateful that they have."

"Manipulate? How?"

"I can hide thoughts, feelings, intentions. I can hide other supernaturals intentions as well. It is the reason I've escaped numerous times, and why I am now sharing your cell."

The hours with the Prophet melted by as he told Kirios of all that was happening above. Many battles had been fought, much blood shed. The race of Asclepians was all but gone, and the few who were left had hidden themselves away so no one knew who they were. Soon, the Prophet whispered sadly, there would be none left.

"How long have I been down here?" Kirios asked.

The Prophet remained silent for so long, Kirios was unsure he would answer.

"Sixty years, my friend. Sixty years."

A noise of distress escaped his mouth before he could control his response, and he sensed the Prophet's sympathy. "I am sorry."

Kirios shook his head, blinking back tears of defeat. It wasn't his fault, he told the Prophet silently.

"It isn't your fault," the Prophet replied. "Not your fault."

Kirios squeezed his eyes shut in agony. "If not my own, then whose?"

"No one's. We are all at the mercy of the will of the gods."

* * *

WHEN PERHAPS A FEW DAYS PASSED, the Prophet turned to him, his eyes bright from sleep deprivation. "I must tell you the reason why I arranged to be in prison with you."

Kirios grunted. So the madman had deliberately gotten himself thrown in prison.

"I've had visions of you, Kirios. I am here to save you."

"Why?" Kirios frowned. What was so special about him?

Tears glistened in the young seer's eyes. "Oh, Kirios. This awful war ... it's going to haunt our world for centuries."

The hopelessness of it threatened unsuccessfully to end a life that couldn't be ended. "Centuries?" he gasped.

"For centuries. At the end of the second millennium anno Domini, Gaia will set in motion events that will lead to the end of this war."

Second millennium anno Domini ... dear Gaia!

"A child will be born into the end of the twentieth century ... a child with blood of both covens running in her veins—a half lykan, half magik who will bring this war to a conclusion."

Kirios shook his head in amazement. "What has any of this to do with me?"

His eyes blazed, his face taut with emotion. "I see you in that future. You are an important element of that future." With that, the Prophet seized a hold of Kirios's head and pressed Kirios's open mouth to his neck, forcing the vampyre to drink from his blood. Sixty years of starvation ... force was not really necessary.

Kirios groaned with exultation and sank his teeth through the soft flesh of the Prophet's neck, drinking and drinking until the blood flowed into every cell of his being, blood unlike any other he had tasted. He jerked back careful, even when so hungry, to take only what he needed. He underestimated his sudden speed and smacked his head off the wall. He barely felt it. Kirios gasped, reaching up to feel his skull ... no mark, no blood. Nothing. He laughed, and the Prophet smiled, shuffling back into a sitting position.

Kirios stared at his hands, looking for some sign in his skin to explain this entirely new feeling in his body. He felt stronger than he ever had before.

"What have you done?" he asked.

The Prophet shook his head. "The gods ... they made me special. My blood ... it has changed you. You will be faster, stronger, and you will be able to mask other supernaturals' trace."

"Why?"

"I do not know. I am only doing what I've been led to do in my visions."

Kirios nodded. "I understand. But what am I to do with this?"

The Prophet shrugged. "Whatever comes naturally to you, my son."

The seer struggled to his feet and Kirios rushed to help him. "I have taken too much."

"No, no. You did fine. Most vampyres do not have your restraint."

"What are you doing?"

"Getting you out of here."

At that, he yelled at the top of his voice, screaming for help. When they heard the shuffling of feet drawing closer, the Prophet turned away from the entrance so their captors would not see the neck wound, only the blood on his hands. Kirios lay on the ground, his mouth wiped clean of the blood, pretending to be as weak as ever. It was a masquerade that would end once the Midnights looked close enough to see the fullness in his body, the healthy sheen of his skin and hair.

"What is all this yelling?"

"I've been hurt," the Prophet grumbled.

"Let me have ... dear goddess, man, what the Hades have you done?"

"I slipped. I'm bleeding badly."

"Can't you fix that yourself?"

"You haven't fed me for days. I don't have the energy."

"Fine." The first magik turned to the other. *"Take the spell down."*

There was only a moment's silence and then a rush like waves crashing onshore.

"Go, Kirios!" the Prophet yelled.

He was gone before they even knew what had happened, running like the wind itself, brushing by blurred magiks and out of their citadel. Yes, he was a different creature from the one that had been thrown into the prison. He was an altogether new breed.

* * *

PARIS, 1385

"I HAVE SOMETHING TO TELL YOU."

Kirios narrowed his eyes on the beautiful woman in his bed. Her long, elegant lines were enticing as all Hades, and any other time he would have been perusing them languidly. But her tone was not something to be dismissed. The faerie in his bed had been keeping secrets from him.

"Are you going to spoil the party, love?" he asked lazily, disguising how tense he had grown. The party he referred to was the one going on as they spoke. The young Charles VI of France had just been wed to his even younger bride, Isabeau of Bavaria, and France was holding its first-ever court ball to celebrate. The faerie in his bed was a Daylight spy he had met a few years ago when tracking a rogue vampyre. She had been gathering evidence that the vampyre was a dog working for the Midnights, and the two of them had collided on the hunt. Collided and then fallen straight into bed with one another.

Theirs was a casual relationship, but one of mutual respect and trust. Or so he had thought. She told Kirios the coven had reason to believe the Midnights would use the celebration of the king's *marriage as an opportune time to attack the Daylights, who had set up one of their largest branches of the coven in Paris. Kirios had been in Scotland at the time, hunting a particularly nasty lykan with his gang of hunters, when the faerie appeared, asking for help. He gladly acquiesced. They'd just heard word that Richard II of England was sending a small army invasion force against the Scots, and Kirios didn't want to get stuck in the middle of his idiocy. It seemed he was forever dodging the battles involving the English and the French. Now, after twenty-eight years, the English were trying to pull the Scottish back into another damn war.*

Dear Gaia, one war was enough for Kirios.

His people had assured him they could find the lykan without him, and off he'd gone. It was, after all, a break from the tedium of hunting rogue Daylights. He much preferred the chance to cut down Midnights, whether magik or faerie, loving the complete shock on their face when they realized he was impervious to their magik—another beautiful gift from the Prophet's blood.

"We did not just meet by chance," she said softly, drawing the bedcovers over herself nervously.

Kirios shook his head. "I'm not sure I understand, Saffron."

"I was captured within the stronghold of the Midnight Coven when I was spying. I was careless. Or maybe I wasn't. He was a Cassandrian and knew I was there. He told me to call him the Prophet. That he had seen me in his visions. That I would play a part in bringing the war to an end ... seven hundred years in the future." She shook her head in amazement. While she spoke, Kirios's pulse raced.

He stumbled over to the bed and plunked down beside her, his eyes wide with excitement. All these years and nothing. He'd almost gone crazy with frustration because nothing had pointed him in the right direction. Finally, here was something.

"Only the strongest of us live that long now, Kirios. He says I am strong too."

Kirios chuckled and stroked her cheek. "I'm not surprised.

You're just a baby and already you're one of the greatest spies within the coven."

She blushed. "You think so?"

He tsk-ed. "No more compliments for you until you tell me what else he said."

"He told me about you. Nothing more ... just where to find you."

"Why didn't you tell me this when we first met?"

"I was afraid. I didn't know if I could trust you."

"And now ..."

She laughed. "Kirios, I brought you all the way to France with false information to speak with you about this."

He snorted. So that was why things had been so quiet around here, why they couldn't find any signs of an imminent attack from the Midnights.

"Why did you not speak with me in Scotland?"

Saffron bit her lip and ducked her head, her long, silver-blond hair falling in front of her stunning face. "I wanted to be on home ground for such a declaration."

Kirios struggled not to laugh at her logic. "Of course. How silly of me."

She shrugged off his teasing and looked up at him with wide, pleading eyes. "Why did he tell me to find you, Kirios?"

"Because he once visited me too."

With that he told her all he could, about the Prophet, about his visions, of what he thought Kirios's help would do. And now Saffron too.

"So." She frowned in thought. "What does that mean for us?"

"I think it means that you and I are stuck with one another for a very long time."

* * *

St. Petersburg, Russia, 1725

. . .

23

KIRIOS WAITED IMPATIENTLY FOR PETROVSKY, *burrowing into his fur coat. He wasn't cold. He was never cold. But the city was charged with apprehension. Peter, the emperor of Russia, had died the night before, and with no heir apparent, a sense of foreboding hung above St. Petersburg like an omen of what was to come.*

His ears perked up, and he spun around at the sound of approaching footsteps. Petrovsky.

"Reuben," he muttered, coming toward him. Kirios had caused a lot of suspicion over the years; legends of a vampyre who couldn't be hurt by magik had circulated. He'd found it necessary to change his name and stay out of the magiks' way so the legend could die. His instincts told him he should remain a shadow until the time was right.

"What took you?"

"Anna's father. He thought we should properly mourn the emperor."

Kirios frowned. "I forgot he's quite involved in human affairs."

Petrovsky nodded. Theirs was a strange and unexpected friendship. A few years back, when Kirios had been on a hunt in St. Petersburg, he'd come across this young Midnight trying to help a Daylight. At first he couldn't believe what he was seeing, so he stalked him for a while. Petrovsky was of lower-class descent among the Midnights and seemed to go out of his way to find Daylights, spending his nights searching the underworld of St. Petersburg with the determination of a bloodhound. Finally, Kirios, concerned for the overeager young magik who was most certainly going to be killed by the supernaturals who intrigued him merely for being a Midnight, had enough and revealed himself to the boy.

Petrovsky was fascinated by other supernaturals, had no ill-feeling toward them whatsoever. And for some reason, Kirios believed him. Petrovsky hated the mindless prejudice of the Midnights who had never treated him well anyway, and like a young soldier desperate to join the war, accepted Kirios's command. A Midnight working for the Daylights was an unimaginable gift.

First Kirios had masked Petrovsky's trace so that the Head of the Midnight Coven would never know his true intentions, and then he'd set about making the boy wealthy. Kirios spread rumors that Petrovsky had killed many Daylights and that, alongside the boy's quirky charm, made him a great favorite with the Head of the Midnight Coven. Certain sacrifices had to be made to prove himself. Petrovsky had to kill some Daylights, but Kirios compartmentalized that issue as a necessity of war and was proven right when Petrovsky was given a position on the Council. It was not long after he married Anna, the daughter of a prominent Midnight and a member of a very old, influential family within the coven.

"I came here because you said you had urgent news," Kirios reminded him.

"I am sorry. I could not get away."

"Fine. What is the problem, Alex?"

Alex grinned. "Anna. She is with child."

The vampyre's pulse leapt. Yes. This was it. This would help change everything.

"Then we must work out a plan."

The young man smiled cheekily. "I thought that was what you would say. You want to teach him, don't you?"

Kirios nodded. "We have to. Your children must know the truth of this war, Alex."

Petrovsky grew very serious. "Of course, Reuben. No child of mine will be contaminated with Midnight insanity."

* * *

NEW JERSEY, USA, 1950s

"HOLY—" Kirios yelped, his glass of blood going everywhere as he jumped. His gang of Rogue Vampyre Hunters were all out and about in New York, prowling the night for their varied predators.

He was taking a moment for sustenance when a familiar magik popped up before him, inches from his face.

The Prophet smiled sheepishly and took a few steps back. "Sorry, I've never quite got the hang of a communication spell."

Kirios shook his head. "What ... how?"

The Prophet looked like a sixty-year-old man now, but his bright blue eyes convinced Kirios that the magik in front of him was definitely the seer he hadn't seen in almost two thousand years.

"Still as articulate as ever, Kirios. Or is it Reuben now?"

He nodded shakily. Not many things could unsettle him, but the sudden appearance of this guy definitely did. "What are you doing here?"

The Prophet tapped his head. "Had a few more visions I thought you might be interested in."

Excitement rushed through every cell in Kirios's body. "Seriously? No joke ... things are finally going to happen? Jeez, I almost gave up hope—"

"I liked you better when you couldn't talk."

He scowled at the Cassandrian. "Fine, what's going on?"

The magik raised an eyebrow before settling onto Kirios's sofa. "Nice place you have here."

The vampyre itched to hit the words out of the magik's mouth, but he tried to remember this was the man who'd saved his life.

After a few minutes of awkward silence, the seer finally smiled. "Okay. Here's what's going on. I've seen this girl. A Midnight. The daughter of a Council member, to be more precise. She is, shall we say, against the war. Her name is Atia."

"What has she got to do with anything?"

He shrugged. "Don't know."

"Is she ... the mother of the child?"

"Don't know."

And just like that, he was gone.

Kirios stared open-mouthed at the empty space on the sofa.

"Fucking fortune-tellers."

* * *

SOME FIFTY-ODD YEARS later

HE WATCHED *the girl as she stared up at the moon from her bedroom window, her pale hair like a beacon drawing him in. Kirios sighed. He had found her. At last. After seeing the evidence of her powers at the house in the woods, of what she'd done to her uncle Ethan, Kirios knew that Caia Ribeiro was the one he had been waiting for. All these years. All the mistakes.*

When the Prophet had come to him about Atia, he had followed her, watching her for any sign of what was to come. She was beautiful and powerful. Petrovsky told him she stayed clear of the war, suggesting she was, as the Prophet had said, against it. But her beauty was enough to entice the Head of the Coven, Devlyn, to ask for her hand in marriage. Her family wouldn't let her say no. Kirios had known at that moment, had seen his chance: she was going to be the mother of the child from the prophecy.

So he revealed himself to her, and along with Petrovsky's help, explained all they had planned. Through her they received information direct from Devlyn himself, and he never knew because Kirios masked her trace. Atia helped willingly. She despised Devlyn.

For a number of years, life went on that way, and during them, she mothered two children with Devlyn, playing her role as mother and wife and her other role as spy for the Daylights. Kirios, on the other hand, was growing despondent. He had no idea how to proceed. Atia was supposed to mother the half-Daylight half-Midnight child. And there had been no sign of that eventuality so far.

Then one momentous day, Saffron had come to him and told him about her mistress, Marion, and the affair Marion recently had with a member of a small lykan pack. Saffron felt sure there was something about this pack, something important, and since her instincts had always run true, Kirios listened attentively. She told Kirios of their Alpha, Mikhail, how special and strong he was. He had an aura. At her description, Kirios smirked; if it'd been three hundred years before, Kirios would've put it down to the fact that Saffron was susceptible to a handsome face, but she'd been gravely hurt by a warlock since then and was frosty to almost every man she encountered. So Kirios believed her and set about planning a meeting between Atia and Mikhail. He knew what he had to ask of them was cold and clinical and completely degrading. But if it would bring an end to the war?

Sighing in remembrance, Kirios leaned against a tree, staring at the girl in her room. Perhaps it was his fault. He'd pushed Atia into the decision, settling her anxiety by using mesmerism. He'd never done that to one of his own before. With Saffron's help, Kirios managed to convince them to sleep with one another.

But after a few years of arranged meetings between them, no child was conceived. Kirios's frustration was the least of their problems. Devlyn was not as naive as Kirios would have liked. He was a jealous husband and had been tracking Atia's movements through faeries, despite no sign of duplicity in her trace. By the time Kirios got wind of the information and warned Atia and Mikhail ... it was too late. Mikhail, without giving the details, warned his pack, Pack Errante, but Atia panicked. She killed Mikhail, assuming that Devlyn would have mercy on her. He slaughtered her anyway.

His eyes glazed over with the memories. So much loss. And all for nothing.

Or so he had thought.

When it felt as if it was time to give up and give in, Saffron came to him with the news that one of the members of Pack Errante had arrived home with a magik he believed to be a member of the Daylight Coven. Saffron knew the girl was Atia and Devlyn's daughter, Adriana; she was there to infiltrate the pack under her father's orders. His instincts told him to let Adriana's seduction play out, ordering Saffron to keep quiet.

Kirios smiled softly and raised his gaze back up to the window.

Caia was born.

A feeling of overwhelming anticipation rushed through him. He'd done everything to protect her, masking her trace when Adriana hunted her, ordering Saffron to keep a close eye on her, to make sure Marion was protecting Caia. For a while, his attention had been diverted by Devlyn and his growing tyranny—his unbelievable madness, his camps for behavioral modification for magiks, his desperation to have them under his complete control. Nikolai, the present son of the Petrovsky family, had grown so concerned that Kirios had masked his trace and sent Nikolai in to kill Devlyn. The Midnights had no clue as to who had done it, supposedly a member of Daylight, of course.

And now Caia was the Head of the Coven! He'd laughed when he and Nikolai realized the truth. But the laughter hadn't lasted long. Devlyn's irritating brat of a son had tried to continue his father's work and was too preoccupied with finding Caia and destroying her. His distance from the coven had allowed Nikolai to solidify an important, authoritative position within the coven, but Kirios had worried over Ethan's ever-increasing obsession with his niece. Not that he needed to worry, he thought smugly, watching her, remembering all that ... mess ... he'd found a few days ago in Ethan's lodge. Now Nikolai was Regent of the Midnights and halting attacks against the Daylights under the guise that Ethan's disappearance had weakened the coven. Not to mention he said he was close to completing the Septum.

But what of Caia, he mused, desperate to come out from the cover of the trees to reveal himself to her. He needed to know more about her. He needed to be able to trust her. Somehow, he had to insinuate himself into her life.

The girl. Yes, he thought. The lykan that Ethan kidnapped. Jaeden.

He watched her for a while, yesterday, wondering what on Gaia's earth had happened to her down in Ethan's basement. He could guess, he supposed. He scowled. She should never have had to go through that. And now ... well ... she had a secret too.

As he watched her, he saw her grow visibly upset and items in her room started flying around of their own accord. A telekinetic. Untapped magikal power in a lykan. She was like a two-for-one special. Not only would she be a useful soldier but he could use her to insinuate himself into Caia's life. Another misfit to add to his crew. Yes. Tonight he would send a few impulses her way, suggest perhaps she run away from the pack. Then he would appear—Reuben the vampyre with his gang of hunters. Yeah. He'd make sure Jaeden wanted to join him.

And then he'd have it all. Jaeden. The Septum.

And Caia.

CHAPTER 3

JUST HOW DEEP THE RABBIT HOLE GOES

*R*euben—sorry, Kirios—was *really* old. Like … *whoa* old.

Caia studied him, trying not to appear intimidated. Of course she was.

But she had to maintain control of the situation. As much control as someone in a cage could.

"What I got from that long-winded tale of sorrow is that your family of hippies is responsible for this war, and you, my friend, are a ruthless son of a bitch. Not exactly endearing me to your cause. By the way, I still don't fully have a grasp on what your cause *is*."

"To end the war. I thought I was quite clear on that point."

She held in a long-suffering sigh. "Yes, but *how* do you intend to do that?"

Reuben looked off into the distance, a smug smile in his eyes. "Marita has inadvertently made everything so much easier for us."

Caia snorted in disbelief. "And how is that?"

"Our plan was to take care of the Septum and then get rid of Marita. That could have been a bloody mess, but Marita

31

has betrayed herself to the Council. We just need to take her out, and then once she's out of the picture, I'm sure it will be pretty easy to persuade the Council to our way of thinking."

"Again, what way is that? What the Hades is the Septum? If you're going to keep me in a cage like a gerbil, you can at least do me the courtesy of providing me with some straight answers."

Reuben chuckled and relaxed once more into his armchair, shrugging elegantly. "What cage?"

A jolt ran through Caia at his amusement, and she closed her eyes in disbelief. It better be there when she opened them. Slowly, she craned her neck. No bars. Her gaze flew around her sides and back. No cage. And the bars that had been suspended in front of her disappeared as she turned around to look at Nikolai. She shook her head, laughing low and humorlessly. "For how long?"

"Since Nikolai gave me this chair."

"Aren't you afraid I'll try to use magik?"

He shrugged, apparently his favorite gesture. "Wouldn't you have done so by now?"

Goddess, he was such a smug bastard. She wanted to smack the expression off his face. "I want to know what the Septum is. It doesn't mean I have any intention of working for you. I want to know what I'm dealing with."

"That's smart. Probably the first smart thing you've said or done so far."

Breathe, Caia, breathe. He claims to be impervious to magik. He could be lying, but if he's not and you blast him, Nikolai will blast you before you can blink, and then Reuben will finish you off.

His eyes wandered over her face. "You think before you act. At least that's something."

"Screw you."

"Very mature."

"Oh, and your pointed insults are the height of sophisticated adulthood."

His lips quirked at the corner. Goddess, she hated this guy.

"I'm just pointing out that you haven't shown a propensity for logic in your previous dealings."

Don't let him bait you. Ignore him. Count sheep or something.

Oh, the hell with it! Counting sheep was for insomniacs. "And what the Hades do you know about it, huh?"

Well done, Caia, that's showing him.

"You were planning on taking over the Daylight Coven with the hopes of beginning peace negotiations with the Midnights. Illogical, stupid, and naive."

She bristled. "Maybe you've forgotten, but *I'm* the one with trace powers. I can sense Midnights emotions and motives, and I can assure you there are a lot of them out there who would welcome my plan to end the war."

"Yes, but there are also many who won't. That's why we need to deal with the Septum first."

Arrrgghhh!

"What is the Septum?" she seethed between clenched teeth.

"Not what. Who." Nikolai stepped forward, seeming to understand Reuben was losing her.

Caia blinked. "Who?"

Nikolai settled on the arm of Reuben's chair. "The Septum is comprised of the seven direct descendants of the Daylight and Midnight Coven." He flicked his wrist, and a scroll of paper appeared on the ground before her. It slowly unrolled. On it were seven names and their locations. "What you see before you is information that has taken us a long time to verify."

Caia shook her head. "I don't understand." *Were these the*

descendants of the magiks who bound themselves to Galen and Penelope, respectively?

"Yes," Reuben confirmed.

Her eyes widened. She hadn't realized she'd muttered the question out loud. She took hold of the paper, seeming to understand that something of great consequence was unfolding here. "So these are the direct descendants of the first seven. What makes them so important?"

Her mind whirred with possibilities, but she couldn't even begin to imagine that her theory was correct.

Reuben smiled. "Caia, you're smarter than that. I think you already know."

Taking a huge gulp of air, she tried unsuccessfully to fold the paper without her fingers trembling. "You think … you think you can get rid of the trace somehow through these seven people?"

They grinned at her as if she were a pet who'd just performed brilliantly for them. Nikolai leaned forward, excitement bristling in his movement. "We don't think … we *know*."

"How?"

"Just before you were born, the Prophet came to me again." Reuben straightened in his chair. "He told me that if we killed the seven direct descendants simultaneously—and it has to be simultaneously, by the same method as it has something to do with connecting their energies and the trace—then the trace will leave us. I've always believed the trace has kept the war alive when it should have ended centuries ago. For goddess' sake, lykans and vampyres, for the most part, have lived in peace with the humans for nearly two thousand years. The Midnights have nothing to complain about anymore … they're just trapped with one another because of the trace and the prejudice of the powerful magiks who control it."

Their revelation was astounding. She stared, eyes glazed, at the paper in her hand and let what they were telling her sink in. Reuben was right ... without the trace ... they would all be free.

She would be free.

"You think this is the first step to ending the war, don't you?" She pierced him with her eyes.

The vampyre nodded slowly. "We do this, and we can build a new world."

"What do you need me for?"

Reuben laughed. "You don't get it, do you, Caia? This is what you were born to do."

She shook her head, completely confused. "No ... I ... the Prophet said I'd end the war."

"Oh, you will end a two-thousand-year-old war just like that, will you?" He snapped his fingers. Before she could snarl in displeasure at his mocking, the vamp continued in a softer tone, "Caia, we need you to use that magik mojo of yours to kill the Septum simultaneously. If you do that, and supernaturals are freed from the trace, then technically you will have ended *this* war. The war we're looking at after that is an entirely new one ... one we can eventually bring to an end. But it will take time."

She felt the world spin, and the next thing she knew, she no longer felt the press of the cold, hard floor but was sitting on an armchair that matched Reuben's. The wave of dizziness passed. "Thank you," she whispered to Nikolai.

"It's a lot to take in, we know."

A lot to take in? For almost a year now, she'd believed she was somehow going to bring the war to a conclusion. Now they were telling her what she was meant for was only the beginning. Exhaustion overwhelmed her, hope bursting like a soap bubble.

"I thought …" She cleared her throat. "I thought it would end. Somehow … I thought …"

"A war of this magnitude doesn't just go away, Caia."

She flopped back on the chair, staring at the gray ceiling. "I've been so naive."

"You weren't the only one."

Fear tightened her expression and she couldn't bring herself to look at them. "You want me to kill those people?"

A moment of sharp silence. And then … "Yes."

Tears pricked her eyes. "Three of them are Daylights. And for all I know, the four Midnights are against the war."

The vampyre's cold voice tore through her like a serrated knife. "Their deaths are necessary." She jerked her head and stared at him in disgust, taking satisfaction in his flinch. Reuben shifted uncomfortably. His face grew taut with anger, all boyishness fleeing his features. "Don't you dare look at me that way. I am not a monster. I am trying to end this war. A war I've had to live through for hundreds of years. You've been dealing with this barely a year. Come back to me in two thousand and see how principled you are then."

"Mindlessly killing people is not the way to end a war. I don't care how you try to justify it."

He laughed, his eyes dark cuts of jet that reflected scorn in the light. "What was that you just said about being naive? All wars are fought with death, Caia. Or haven't you been listening in history class?"

Nikolai hastily interrupted before she could retort. "Caia, if it helps, most of the Septum are very old now. A few would probably willingly sacrifice themselves for this."

Her chin lifted at the suggestion. "Fine, get them to agree to it and I'll think about it."

"Caia—" Reuben warned.

"No! You can't just expect me to kill innocent people!"

"It must be done!" He flew out of his chair toward her,

and Caia shrank back, remembering her magik would do her no good with him.

"Reuben ..." Nikolai made a move toward him, watching him very carefully.

The vampyre towered over her, his hands braced on the arms of her chair, his face inches from her. "Stop acting like a child," he whispered, clearly trying to gain control over himself. "There is no choice, Caia. Seven people over millions. Don't you want to be free of the trace? Don't you want all those voices out of your head?"

Bleakly, Caia nodded. "Yes," she whispered. "But I don't know if I can do what you need me to do."

He sighed wearily and retreated, scrubbing his hands over his face. "You need time," he told her emotionlessly. "Think it over."

She knew then she wasn't getting out of here without conceding to at least this request. Both men were determined. One of them had been planning this for a *long* time.

"Fine," she snapped. "But I want a change in scenery. For a start, I want windows."

The Russian smiled like a kindly father. "Of course."

"And I want the pack informed I'm all right."

"No—" Reuben began but was cut short when Nikolai's hand clamped down on his shoulder.

"I know you are impatient to get on with it, but I think we can accommodate Caia in this."

To Caia's surprise, she watched Reuben relax. "I apologize. I have to stop treating you as if you were an enemy. We need this, Caia. Please take your time."

"Putting aside the moral magnitude of what you're asking me to do ... I don't even know if I have the capabilities to take out that many people in one go."

Reuben smiled softly. "You incinerated four magiks only a few weeks ago ... simultaneously."

"You think that was easy?"

"I think some were misguided magiks—not truly evil—and you killed them, without thought, to protect those closest to you. Think on this as the same thing. Killing the Septum will protect the people you love."

She flinched at the reminder of what she'd done, knowing he was deliberately playing on her guilt. "You are a horrible person."

He gave a huff of laughter. "Perhaps I am." He turned then and opened the door. Quietly, she followed as they led her out of the stone room and down a narrow, dank corridor. She might've been imagining things but she could've sworn they were in a castle.

"I don't sense fear from you, Caia," Reuben mused as they strode through the maze of dimly lit halls.

"Should I be afraid?"

"No. Should I?" He grinned.

"Definitely."

Finally, they came to a stop outside one of the many doors they'd passed. Nikolai pushed it open and a stream of light blinded her as Reuben nudged her inside. She blinked, adjusting to the brightness, and her eyes widened at her surroundings. "Wow, this is not what I was expecting at all."

The circular room looked as if it might have once been a tower room. Now a panoramic window spanned a good portion of one wall. The mahogany hardwood flooring contrasted sharply with the soft white walls. The room was filled with modern furniture, including a sectional and a four-poster bed.

Caia moved toward the window, her eyes soaking up the stunning countryside. "That's fake, right?"

Nikolai chuckled. "Yes. But why have windows without a view to go with it?"

"Well, I like it."

He smiled and shared a triumphant look with Reuben.

"Doesn't mean I like you all."

That wiped the smirk off their faces. *Good.*

Reuben cleared his throat. "We'll leave you alone with this." He handed over the Septum.

As soon as they left, Caia flopped down on the sofa and held on to Nikolai's trace as he and Reuben walked through the building. A building that no longer resembled a castle. Glamour. Damn Nikolai. He was way more powerful than she'd like. The building now appeared to be more of a large, stylish mansion than an old castle.

Caia frowned. Nikolai's trace was different. Usually his thoughts were covered in thick smog, and she could only ever get surface thoughts. Today she could feel him more deeply, clearly, in the trace. She remembered what Reuben said about manipulating Nikolai's trace and wondered if perhaps he'd relaxed his control on it to appease her. *Hmm.*

The two men entered a large reception hall that paid court to a grand antique staircase. The staircase descended toward them before pausing briefly at a small landing that branched off into two more staircases like wide, welcoming arms. Almost immediately, a tall, broad figure appeared at the bottom of the far right of the stairs.

"Vanne." Reuben frowned, heading toward him.

Caia gasped, feeling Nikolai's anticipation at Vanne's appearance. He was thinking something must've happened at the Center.

Vanne! Caia began to sweat at the implication. Nikolai was familiar with Vanne? Friggin' Hades! Vanne was one of them? Just how deep did Reuben's infiltration of the coven go?

"We have a problem." Vanne looked frantic.

"We know about the Council." Reuben shrugged him off.

"Do you know Marita is going to have them executed in a week's time?"

Reuben's jaw dropped, an expression Caia was guessing was rare for him. "Is she insane?"

"She is completely unraveling. She won't listen to anyone. She's told Marion that Caia has betrayed them—that's her excuse for holding Lucien and Ryder prisoner. Marion has refused to believe her but was met with a threat of imprisonment herself if she didn't stop her 'nonsense.'"

Reuben swore. "We need the Council if our plan is to succeed. They're too powerful to lose."

Vanne nodded. "There's more. Marita has Caia's pack under guard. They're all holed up at Lucien's home, surrounded by magiks. Lucien, Ryder, and the pack children were all taken. I know Lucien and Ryder are in the containment center, but I have no idea what she has done with the children."

The blood rushed in Caia's ears. That witch had Lucien and the kids and Ryder! Without thought, Caia burst out of the room, racing with an ever-thrashing heartbeat through the mansion toward the trio. She burst into the reception area. "We need to get them back!"

Annoyance flickered across the vampyre's face. "I might have known you were following Nikolai's trace rather than doing what we asked you to do." He gestured toward the scroll crushed in her hand.

At the direction of his gaze, Caia tucked the Septum behind her back. "I'm not doing anything for you unless you help me." She turned pointedly to Vanne. "Fancy meeting you here."

He at least had the decency to look sheepish. "Hi."

"The children," Caia addressed them all abruptly. "She is experimenting on them. When I was at the Center, I followed her into the Altar of Gaia. She has a secret basement lab underneath the altar. I know she's experimenting on lykan children because I saw it for myself, but I suspect she's also experimenting on vampyres."

"What?"

"Aah, something you don't know, Mr. 479 BC."

"Oh good, you *were* listening."

She grunted in annoyance before continuing, "We need to get back to the pack and save them, and then somehow, we need to get into the Center and free Lucien, Ryder, and the Council. And we have to get those kids out of there. I don't know what she's up to, but I have a feeling it's connected to the fact that Jaeden has particular abilities after being tortured by Ethan."

Nikolai looked aghast. "You don't think she's torturing the children, do you?"

Caia sighed. "It didn't look like torture exactly. There were chemicals and test tubes ... who knows. We just have to get in there."

Reuben sighed. "You're giving me a headache. If you calm down, I will come up with a plan."

Her eyes widened hopefully. "You're going to help me?"

"I don't have much of a choice, do I?"

CHAPTER 4

PRISONERS

*T*he ugly truth is, a magik could take a lykan in human form anytime, anywhere. Hence why he was here now, staring at a bright white ceiling, clenching his teeth and fists in rage. When Lucien had woken up in this cell with Ryder by his side, he'd not been surprised to see Marita glaring at them from the other side of the Plexiglas. He *had* been surprised by the first words out of her mouth, however.

"So the little monster is missing?" she hissed in outrage. "And unless you two are extremely good at hiding things from me, you don't have her."

"Why don't you let us out of here, you insane bitch, and then we'll talk." Ryder said.

Marita's eyes narrowed to dangerous slits. "I want to know where Caia is *now*, or I won't be so kind in my experiments on the pack children. Stop shutting your minds to me and tell me everyone who has been in touch with you."

If Lucien hadn't been so shocked by her line of questioning, he would've pounced (an idiotic mistake since the Plexiglas was magikally electrified). His frown of deep concern was unmistakable. "You mean you don't have her?"

"Don't play games with me, Lucien."

"I'm not!" He growled, springing to his feet. "Do you or do you not have her?"

Marita sighed. "No. I don't. I thought you might know something. Now I see you don't."

His mind whirled with the possibilities. Who had Caia? What did they want with her?

Ryder seemed to sense his slow unraveling and answered for him. "She was taken a few hours before your guard arrived. We thought you'd kidnapped her."

"Clearly you were wrong." Marita huffed and turned to the guard behind her. "I want her found. Go back to Lucien's home and look for any evidence of her kidnapping. I will have a look at the trace, see what I can find."

She left without another word.

As he lay there, Lucien's mind tripped over and over again his last moments with Caia, and he began traveling toward dark conclusions. His heart picked up and his only outlet was to let rip a garble of snarling growls that built into a howl. It did nothing to ease his fear over Caia. He felt impotent and lost. Desperate. But he knew those feelings weren't going to get him any closer to finding her. He knew he needed to maintain his self-control if he was going to escape in time to find her before …

At his sudden silence, he heard Ryder sigh from behind him. "After that, at least the Council members know they're not alone down here."

Ryder's words sunk in. *Crap.* Lucien growled. *Crap, of course.*

"What? What did I say?" Ryder asked wide-eyed as Lucien spun on him.

"If the Council can't get out of here, how the hell are we going to? No wonder she stuck us in here together."

"Come on, man, we just need to think of a plan."

What if Caia was already gone? What if one of the Midnights had gotten wind of her existence and had snuck up on her before Caia knew what was happening? What if she was lying somewhere ...

Feeling his chest constrict, Lucien braced himself against the wall of the cell, fighting to catch a breath.

"Lucien, you have to calm down. Jeez, I never took you for the claustrophobic kind."

"It's not that." He scored his nails down the brickwork, ignoring each pop of broken skin and the prickles of blood.

He felt the moment when his friend understood. His stillness caught hold of Lucien and pressed even harder on his chest.

"We'll find her."

"And if it's too late when we do?" At the words he felt the prick of tears, the painful grip of grief clogging his throat.

"She's not dead," Ryder promised. "You would feel if she were gone. And this is Caia Ribeiro we're talking about here. She's a frickin' nuclear warhead. Have a little faith."

The pressure eased a little. "You think?"

"I know."

Slowly, his breathing grew less labored and he turned to Ryder. "Sorry."

"No need. If I thought for a second something had happened to Jae, I would be ripping this place apart."

"We're lucky Jaeden's quick. They couldn't touch her once she was in wolf form. And it looks like Caia was right about Marita wanting her specifically. She was more than a little pissed off she couldn't get to Jae."

Ryder grinned proudly. "Yup, plus she got a few slices in while they grabbed us."

"Sorry you didn't get your wedding night."

His friend shrugged lazily. "We'll be out of here soon enough."

"You really are an optimistic son of a bitch, aren't you?"

"Have to be." Ryder frowned. "She's got the kids. And I'm guessing she's got them in that lab Caia told us about. We have to get out of here and get those kids back to the pack."

"What are you talking about?"

Lucien spun at the voice that had caused Ryder's eyes to narrow in disgust.

"Marion," Lucien snarled. "How nice of you to show up."

Her presence was like a punch to his gut. All these years she'd been a close friend of the pack, one of Magnus's best friends, in fact. Now she had betrayed them just as her sister had betrayed the coven. He was about to spit and vent his fear over Caia and his fury over his predicament in her face, when he took in her appearance. The witch flinched at his tone, her pale features wan and drawn. Her mouth was pinched with strain and her eyes dark with distress.

"I ... I don't know what's going on here, Lucien," she whispered, drawing slowly closer to the Plexiglas. "I can't stay. She doesn't know I'm here."

As the truth of the situation hit him, he deflated, his anger just as suddenly replaced with reluctant sympathy for her. "She's threatened you?"

Marion nodded. "With imprisonment."

"You know the Council didn't do anything wrong."

She threw up her hands. "Lucien, I don't know anything. I thought I believed her about the Council ... maybe ... I don't know. But taking you and Ryder? Telling me Caia betrayed the Coven?"

Lucien growled, rushing forward. He almost blasted into the Plexiglas without thought, but Ryder was fast, grabbing hold of his shirt and tugging him back. "Caia didn't betray the coven. She found out your sister was playing with the dark side."

Marion shook her head, her wide eyes filled with fear and confusion. "No. No. She couldn't be ... we ... our family are the ones who put the coven to right."

"Then why did she take the pack kids?"

Marion frowned. "What do you mean?"

Lucien snorted. "You're telling me you didn't see us come to the Center with all the pack kids in tow?"

"I missed your arrival."

"That's a nice way to put it. Almost as if we came here by choice."

"Lucien, I'm so sorry. Maybe if I could speak to Caia—"

"CAIA'S GONE!" he roared, causing her to stumble back in shock.

"Lucien," Ryder cajoled, pulling him back. Ryder turned more gently to Marion. "Caia was kidnapped before we were. Not by your sister. We don't know who has her."

The witch stiffened. "How is that possible? Are you sure it was kidnap?"

Ryder snarled this time. "Her blood was at the scene of the *kidnap*."

"Oh goddess," Marion gasped, running her trembling hands through her wild hair as she digested the news. Finally, she looked up, her face taut with determination. "I'll find her."

"So your sister can have her killed?" Lucien spat.

Marion appeared appalled by the idea. "No ... she would never ..."

"Before you go making any statements of assurance on your sister's high moral standing, why don't you go into the Altar of Gaia. To the right of the statue, you'll find a small metal stud embedded in the marble flooring. The slab opens up, revealing an entrance to an underground lab, where your

46

sister is running illegal experiments on lykan children. Possibly even vampyres."

A bit of her usual fire flared in her eyes. "I don't believe you."

"Would you believe Caia? She's the one who found it. That's the reason she went to the Council. They were investigating her claims. I guess they found out it was true. Otherwise why would Marita have them imprisoned?"

She shook her head, dazed ... "No," she whispered.

Lucien sighed and stepped slowly toward her. "Marion, please. We need your help. Please just check it out. If we're right, you have to get us out of here. We have to free the Council and those children."

At her continued silence, Lucien pushed, "Please, Marion ..."

"I have to go," she blurted, and as suddenly as she had appeared, she was gone.

Ryder looked over at him. "Do you think she'll check it out?"

Marita was still Head of the Coven, and despite the controversy over her imprisonment of the Council, a majority of the Daylights at the Center still seemed to trust her. It didn't help matters that she'd won them a number of great victories over the last few months (all of which were Caia's doing, but most Daylights didn't know that). She was a powerful being, and one with a hell of a lot of support. It would be foolish to go against her. Especially a Daylight. She could see the treachery coming in the trace if she thought to look. And he was guessing Marita was keeping a close eye on the major players, including her very own sister.

Lucien dropped to the floor, pressing his back against the wall. "I don't know. Marion is a brave woman, but sometimes going into battle is easier than facing the awful truth."

* * *

LIFE AS A LYKAN was growing increasingly dull. For instance, there were very few ways to express yourself—there really was only so much growling and snapping you could do. Jaeden huffed and once more circled her mother's legs. She felt the stroke of her mom's fingers through her fur and relaxed a little. Yes. She needed to relax so she could come up with a plan. Her wolf eyes took in the pack, excluding all six of the pack children who'd been taken. She growled again, worrying over the fate of her beautiful, innocent niece, Jaela, and Jaela's three cousins.

Sebastian's parents sat in the corner clinging to one another, the remainder of their family—Seana and Sunday—also taken, leaving them momentarily childless. A sort of numbness seemed to have descended over them, and Jaeden let out a small howl in sympathy. Her mother's hand swept through her coat again and she trembled, trying to rein in her anxiety. She had to think. *Think.*

The pack was stuck inside Lucien's house, with a spell around it keeping them trapped inside. She could smell five magiks surrounding the house. There had been more when they first came. Marita used her opportunity well, descending on her and Ryder's mating celebrations as soon she realized Caia wasn't going to come so easily.

Caia, she whined. She could still smell her blood on the car outside. What had happened to her friend? And it was bad enough being parted from Ryder, their night stolen from them, but for the pack to lose their Alpha ... on top of having the children taken and not knowing why (although she had the unsettling feeling it had something to do with the lab Caia said she'd found). The pack was shaken. Frightened. Desolate, without the guidance of their young leader, and in no frame of mind to take on the Head of the Coven.

They all feared the worst, but Jae would know if something had happened to Ryder. He was going to be okay. He and Lucien were together, looking out for one another. Still … she would feel a lot better if she had some kind of plan to get him back.

Hmm.

Jaeden padded away from her mother and wandered into the kitchen. A magik stood on the porch, but he was a few meters from the kitchen doors.

She was fast. Perhaps not as fast as Caia and Lucien, but fast enough to get past the magik.

Plus, it wasn't like he could do anything to her while she was in lykan form. Her head swiveled and she gazed toward the hallway. She wished she could tell her parents where she was going.

Bracing herself mentally, she hopped up onto the kitchen table, backing toward the near edge.

One. Two. Three.

She sped along the long wooden tabletop and as she neared the end of its length, she leapt, pushing her wolf body with enough force to smash through the glass of the kitchen door. Ignoring the fragments that sliced through her skin and clung to her pelt, Jaeden shot down the porch and into the woods, delighting in the outraged shouts of the magik behind her.

Five minutes into the forest, she felt guilty leaving the pack when she was their only defense, but she needed to get to Vil and Laila. Three heads were better than her lousy one, especially when it was clouded with fury and fear.

She followed the woods along the highway. Then there was the difficult task of keeping out of sight as she made her way through town. Garbage cans and cars came in handy, but when she turned up a back alleyway a few blocks from Ryder's apartment building, she surprised a drunk who mistook her for a dog. He kept scrambling at her and even managed to grab her tail. With a huff of unease, Jaeden swiped at his trouser leg, creating shallow scratches across his skin. He howled as though he had been shredded, and Jae used the moment to bounce off the wall and soar behind him, dropping to the ground with ease before running out the other end of the alley.

Making it to the apartment led to another problem. She had to wait forever for someone to come out of the building to get in; sneaking past as if invisible was impossible. The woman who opened the door shrieked in terror, clearly not mistaking her for anything other than what she was. Jaeden raced up the staircase and slammed into Ryder's door, hoping Vil would be suspicious enough to check the peep-hole. That woman would be calling animal control, and Jae really needed to be back in human form before they got there.

Her racing heart almost stopped when the door peeled away from the jamb slowly and cautiously. She didn't give him a second to hesitate. She threw herself into the gap and past him with her lykan strength and gave a wolfy laugh at Vil's shocked "Hey!"

She shot past a startled Laila, who dived out of her way, and loped into Ryder's room, his scent enveloping her and bringing her anger back to the surface.

She missed him.

He'd only been gone a little over twenty-four hours, but she missed him with every molecule of her being. She wished he were here. Helping her through this. She whacked the door shut for privacy and began to change, reveling in the burn and crack of the transformation. Finally, she lay in human form, her body drenched in sweat. That was the fastest she'd ever gone through the change.

At the sounds of Vil and Laila's anxious whispering, Jae

struggled to her feet and rummaged through Ryder's clothes. She found a large *Death Cab* T-shirt and a pair of shorts, the waist of which was held up with one of his belts. She opened the bedroom door only to be confronted by Vil, who in his nervousness shot out a stream of energy. A wave of nausea overcame her.

"Jaeden!" he yelped, and the overwhelming feeling disappeared. "I'm so sorry ... we just ... I was ..."

"It's fine," she assured him, brushing off his apology. "I get it. It's okay."

"Are you all right?" Laila approached cautiously. "Something ... is wrong ... yes?"

"You bet."

After ushering them into the living room, Jaeden explained the full scope of the situation.

Vil paled considerably. "What are we going to do?"

Jaeden looked at them wide-eyed. "I don't suppose you guys would consider helping me take out those guards?"

"Of course."

"What? Are you crazy?"

Their replies came in unison. Jaeden laughed. She wasn't surprised. For all her gentleness and appearance of fragility, Laila was brave and strong from her experiences. Vil ... well, he just didn't want anything bad to happen to Laila.

A new voice entered the fray. "Yes. She is crazy. But that's why I've always liked her."

She gasped along with her companions and turned to find Reuben standing in the doorway. Oh, Reuben, thank the gods! He would help. He could get the gang. Just as these thoughts rushed through her, and just as she was about to throw her arms around him in delight, another figure stepped into the doorway. Smaller. More feminine. But just as familiar.

Jaeden lurched to a stop. Thank goddess.

A slow grin spread across her face. "Caia?"

CHAPTER 5

SACRIFICE

*I*t was strange to find herself at this age so lost and afraid. It was strange to find that she was so unsure at any age, as she'd always found confidence in who she was and the powerful family she belonged to. Marion trembled, drawing in a deep breath as she sank into a wooden pew in the front of the statue of Gaia. Having spotted the metal stud in the marble flooring that Lucien had spoken of, Marion was now taking a moment to decide what to do, if, in fact, there was anything she could do.

That morning Marita had held a meeting in the largest of the training rooms, requesting the presence of everyone who lived, worked, and trained or served at the Center. There had been much upset when Marita had imprisoned the Council. Some fighting broke out, but they'd managed to deal with the people responsible and had put them out of the Center. All portals known to outsiders were shut off after Daylights (the families of Council members, to be exact) had gotten into the Center with the sole purpose of rescuing the prisoners.

There would be more rescue attempts, they were sure, as the news took its time to reach other Daylight supernaturals around the world. Marita had to act fast to prove the Council's treachery ... or a war within the coven would begin.

Luckily for Marita, none of the Daylights so far had taken the time to organize, and their attempts were shut down immediately by Marita's soldiers. But unrest within the Center itself was growing anew. Marion had wanted it to, had wanted some sense shaken into her sister. How could Marita hold Pack Errante against their will? How could she hunt Caia? It was ... insane.

The meeting, however, had done nothing to soothe Marion's fears. Although there was discontent, primarily among Caia's friends within the Travelers and lykans, Marita had managed to contain the threat of riot by announcing her plans to create a new Council—assuring everyone she had no intention of turning the Daylight Coven into an autocracy. Moreover, some seemed willing to accept her claims that Caia was working for the Midnights and that she had convinced the Council, with her supreme powers, to work against the Daylights.

Why wouldn't they believe her? Marita was part of a noble family and had been their faithful leader for years. And more importantly, it was becoming apparent there were still a great many Daylights who were just as ruthless in their beliefs as she was. They would do anything to win the war, to destroy Midnights, and it was only now Marion was realizing that meant sacrificing their own. How could Marion possibly stand against her sister and such odds?

But this ... if Lucien was speaking the truth about the children? Oh goddess. Who was she to trust? Her sister was clearly maniacal at this point, and Caia had been lying to her for weeks.

You have to look. You have to know for yourself.

Heaving the weightiest of sighs, Marion stood. Her legs trembled so badly, she had to grasp the pew behind her. She took a moment to bolster her courage, to remind herself of *who* she was, how strong she'd always been. She couldn't let her strength desert her now ... now when she needed it most.

With tentative steps, she stood above the marble slab. Very slowly and gently, she pressed her finger on the near-invisible stud.

Whoosh!

She watched, silently horrified, as it opened, a blast of cool air whipping across her skin. Peering down into the subbasement, dread settled in her stomach. Quietly she made her way down the ladder attached to the wall and found herself standing in what looked like a hospital corridor. Like a surreal nightmare, it felt as if she wandered forever through white hallways, garishly lit with fluorescent lighting, her heeled boots echoing ominously as she approached what was sure to be an unwanted reality.

The next corridor she turned down was different from the others—wider. A door sat adjacent to a large viewing window.

Another door farther up the corridor on the opposite side, another window.

Her chest reverberated with the pounding of her heart, and she clutched her stomach at the welling of nausea and fear. Her heart raced out of control and then stopped as the words on the door shot through her with the impact of a shotgun blast.

Laboratory 1: Lykanthrope.

Oh Gaia, no. *No.* She squeezed her eyes shut. No, her sister couldn't be capable of this.

Anger, unlike anything she'd felt, mixed with the cruelest of disappointment, surged through her. She took the door-knob in hand and thrust it open.

"Hey! You can't be—" A magik in a lab coat rushed at her,

only to be cut off as she blasted him against the far wall with enough force to render him unconscious. He slumped helplessly to the ground, papers flying up and then fluttering slowly to the floor around him. Tears filled her eyes at the sight before her. Seven frightened children stared back, wide-eyed and pale, from within cages.

"Marion?" a child whispered, and she stumbled in recognition. It was Seana Trey, and in the cage next to her was Joaquin Barton. They were Pack Errante kids. Oh Gaia. Oh Hades ...

"I didn't want you to find out like this."

Marion whirled to face her sister whose eyes seemed to plead with her.

"This isn't what it looks like."

"Where are the others?" Marion asked numbly. "Where are the other pack children?"

"They're safe ... in another lab farther down."

"Safe? How so? They're being experimented upon! This is completely immoral, not to mention illegal!"

Marita sighed. "Illegal to whom? There is no longer a Council, Marion. I am the law now."

"What are you doing?" Marion cried. "This isn't you. You wouldn't do this. You wouldn't torture and experiment upon innocent children!"

Marita flinched. "I'm not torturing them."

Marion gazed at her, aghast. Had her sister gone completely mad? "What do you call putting them in cages?"

Her sister's shoulders slumped, her marble poise deserting her under some invisible crushing weight. "Certain sacrifices have to be made, sister. Don't you see? Before Caia, the Midnights were winning."

"Oh goddess, Marita, if Father knew who he had left to the run the coven—"

"Father!" Marita spat. "*He* was the one who told me things

needed to change. *He* was the one who told me we needed to be more ruthless in our dealings." She smirked as if enjoying her latest revelation. "Father was the one who left the plans for the laboratories. He believed that experimenting with genetics was the only way to win the war. And he was right. If the Midnights were winning before Caia, with her ... we will be destroyed. But these children are the key."

Marion shook her head in denial. "How on earth could he think that? How can you?"

"Because he was proven right."

Marion stared at her blankly.

Her sister smiled. "Jaeden. She has telekinetic abilities, has had ever since her time with Ethan."

"He tortured her! Do you intend to do the same to these children?"

The look of outrage she was hoping to see appear on Marita's face at the mere suggestion did not, and in that moment, it felt as if her entire world was shattering into a million pieces.

"I am hoping it will not come to that. But if it does ... so be it. We need an army of Caias to win, and if we can't have that, then the next best thing is an army of Jaedens."

"This is madness. We were winning. With Caia on our side, we were winning!"

"No! That filthy Midnight bitch was never on our side! She went to the Council to have me killed so she could be Head of the Coven! Head of *both* covens, Marion ... do you have any idea how powerful that would have made her?"

Marion felt the tears running down her cheeks. "She went to the Council because of what she found down here. She would have saved us, Marita. It was prophesied—"

"It was not! It was prophesied that her birth would bring an end to the war ... it didn't say how."

Marion shook her head. "It doesn't matter. She would

have saved us. Now we'll be lucky if she doesn't turn to the Midnights for what you've done. Let them go. Let the Council go. We'll plead your case. It'll be alright. I promise."

Marita's pinched expression gave way to disgust. She glared at Marion with such rage that Marion knew ... for Marita, there was no going back.

"You are either with me, or against me."

Marion straightened, her steel spine finding itself again. "Then I'm against you."

For a moment an utter sadness flitted across her sister's face. And then it was replaced with anger. "Then I'm afrai—"

Marion didn't give her time to finish. She gathered all her strength and pushed her energy force out at her sister, knocking the witch off her feet and out the door, only to smash her against the opposite corridor wall. With a sweep of her arm, she created a high wall of fire across the doorway and turned to the children, melting each lock on the seven cages.

The children were frightened by the height and heat of the flames at her back, and she found herself hurriedly coaxing them out of their cages. What she was about to do, no one had ever survived ... but the children ... the children would be alright. There wasn't any other way.

"Marion!" her sister shrieked.

"Hold tight to me," she urged the children, grasping them roughly to her, making sure each little hand clasped her arms.

The pain was excruciating. A communication spell should never be used to transport more than two beings; the kind of power needed to do so could rip a person apart, and that, coupled with the fear of hurting the children, only made the agonizing burn that much more intense.

At the sudden silence, she opened her eyes and gasped in relief. They had made it. Saffron blinked back at her from her perch on the sofa. They were in Saffron's home, a place she knew Marita could never find in her trace. And Saffron was incredibly choosy about who was invited.

One of the children brought her attention back to them as he threw up on her boot.

"What?" Saffron yelped and moved toward them. She blurred across Marion's vision, and the room turned itself upside down. She burned like ice all over. The pain. It was just too much.

"Marion!"

Her body fell apart, her mind with it, and she descended into the darkest of peace.

* * *

CAIA ALMOST JUMPED BACK in shock as Jaeden rushed at her but was pleasantly surprised as her friend's arms pulled her into a suffocating hug.

"Oh gods, am I ever glad to see you!"

Caia smiled and gently pried her back to arm's length. "Blame Reuben for my sudden disappearance. He's the one who kidnapped me."

Jaeden hissed at the revelation and turned to stab Reuben with her ferocious glare. "What exactly does that mean?"

Caia momentarily ignored her to smile at Laila and Vil, quietly watching them all. "You guys okay?"

They nodded.

"Caia?" Jae demanded.

"Sit down. Please. This needs to be quick."

It took longer than she'd hoped to explain everything, especially with Reuben jumping in to fill in the parts she'd missed. She finally got through the tale when his cell rang and he went off into the other room to speak with Nikolai.

When he returned, he hadn't looked concerned, so Caia continued on.

While Vil and Laila looked on with growing fascination, she could see Jaeden turn a shade darker with rage as the tale unfolded. When Reuben explained how he had masked Vil's trace so Marita couldn't find them, Caia almost rolled her eyes at the hero-worship in their gazes.

"Wow." Vil smiled at Reuben, his pale eyes glittering. "You masked my trace? Thank you."

"From us both," Laila added sweetly.

"Hey, hey!" Jae jumped to her feet, a growl burrowing out from the back of her throat. "Don't thank him!" She turned on Reuben, her eyes brimming with outrage and hurt. "You tricked me. Lied to me. *Used* me!"

Caia was unsurprised by his stoic nod and matter-of-fact response. "Yes."

Jaeden stilled.

Oh goddess, Caia groaned inwardly.

"Yes?" Jae whispered. "Yes? That's all you have to say? I could kill you!"

As she lunged toward him, Caia threw up an invisible barrier between them, causing Jae to bounce gently off it. She snarled and whipped around to glare at her.

Caia shrugged wearily. "Believe me, it's for your own good."

"Like he would dare hit me back."

I wouldn't be so sure. Caia raised an eyebrow, and they both looked at Reuben who shrugged. "If the attack is unprovoked … I hit back."

"Unprovoked," Jae spluttered.

For Gaia's sake.

"Jeez, Reuben, could you at least try here?" Caia pleaded.

"OK, maybe she's been a little provoked."

"You used her. She thought you were her friend."

"*She* is standing right here," Jaeden snapped.

Reuben shrugged again. "I *am* her friend. It was just … necessary. I don't apologize for what is necessary."

Jae snorted. "Oh." She crossed her arms over her chest defensively. "So, coming on to me was necessary, was it?"

Caia hadn't known about that part.

Reuben grinned. "Nah, that was just fun."

"You're a creep."

"I've been called worse."

Sure that if she let them, their argument would continue on into the wee hours of the morning, Caia stood to interrupt. "If we're done, may I suggest we get a move on?"

"Please." Reuben nodded.

Jaeden didn't look very happy about her grievance being dismissed, but she nodded reluctantly, along with Vil and Laila, and sat back down again. "What's the plan?"

Taking a deep breath, Caia laid it out for them. "First, we approach the families of the Council members who have been imprisoned. Believe me, they will be happy to help. Second—"

"Wait," Vil interrupted, "I know Reuben is masking my trace, but how can we contact all those people without Marita being alerted to it?"

The vampyre's expression didn't change. He responded blandly, "I'm masking a number of traces at the moment. Another few shouldn't be a problem."

"Another few," Jaeden grunted. "We're talking about at least ten magiks."

"More, actually." Caia sighed. "After we gather some magiks from that group, I'm going to approach the MacLachlans for help. Including Phoebe, they have another four lykans among them capable of fighting. After that, we're returning to Lucien's, where Reuben will mask the trace of the guards and the entire pack so Marita won't be alerted that we've taken the guards out and rescued the pack."

"That's at least forty people. How—"

"Maybe more," Reuben interrupted, irritation bubbling under his tone. "It's not a problem."

"Oh yeah, I forgot, you're like a million years old or something. It's completely gross how decrepit you are ... thank goddess I didn't go down that road. Ugh, can you imagine—"

"Jae," Caia warned, and her friend's eyes glittered darkly, as if Caia had betrayed her. "I know you're angry. You have every right to be. But I need us all acting as a team if we're going to do what we're about to do."

"Which is what exactly?" Laila inquired quietly.

"We're going to break Lucien, Ryder, the pack children, and the Council out of the Center's prison ... and then we're going to take the Center from Marita."

"Holy—"

"No frickin'—"

"Oh my—"

"Be quiet," Reuben's cold voice rumbled around the room like an earthquake. Silence settled in its wake.

Caia rolled her eyes at him but refrained from commenting. "We can do this. Vanne told us that I still have a few followers in the Center, including a lot of the Travelers. He's very kindly reopened the portal at Magic Fitness so we can get in. We'll go over the strategy for takeover once we have everyone assembled and ready to fight."

"You really think this will work?" Jaeden bit her lip nervously.

"As long as we can get the Council out, yes."

Suddenly a blur of color erupted in front of Ryder's television and Saffron was before them, her usually expressionless face twisted in rage ... and grief.

Reuben was the first to shoot out of his chair.

"Saffron?" he queried, striding toward her quickly. She braced a hand against his chest, her fingers curling into his shirt. Her uncharacteristic display of emotion put Caia on immediate alert.

"Reuben," she hissed, her wide blue eyes searching his. "It's Marion."

Caia felt her breath leave her. "Marion. What about Marion?"

Saffron realized they weren't alone and let go of Reuben's shirt. She didn't move away from him, however, their body language betraying their close relationship. "Caia." She nodded deferentially at her. "Marion is ... I tried everything but ..."

"What's happened to her?" Caia demanded, fear pulsing through her veins. Not Marion, not Marion. Please ...

"The children told me she found them in their cages in some lab. That Marita appeared and Marion fought her before bringing the children to me via a communication spell. I was just lounging at home when she appeared before me with five children gripping onto her. And then she collapsed. She ... couldn't withstand the energy depletion created by traveling with five other beings."

Grief marred Saffron's every word, and Caia shook her head in denial. "No. Take me to her."

"Caia—" Reuben tried to interrupt.

"No!" she yelled, angry tears blurring her vision.

"She's gone, Caia," Saffron whispered, her own tears rolling quietly down her cheeks. "She's dead."

CHAPTER 6

COMPARTMENTALIZING

"*I* can't take much more of this man." Ryder's grumble reached him from his place on the floor. The Hunter was sitting with his back against the cold brick wall, his knees drawn to his chest and his head tilted back to stare blankly at the ceiling. Lucien wondered if the ceiling was any more interesting than the blank wall he was staring at from his seat on the metal bench at the back of the cell.

Another few hours passed, and yet it could have been days. Their constant worrying over Caia and the pack had filled the cell with so much tension, Lucien was sure one spark would blow the whole place up.

"I can't hear anyone else down here. Can you?" Lucien asked softly.

"Nope. Not a damn thing."

Lucien grunted. They had tried to let the change happen, to shift into lykan form numerous times, but there was no getting past the spell cast around the cell preventing them from doing it. This helplessness was sure to drive him crazy. If not that, then the constant images of Caia would. He growled and threw his memory of finding her blood on the car out of his mind.

"Lucien?"

"I'm fine."

"Uh-huh. Just think about other stuff."

Despite his dismal mood, he found himself smirking at his friend. "It is scary how well you know me."

Ryder chuckled. "Nah, it's just scary how other people think you're *actually* hard to read."

Scowling, Lucien scoffed, "I am hard to read. I've perfected *being* hard to read. If I weren't, Caia wouldn't have taken so damn long to come to her senses now, would she?"

"Not to criticize your mate, but she's kinda dense when it comes to you. I mean … she's attracted to you for a start."

"I could say the same thing about Jaeden."

"When Jae agreed to be my mate, she provided the world with an example of her supreme intellectual and emotional superiority."

Lucien snorted. "I'd like—"

"Ssh," Ryder interrupted, gesturing for him to be silent. He jumped to his feet noiselessly.

Immediately Lucien's own ears perked up, and he heard approaching footsteps. They shared a wary glance just before Marita appeared. His heart, seeming to perceive something he didn't, pumped loudly in his chest at the sight of her. Usually so together, so coiffed, Marita stood before them somewhat disheveled, her eyes filled with a war of emotions.

"I've come to update you," she informed them crisply, hollowly. "My sister, under your suggestion, found the laboratory. She was … unwilling to reach an agreement with me and foolishly tried to fight me off." She stopped as if trying to compose herself, and when she looked back at him, he was almost knocked off his feet by the fury he saw there. "She took the children on a suicide mission."

Ryder tensed. Lucien cleared his throat, hating to ask. "What does that mean?"

Marita hissed like a snake readying to strike. "She did a communication spell with five children clinging to her. I know her destination was her faerie Saffron's, where, despite much investigation, I've never been able to find—treacherous bitch. I know she reached there." She stiffened and bleakness flashed across her eyes before disappearing altogether. "I know the children survived. I know she died. The spell is too much for any witch or warlock, no matter how powerful."

What? Was she saying?

"Is …" He shared a brief look of horror with Ryder. "Is Marion dead?"

Marita nodded, her lips pinched cruelly. "Thanks to you."

His blood boiled. "Thanks to me? Thanks to *you*! What am I supposed to tell Caia? I will kill you for this! I will—"

His last words were cut off as he was blasted against the wall, his head connecting with eye-watering accuracy on one of the shelving units. He slumped to the floor trying to focus his vision. In all that pain, all he could think about was how devastated Caia was going to be. Marion meant the world to her.

"I don't care what Caia thinks," Marita clipped. "She was *my* sister. This is *my* pain, not *hers*! Any thoughts I had of granting mercy to that little perversion of nature you call a mate is gone now. She is the reason our coven is falling apart, that my sister, one of the greatest magiks of our time, killed herself trying to save some low-bred lykan pups!"

"Do you hear yourself?" Ryder countered as Lucien got to his feet. "You sound like a Midnight."

Marita flinched. "How dare you? I have no racial prejudice against other species, but no society, natural or supernatural, can survive without class order. My sister, a witch of noble lineage, should not have had to die for five common lykans."

A growl erupted from Lucien's chest so abruptly, he was just as taken aback as the insane witch in front of him. "Your sister was a hero. She upheld her place within your 'noble lineage' as you call it. You … have shit all over it. And you can bet when you travel to the Underworld, the dead won't be as understanding as the idiots in this Center pandering to your lunacy."

Marita made no comment but Lucien was satisfied by the pallor of her skin. She narrowed her eyes and straightened her shoulders, pretending his words hadn't affected her. "I just came to warn you that your time is nearly up. I will be executing the Council in a few days and with them … I will be executing you. By then I hope to have found your precious mate so she can witness your death. Before I send her to her own."

* * *

SHE COULDN'T CATCH her breath. She could feel the others hovering outside the bedroom door, their worry and grief adding to the thick claustrophobia she felt clawing at her throat. How could Marion be dead?

A sob caught in the back of her throat, but she refused to let the tears spill. They all thought she was in here crying her heart out, but in truth, she was trying to plug the hole the death had made in it. She was trying to force her brain to switch off, to pretend that Marion was alive, that she hadn't died protecting the children *Caia* had left alone down in that lab. Oh goddess, it was like losing Sebastian all over again.

No, she snarled at herself, shaking her head as if she could empty the thoughts right out of her ears.

"Caia," Reuben's cool voice filtered through the door.

She took a deep breath. She could do this. She had no other choice but to do this. Slowly, she made her way to the door and peeled it open, unsurprised by the four anxious faces staring back at her. Caia frowned. "Where is Saffron?"

Jaeden's lip trembled a little. "She's gone back to look after the children. She's keeping them safe while we ..." She stopped, her huge blue eyes glimmering with pity. "Caia, are you going to be okay ?"

She shouldered past them, quite a feat considering how small she was compared to the three of them acting as a wall. "I don't want to discuss it."

"But Cy—"

"I said I don't want to discuss it." She whirled on them, completely unaware of how much she looked and sounded like a young queen commanding her army to obey. Jaeden stiffened a little but nodded, clamping her mouth shut. Reuben stared at Caia in admiration (unnerving, to say the least) while Vil looked uncomfortable. Laila, however, slowly moved toward her and Caia braced herself. If the girl said anything comforting, she knew she was going to fall apart. But the Midnight merely placed a soothing hand on her shoulder and said, "We should go to the Council members' families at once, Caia."

At her touch, an almost medicinal peace flowed through Caia, and the lump at the back of her throat eased, her lungs opening to allow the air to flow freely.

"You're right." She nodded, feeling far more confident she could continue on with the plan, despite her grief.

Jaeden strode forward, the pity gone from her face to be replaced with a far more familiar determination and mulishness. "We aren't going anywhere until we rescue the pack."

"Jaeden—" Reuben began to warn her, but Caia help up a

hand to quiet him. She took a brief moment to enjoy the little power she had over the formidable vampyre.

"She's right." Caia nodded. "We're taking the pack back first."

"That gives us less time to gather the families of the Council and the MacLachlan pack."

"How so?" Jae glared at him.

"Because Marita must be checking in with her guards that surround the pack. What happens when she checks in and she gets no answer?"

Jae curled her lip sardonically. "What … you can't muddle their trace with that masking trick of yours so that she thinks everything is alright?"

"Uh …" Reuben stopped and scowled at her. "Yes. I can do that."

Jaeden chortled at her little victory. "Not so much with the smarts, are you?"

"I've just been given very trying news. Marion was a good person and a portentous ally. Forgive me if I'm not thinking straight."

At the mention of the witch, they all tensed, waiting for Caia to react. She glared at the vampyre. "The big bad vampyre, who would sacrifice his own children for this war, actually feels grief?"

His dark eyes narrowed and he looked nothing like a young gang leader and very much like a dangerously old being that could rip them apart in seconds. "Don't provoke me, Caia. I am not in the mood."

Caia stared back stonily. "Neither am I. So let's move."

CHAPTER 7

AMBUSHED

*B*irds twittered and squawked in the trees, insects buzzed around her ears, and the wind rustled every piece of foliage its fingers brushed against. Her pounding heart provided the back drumbeat to their musical surroundings, and as her pale hair got caught gently in the breeze, Caia was sure the guards surrounding Lucien's must be able to hear and see them hiding in the sullen cover of the woods. She glanced back at Laila and Vil who had refused to be left alone at Ryder's apartment. Caia had given into their wishes because she was sure she would need Vil at some point. For now, however, she had them hiding behind a couple of trees, farther back from herself and Jaeden.

"Where is he?" Jae hissed, her hands clenched into fists.

Caia raised a finger to her lips, her eyes telling her to be patient.

"It's done."

They both jumped, startled, and turned to find Reuben inches from Caia. She stepped back, uncomfortable with his nearness. He was possibly the most unnerving person she'd ever met. By "it's done," they both knew Reuben meant he had successfully manipulated each of the five guards' trace, so that if Marita tapped in to see if everything was all right, she would find nothing but a mixture of bored thoughts and loyal determination to do a good job. Moreover, he was masking the trace of the entire pack so Marita would think they were still under guard. Caia almost shuddered in apprehension at the thought of the vampyre's seemingly unlimited abilities.

"OK." Caia nodded, drawing a breath. "Are we ready?"

After a successful attack on Midnight magiks in similar surroundings a few weeks ago, Caia had assumed her nerves over going into battle again would be few, but it seemed she still had enough butterflies in her to open a riotous farm. Jae nodded militantly and quickly stripped, Reuben watching avidly. Rolling her eyes, Caia reached up and grabbed him by the chin, forcing him to look away. He grinned unabashed and turned his attention to her face. She tried not to squirm under his penetrating gaze, but she would give anything to know what was going on in the vampyre's mind.

At the cracking of bones, Caia felt a rush of unexpected envy. She used to love the feel of the change, the burning, the breaking and bending. Now she changed so fast, all she ever felt was a quick flush of hot energy. It left her with that irritating feeling of when your back aches and you know if you could just crack it, you'd be satisfied.

Something wet touched her hand, and she looked down to see Jae nuzzling her nose into her open palm. Caia smiled reassuringly down at her and gave her the nod. Wolf Jae turned in an instant and rushed through the woods in a blur. They heard the distant cry of two guards, and they were off.

She wasn't as fast on two legs as she was on four, but Caia was faster than the average human. Reuben ... was a streak of movement. Caia knew he was heading for the magik guarding the back porch. As she raced around the edge of the house, she saw he had a hold of the magik by the neck. A loud sickening crack reached her ears. *Oh my.*

She squeezed her eyes shut briefly and then forced her flight to the driveway to confront the two magiks Jaeden was momentarily distracting. Their cries had alerted the other two guards, and they were heading toward them from opposite ends of the grounds. Pushing away any gentle feelings, Caia pressed her magik into the approaching guards' lungs and they both collapsed, clutching their chests as water filled their airways. Seeing the downing of their comrades, the other magiks turned on Caia. Jaeden took that moment of distraction to lunge at the one closest to her.

Flooring him, she swiped at his face with her claws, eliciting a piercing scream of agony that was quietly culled by her jaws as they clamped onto his throat. The other warlock seemed to hesitate, deciding whether to save his friend or deal with Caia. His decision was made in seconds, and he turned on Caia. She threw up a shield to stop whatever energy he was pushing her way. His face mottled red with determination, his black eyes blazing with fury.

A blur shot past the two magiks she'd suffocated and came to an abrupt stop behind the one trying to get past her shield with what she was sure was air magik. The blur cleared into Reuben, and his large hands gripped the warlock's head before giving a forceful tug that removed it from his body. Caia watched in horror as his body fell away from the vampyre in a loud thump across the gravel. Reuben sneered and let the head roll from his hands to land in the bloody pool that oozed from his victim's decapitated corpse.

It was only as he turned to look down at Jaeden that Caia remembered her. Jae was hacking up the blood of her own victim, and Caia knew all too well how disgusting the taste and feel of death was.

"What now?" Caia gestured a little shakily to them.

"Marita wouldn't have felt the attack but won't she feel their deaths? Won't it be like ... white noise?" She felt a little stupid for not having thought that part through ... more than a *little* stupid, really.

Reuben's lips twisted as if he was insulted by the mere suggestion he would've been idiotic enough to not have thought out every second of the attack. "The manipulation can last past death as long as something of their physical body remains."

She shook her head in amazement. "If Marita ever knew of your existence, you would be enemy number one, you know that, right?"

He snorted. "Caia, she does know of my existence. She would just prefer to believe I am merely a legend, a myth ... makes it easier to sleep at night."

"If you're so powerful, why didn't you take over years ago?"

Reuben laughed, his eyes glittering darkly. "This really isn't the time for that discussion. But the short answer is ... I'm just not interested."

Laughing, Caia strode past him, stroking her fingers through Jae's pelt in comfort as she walked into the house.

"Caia!" Magnus yelled. He'd obviously detected her scent amid the sounds of the disturbance outside. The thundering of feet could be heard from all over the house as people rushed to the entrance.

Magnus was the first to reach her, and she was dragged into a crushing hug. She felt his lips in her hair and the shudder of his relief, and as she breathed in his familiar scent, Caia felt a rush of painful affection. Marion. She'd been one of Magnus's closest friends. Caia would have to break the news to him.

"Uncle Magnus." She burrowed deeper into his chest.

The exclamations of the pack got louder when Jaeden and

Reuben entered. Caia managed to pull back from her uncle's tight grip to see Dimitri and Julia hovering over Jaeden, aghast at the blood on her muzzle. Christian and Lucia stood close by, clinging to one another, grief over the kidnap of their toddler tightening their features.

"Caia!" She felt herself being yanked out of Magnus's arms and into Irini's. At the feel of her sister-in-law's trembling, Caia felt a rush of emotion she wasn't expecting. All the years Irini had looked after her, Caia had wondered if the lykan had resented her existence. But her tight hug, and the way she pulled back to brush the hair from Caia's face, told her something she had missed all this time. Irini cared for her, truly and deeply. She smiled tremulously, not sure if she could handle any more sentimental outbursts.

"We were so worried," Irini whispered, her eyes bright with unshed tears. Aidan stood by her side, his hand on her shoulder. "Lucien was … I've never seen him so …"

Caia blanched. "He must be thinking the worst."

"Caia, he's been taken," Aidan announced, causing the riot in the hallway to dissipate. "So have Ryder and the children—"

"I know." She nodded, turning to look at them all.

She didn't have a chance to say anything more before she Ella embraced her. "Caia, I am so sorry." The words tumbled out of Lucien's mother's mouth in an incredible flood of remorse. "You were right about Marita and everything and we—"

"Yeah, we're so sorry—"

"Can you—"

Feelings and apologies engulfed her as the pack urged her to forgive them for not believing her about Marita. She tried shushing them but to no avail. They were determined to have their say, and they were far louder than she was.

"Quiet." The vampyre didn't raise his voice, but the pack puttered to a stop and stared sullenly at him.

"You remember Reuben?" she asked wryly.

He nodded hello.

"I know about the kidnapping." Caia turned to the pack. "I know about everything."

CHAPTER 8

ALPHA

*A*s Magnus excused himself, Caia's eyes followed his tall figure as it lurched out of the kitchen and onto the porch, disappearing into the yard and then the woods. Ella and the pack stared after him solemnly while Caia fought the Marion-shaped lump of grief at the back of her throat. At the sound of Magnus's harsh howl in the distance, she stumbled back from the gathering and hurried upstairs, into the room she shared with Lucien.

Spotting Lucien's shirt strewn across the sofa in the corner, Caia rushed for it, pressing the fabric to her face so his scent flooded her nostrils. She promptly burst into harrowing sobs and collapsed on the sofa. As she struggled to breathe through the burning agony, she wished more than anything Lucien were here, to help her through this. There had always been the chance that once her war with Marita had begun, Caia would have lost Marion anyway. But at least she would've been alive and thriving, helping to keep the coven tempered with her goodness. Now, to exist in a world where there was no Marion was to exist in a world without light. And more than ever, Caia needed that light.

A cool hand clasped her shoulder, eliciting a sharp thump from her heart. She looked up to see Reuben staring down at her kindly. There wasn't even enough time to be surprised by the concern in his eyes before she was pulled out of her seat and enfolded in his arms. Shocked at his display of sympathy, of solicitude, she tensed against him. He tightened his hold and pressed her head against his chest, soothing her with quiet words.

"You're allowed to cry, Caia. She meant a great deal to you, to everyone. In this war you will see a lot of death, and feel much grief, but you have to *let* yourself feel it. If you stop allowing yourself to, you will stop caring about why you are fighting in the first place." He placed a soft kiss on her forehead. "I know I seem ruthless ... and I can be sometimes ... but I still care. I need to."

Tears rolled quietly down her cheeks as he spoke, and as his voice faded to silence, she could no longer stop, burrowing her head deeper into his chest and soaking his shirt with her salty, uncontrolled sorrow. When at last she had quieted and stopped shuddering with the force of her emotions, reality intruded and Caia pulled back from him, instantly uncomfortable with her outburst. And as her gaze locked onto his dark, unfathomable eyes, wariness sprang between them. Caia was frightened by her need to trust him, and he seemed unnerved by the idea that he might just trust her.

"I'm sorry," she apologized shakily.

Reuben sighed, and she felt him brush her hair back from her face. "It's fine. You needed to do that to get on with the rest of today."

She nodded, her eyes glued to the floor. "We should go to Alfred Doukas's home." She referred to the Council member she was acquainted with. "Enlist his family and get them to organize the others."

"Vil can take you to them. I think we should hurry this along."

She looked up at him now, her eyebrows raised in surprise. "What did you have in mind?"

"I'm going to call on Vanne. He and I are going to the MacLachlans while you deal with the Council. With Vanne's help, I'll be able to convince Alistair MacLachlan and his daughter to join us. We should arrange a time for us all to meet at the portal."

Caia frowned. "Can Vanne get away from Marita without raising suspicion?"

The vampyre chuckled. "Of course. When I whistle, he comes running. End of story."

She guffawed. "You really are sure of yourself, aren't you?"

"I've had over two thousand years to perfect arrogance and acquire a solid arsenal of diverse weaponry to support that arrogance."

Before she could mock his cockiness, the door to the room blasted open and Jaeden strode in, now in human form and fully clothed. She curled her lip at Reuben and turned her attention and respect to Caia.

"Saffron's arrived with the children. Two of them are Joaquin and Seana. Cera and the Treys are in hysterics." She paused so they could hear the commotion rumbling up through the floors from the kitchen. "The other three kids aren't ours." Her lip trembled. "Jaela and the others must still be at the Center. Anyway, Vil's going to take the kids home one by one."

Caia glanced at Reuben who was frowning. He seemed ready to dispute that decision when Caia subtly shook her head at him. She looked to Jae who seemed to be watching them both with narrowed eyes, a quizzical furrow between her eyebrows.

"That's fine. But tell him to hand the children over and leave. We don't have time for explanations, and I need Vil to take me to Alfred Doukas."

"OK." Jae grimaced. "But isn't that a little mean? These people deserve to know what happened to their kids."

Reuben rolled his eyes. "Then pin a note on them."

Caia winced at his insensitivity and the volcanic look on Jaeden's face. Before Jae could erupt, Caia stepped in between them. "Ignoring his charming delivery, Reuben has a point." She sighed wearily. "I don't like it very much, but maybe we could return them with a note explaining everything, for now."

She wasn't sure Jae was going to respond. And then she snorted in disgust. "Don't spend too much time with him, Cy. You're starting to think like him. And remember, if he can mesmerize me with his voodoo crap, who's to say he won't do it to you?" With that, she spun on her heel and left the room.

Hmm ... she hadn't thought about that. Was that what Reuben was doing? Wafting his powers over her so she felt like she could trust him? She slanted her gaze at him and noticed with some annoyance he was smirking, as if he knew exactly what she was thinking.

"I haven't manipulated you. I swear."

"And I'm supposed to take your word on that?"

He shrugged. "I don't care one way or the other."

As he walked away in Jaeden's wake, Caia squeezed her eyes shut. She needed Lucien back. Everything would be okay once she had Lucien back.

* * *

"It's a good thing you called me out of there when you did," Vanne stated in a deeply chilling tone, his powerful energy crackling and sparking in the air around the house. The pack was scattered in different rooms, but the Elders were in the living room watching a distraught Vanne pace in front of the main window. Alexa stood next to a grief-stricken Magnus pretending to give comfort, when in fact it was clear she was fascinated with not only Reuben but the Head of the Daylight Coven's husband.

"I nearly killed her," Vanne choked, coming to a stop to stare numbly at the floorboards. "When she told me about Marion ..." He shuddered, shaking his head. Intimidating though Vanne may be, Caia couldn't help but reach out to him in comfort. She squeezed his shoulder lightly, and he glanced down at her, his eyes terrifying and glassy with unshed tears. "I've always loved her best, you know," he whispered. "I courted her first before ..."

"Before I asked him to join me and break it off with Marion. To win Marita over instead so we could spy on her," Reuben answered for him, his voice dead. Caia glanced sharply at him, marveling at the hint of guilt and regret she saw in his eyes.

An ache spread in her chest for Vanne. For him to have loved Marion while he slept with her sister? To be so close to the day when he would no longer have to pretend ... and now the one person he wanted to share that day with was gone. Tears splashed over her lids and she sighed in frustration, turning her back to the room and swiping at them angrily. She couldn't act like a silly little girl. She had to be strong for them all.

She sucked in a deep breath and turned to face them. "Can you do what we asked? Can you go with Reuben to the MacLachlans?"

Vanne nodded. "I'm friends with Alistair. However ... it may take longer than just a few minutes to convince them. Phoebe is well educated on magik. She'll suspect I'm another magik using glamour to look like me. Such an incident happened at the Center only a few weeks ago," he reminded them, throwing Caia a look that managed to be sardonic despite his pain-filled eyes. He was referring to when Caia had glamoured Vil to look like Vanne to rescue Laila from the containment center. "Glamour lasts roughly thirty minutes. Phoebe knows that. So we're going to have to sit that time out until they're convinced I am who I say I am."

"That's fine. I imagine it will take longer to gather the family members of the Council who are willing to fight," Caia said.

"That reminds me—" Vanne tugged at something in the back pocket of his suit trousers. A white paper appeared in his hand and he gave it to Reuben. "A list of the family members who tried to get in and were fought off by our guards." He sneered. "Marita told them not to use deadly force … the idiots bought it, that holier-than-thou crap." His tone vibrated through her like an apprehensive shiver.

Knowing what she now knew didn't stop Caia from being disturbed by this version of Vanne. He was a mighty good actor. Every time she'd met with him and Marita inside the Center, she could've sworn he was a loyal husband and devout Daylight. Ignoring the impulse to gape at him as if he were nuts, Caia held out her hand to Reuben. "I'll take that."

He chuckled and threw her a flirtatious look, nibbling on his lip piercing. He took a moment before he handed over the paper. "Getting awfully bossy, aren't we?"

Ignoring him and the numerous frowns thrown his way by the Elders and a disgruntled Alexa—who had so far been trying to catch his attention (even imminent war couldn't stop her natural predilection for hooking up with the newest, hottest being around)—Caia quickly scanned the list. There were quite a number of names here.

"This should do, actually," she murmured, knowing

everyone could hear her anyway. She looked up as Jaeden entered the room with Vil and Laila. "Vil, we should go. Vanne's provided us with a list of names to give to Alfred Doukas's wife. She should be able to gather them to us pretty quickly."

Vil nodded but she noticed his hand tightening in Laila's. Before she could reassure them, Alexa stepped forward, a little pout she'd perfected years before playing on her luscious mouth. "I wanna help."

Caia, as well as everyone else, stared at her, dumbstruck.

"You ... want to help?" Ella queried, quietly disbelieving.

Alexa narrowed her eyes. "What, like I'm useless? I can fight, you know ... I have a sharper set of claws than any of the bitches in the pack."

Well, that I believe. An offer of help, however unexpected, wasn't something Caia was about to turn down. "OK. If you're sure ... Alexa, you can come with us to the portal. You can help us fight at the Center."

A shadow cast across the room as Alexa grinned excitedly at the thought. Standing in the doorway was Morgan with Malek, Morgan's dark eyes burning into Caia.

"If Alexa is going, I'm going," Malek puffed, crossing his arms over his large chest defiantly, smirking at his older sister.

Morgan whipped on him with a fierce growl. "You're not going anywhere." His next lip-curling comment was directed at Caia. "And neither is my daughter. You are not Alpha here, and you do not get to decide whether my underage children hit a battle zone for you!"

After years of perfecting a blank expression, Caia managed not to flinch under his outrage, but inside she felt dumb and guilty. "You're right. I'm sorry."

Before Alexa could mount what was clearly an oncoming

—and loud—protest, Reuben slid forward to face Morgan. Standing a few inches taller, and just as broad, the vampyre made his displeasure known in every nuance of his body language. "You don't speak to her with anything but respect, do you hear me?"

The older lykan was not intimidated one bit.

"Guys ..." Caia tried to intervene, glancing helplessly to Magnus and the Elders who watched in fascination. *Fricking lykans!* They just loved the show of dominance crap.

Morgan sneered, his eyes wandering over the vampyre in disgust. "And who the fuck are you to tell me how to talk to her?"

Ella gasped at the profanity and made to stand up, but Dimitri held her back. Caia glared at him but he shrugged as if to say, "Sorry, but I wanna see what happens."

Reuben took another step closer and Malek glanced nervously between his father and the outsider, wondering if he should step out of the way.

"I'm just a being that could tear you a new one in two seconds flat. But I can see I would actually have to do that to earn any respect from you. So why don't I remind you that Caia is your Alpha's mate and should be afforded the respect you're refusing me."

At that, Morgan lowered his eyes, and Caia knew Reuben had gotten to him. "You're right." He looked up and gave her a slight nod, his eyes dimmed but not defeated. "I'm sorry. But I can't have my children in this war, Caia."

"I understand," she replied softly. "I'm sorry I didn't speak to you about it first."

"Uh, hello!" Alexa called, taking a step closer to Reuben with a flirtatious shake of her hips. "I think, Daddy, you're forgetting one thing."

Morgan raised an unimpressed eyebrow at her.

"I'm an adult. I don't need your permission." She smiled up at Reuben. "I'm still in."

"You still live under my roof, so you will do as I say."

"No—"

Sensing a huge disagreement brewing, Caia stepped forward. "Alexa, your father is right. I don't think you've thought this through. You will be fighting to the death—and fighting magiks. The closest you've gotten to fighting is tussling with the pack."

She whirled on Caia so fast she almost gave Reuben whiplash with her long, thick hair. "I can't believe you of all people are trying to stop me."

Jaeden growled. "And what does that mean?"

"Can't she talk for herself?" Alexa cried, gesturing toward Caia. "Jeez, you've got so many champions, it's a wonder you need to fight at all. Speaking of which … *you* had no fighting experience when you went in after Ethan. And you let Jae take those guards on outside."

"Jaeden hunted with me for months before that and has become a proficient fighter," Reuben reminded them quietly. Jaeden began to smile at him in thanks and then seemed to remember at the last minute that she hated him.

"Arggh!" Alexa spun and glowered at her father. "Daddy, let me do this! I am fed up with being a useless pretty ornament … uh, one, by the way, who didn't even land the pack Alpha or Rogue Hunter!"

Wow, you had to admire her honesty. She didn't give a rat's ass who knew how shallow and ambitious she was.

"Oh dear goddess," a soft female voice entered from the hallway—Alexa's mother, Natalia. Alexa was the spitting image of her mother, and they could easily pass for sisters. The only difference being that Natalia wore her thick, dark hair cut short, and whereas Alexa's eyes were constantly spitting fire, there was a gentleness to Natalia's. At the moment, that gentleness was replaced with weary indignation. "Please don't tell me you want to go off on this suicide mission because you think it's the way to gain a mate?"

Malek snorted but Alexa shrugged, apparently not embarrassed that this conversation was occurring in front of not only the Elders but Reuben and Vanne. "It's not just that! Okay, maybe I thought about it … Caia and Jae have done pretty well for themselves, and they're not as pretty as me so I have to conclude that it's their willingness to fight—"

"An admirable quality but one that I don't want my daughter to share." Morgan sighed.

"But I do," Alexa whined. "Daddy, I feel useless and stupid. But Caia is giving us a chance to do something amazing … something important! This is bigger than finding a mate. This will, like, totally change everything."

They were all stunned by her sincerity. And as Caia watched Alexa plead with her father, she decided right there and then to start acting like a leader. This was a decision she was taking away from him. Alexa wanted to do this. She deserved the chance to show them all what she could do.

"Then you're in," Caia said quietly, and all eyes turned to her.

Alexa's were bright and for the first time, she threw Caia a genuine smile. "You really mean it?"

"I really mean it."

"No!" Morgan yelled. "I swear to you, Caia—"

Before Reuben could make that next unmistakable move toward him, Caia was across the room with a speed that surprised her as much as it did them. She stood in front of Reuben facing Morgan down, as much as she could at her diminutive height.

Caia scowled at him and used a little of her magik to force him back from her. She could tell by the widening of his eyes that he felt it. "Alexa wants to fight. She's a grown-up and it is her decision, not yours. And Reuben's right ... when Lucien and Ryder are absent, then the Elders and I are in charge. Last time I checked, you weren't either. The Elders have raised no concerns over Alexa's involvement so that leads me to believe they think she should be allowed to make up her own mind."

A rumble of grunts from the Elders confirmed that.

"I suggest you swallow that decision gracefully—"

Malek stepped forward, interrupting, "I wan—"

He snarled as Caia pushed him back but she was unimpressed. "Don't interrupt. Your father said no. You're still underage, Mal."

Morgan looked as if he wanted to strangle someone. "You'll understand when you have your own children, Caia."

She sighed, trying desperately to hold on to the hard-ass act. "Morgan, if I don't get enough people to help me fight Marita ... we won't have a future, let alone the possibility of little Caias and Luciens running around underfoot."

He gazed at her in strained silence and then nodded curtly before leaving the room with his arm around his wife. Malek followed in their wake, disgruntled mumblings trailing him.

Caia turned to face the room. "I feel like I've been run over."

"You handled that like a leader." Reuben nodded, and she could've sworn there was pride in his eyes. Vanne looked sad, and Caia knew he was thinking about Marion. The Elders were a little shell-shocked, but Jae, like Reuben, smiled smugly.

"You kicked ass."

She felt a hand on her arm and looked up to see Alexa smirking. "Thanks. I mean it. I'm totally pumped to do this."

Caia glanced over Alexa's long nails and saw her as a

lykan, a strong, lithe black wolf with powerful form. "I have no doubt you can take care of yourself."

Vanne coughed, drawing back their wandering attention. "As interesting as this little window into pack life has been, I do suggest we get a move on."

with powerful form. I have
ame of you.

having back their whimpering amad[...]
window and pick it up has been
[...]

CHAPTER 9

GAME ON

*T*his was it. Caia glanced around at everyone gathered outside Magic Fitness. She couldn't believe who had turned up to pull through for this coup. Phoebe MacLachlan stood hands akimbo, muttering instructions to three burly male MacLachlans whose faces were pinched with concentration. Alfred Doukas's eldest son gathered with nine other representatives of the Council's families, all ready to take on Marita and her soldiers. Their fury crackled around them like the sky before a lightning storm.

As for Pack Errante, Caia had Magnus, Alexa, Jaeden, Christian, Lucia, Aidan, and Irini. The others had been left behind under the protection of Ella, Dimitri, and Morgan. As for Vil and Laila, Caia had sent them both back to hide out at Ryder's apartment. Reuben and Vanne stood off to the side with their heads together, and Caia watched them suspiciously.

"Something we need to know, boys?" she asked in irritation.

"No." Reuben shook his head. "Just going over the plan one more time."

"Everyone knows the plan. You create a distraction in the reception area while Jaeden and I head toward the containment center. You follow when you get the chance. Lykans use their noses to follow our trail, magiks use the lykans to follow their trail. Okay?" She looked around, waiting for a nod of agreement from all.

The magiks from the Council members' families stared at her in awe, and she could tell they were thinking, "Who the hell is this kid?" Nothing for it now, though. They had agreed to this.

"OK. Let's get off this street before someone calls the cops," she cracked. It was dark and there was no one around. She hoped. Caia turned back to the door and used her magik to pop the lock. Like quiet mice in a churchyard, they all made their way inside and followed her to the room with the portal.

"Lykans."

All except Jaeden began the change, magiks and everyone else looking discreetly away as they undressed and underwent the bone-cracking transformation from human to wolf. After what seemed like forever, the last of them finished.

"Vanne." She turned to find him. He brushed his way forward with Reuben. They had decided it would be best if he and the vampyre went first because no one would attack Vanne, giving them the element of surprise when the others arrived at their backs.

With that, he put his hand to the glass, and it shimmered and congealed, turning into what looked like liquid mercury. Without another word, he disappeared into it with Reuben holding on to his shoulder. Once they were through, the glass resolidified. Ignoring the flurry of butterflies in her stomach

—and the fact she may be sending these people to their deaths—Caia placed her own hand on the glass and reopened the portal. When it was ready, she ushered them all through.

At last it was just her and Jaeden.

"You ready, Cy?" Jae whispered, her usually tan face pale with fear.

She shook her head numbly at her friend and clasped Jae's hand tight. "Nope. We've got to be brave, though."

"I will if you will."

They both drew in a huge, shaky gulp of air and stepped into the mirror. She barely had time to get used to the feeling of traveling by portal when the shouts and screams hit her ears. On instinct she dropped to the ground, pulling Jaeden with her, and a blast of power flew over their heads and splintered the wall at their backs.

Heart pounding, Caia looked up to see the Center's reception area was already a battleground. Lykans were in the middle of chewing up magiks, battling it out with lykans from the Center and bouncing off protective shields. Water, fire, and earth exploded everywhere, mixing with blood and the pressure in the atmosphere created by air magik. She swung her gaze around to see their way out of the reception was blocked by two magiks fighting off a lykan.

"Reuben!" Caia yelled to the vampyre. He was choking the life out of a younger vamp as if he were merely a rabbit caught in a trap. He grunted in question as he shook the boy and let him drop. She indicated the blocked pathway, and he nodded. His body was a blur as he crossed the room and shot his entire weight into one of the magiks. The warlock barely had time to scream as his body flew backward into the wall with such force, the brickwork cracked around him. He stuck there almost comically for a minute before collapsing to the ground. Reuben said something to a lykan—Alexa, it seemed—and she tore off after the injured magik to finish him off.

"Jeez, I never knew he could move that fast. The son of a bitch never moved that fast, not once when we were out hunting," Jae whispered loudly in her ear.

Caia smirked. She wasn't surprised Reuben had been careful to keep quiet about how powerful he really was. It was probably one of the many reasons he'd lived as long as he had. She waited and readied herself as he took the other magik in hand. "OK, you ready? We have to move quick."

Jae braced herself like an Olympic sprinter and gave a determined nod.

"Go!" Caia yelled, and off they shot, dodging fighting supernaturals and trying to ignore the howls and snarls and screams, praying that their side were the ones winning.

They never slowed, even as they made it out of the reception and into the quieter corridors.

"The elevator," Caia puffed, already feeling the burn in her legs.

They'd almost made it when, out of nowhere, a tall, broad-shouldered vampyre rushed around the corner, his lips drawn back so they could see his lengthened fangs. He swooped on Caia but Jaeden was already in front of her, unsheathing a steel ax from a belt she'd strapped to her hip. Caia watched in awe as Jae ducked the vampyre's punch and jumped over his side swipe, smashing her elbow into his face in the same motion. Dazed, he staggered back, allowing Jae a few more punches, including an uppercut that sent blood spraying from the vampyre's nose.

Caia was sure Jae was about to be declared the winner when, with a terrifying hiss, the vamp blocked another of her punches and grabbed her arm, twisting it behind her back to secure her in a chokehold. Caia didn't even have time to aid her before Jaeden used her telekinesis to thrust him from her and pin him to the wall. She was on him in a second, slicing the blade of her ax into his neck with such force, it tore through his skin and bones and lodged into the wall behind him. His head rolled off his body and onto the floor before bouncing to a stop.

Blood and all sorts of nastiness oozed out of the top of his decapitated corpse. A sudden need to vomit overwhelmed Caia. She was never going to get used to the violent art of decapitation.

Jaeden meanwhile whistled as she cleaned off her ax on the vamp's leather duster and slid it back into place on her belt. She smiled brightly at Caia and headed toward the elevator. Caia followed, glancing back at the dead vampyre in revulsion as his headless body fell forward. She hit the button on the elevator and turned to her friend. "You are way too comfortable with what you just did."

Jaeden shrugged. "Vampyre Hunter, remember."

"Uh, bringing up your foray into illegal activities is not reassuring."

They stepped into the elevator and while Caia pressed the button that led to the containment center, Jae grinned. "You are too sensitive, Cy. You need to just shut down and get the job done. I thought you'd have done this stuff before."

"Yeah, but ..."

"But what?"

"You were like ... really good at it. You know, quick, efficient. And you seemed to ... I don't know ... like it."

She shrugged, wiping the sweat from her forehead. "It's kind of exciting."

Caia snorted. "Yeah. Well, I'm sure it'll still be exciting in ten years' time."

Disgust and horror crossed her friend's features. "You think we'll still be doing this in ten years?"

"This or something like it, according to Reuben."

"What the hell do you mean?"

"Apparently we've all been naive to think I'm somehow going to end a two-thousand-year-old war in a year."

Jaeden grunted. "When you put it like that ..."

"I know, I know. He's right. I'm an idiot."

"We're all idiots. Let's just get through this and worry about tomorrow, tomorrow."

The elevator binged and the doors slowly slid open. Caia moved to step out and looked up.

Her cheeks flooded with heat; her entire body froze. *Oh, holy Artemis.* Now they were in for it.

Without another thought, Caia shoved Jaeden back into the corner of the elevator, jumped out of it, and hit the button to send her back up.

"CY, NO!" Jaeden screamed at her in outrage as the elevator slammed shut, leaving Caia to face Marita and the five magiks before her by herself. They had positioned themselves in the reception hall of the containment center, the center itself locked tight behind them. There was no way she was getting into it unless she went through these guys first.

Marita's face twisted with an amalgamation of emotions. Grief, hatred, disbelief ... more hatred.

Caia's mind raced with some way to stall, counting on conversation to save her somehow. But it seemed Marita was all out of conversation. Before she could protect herself, a blast of power sent her rocketing back into the elevator doors, her head jarring off the steel with a sickening sharpness that shot all the way down her spine and into her toes.

She crumpled toward the ground and hadn't even made it there before she felt the world spin, the air rushing through her hair and skin as she was thrown across the room, her feet brushing the ceiling before the energy released her and she dropped like a dead weight, smacking into the floor with enough force to ricochet her chin off the ground. With the impact, the air rushed out of her lungs and she clawed at the floor in panic, desperately trying to pull in oxygen. Ignoring the throbbing of her chin and the blood that trickled out of her mouth, Caia spat a tooth out and wheezed. Through a curtain of her hair, she saw the magiks approach.

"Have at her," Marita said softly. "Make it slow."

Fire erupted along her arms and legs, the flames licking her skin, the agonizing pain of her crackling flesh like nothing she'd ever experienced before. Caia screamed in release, tears streaking her face, the vomit-inducing smell clogging her nostrils. And then the water filled her lungs and she couldn't breathe, couldn't scream, could only writhe in unimaginable torture. Oh goddess, she couldn't think. She needed to think!

"CAIA!" She heard Jaeden distantly and her heart almost stopped. No! She wouldn't be stupid enough to come down here! She twisted in an effort to catch sight of her friend and then watched her in utter amazement. Jaeden stood like an Amazon, rage mottling her pretty features.

Before Marita and the magiks had time to blink, they were thrown back by Jaeden's telekinesis. Their magik ceased the attack on Caia as they themselves collided with hurricane force against the containment center entry doors, buckling the metal. And before they could get to their feet, five lykans shot out of the elevator, their muzzles pulled back, some covered with blood and gore.

They looked ferocious and feral ... and ready to rip Marita apart. With a howl from the leader who Caia joyously recognized as Phoebe, they tore after the magiks. Marita's eyes widened in shock as Phoebe headed directly for her. But the lykan didn't get within an inch of her. With one last look of determined retribution, Marita disappeared before their eyes. Three of the other magiks followed, but two of the females weren't quick enough and the lykans converged on them as a pack.

"Caia!" Jaeden ran to her as she tried to get up. Jae grabbed her arm, and the pain set off another stream of screams and curses.

"I'm sorry, I'm sorry … oh gods, look what they've done. Oh, Cy …" Her eyes swept helplessly over her friend.

Jeez, she must look a mess, she thought wearily.

"It's fine," Caia croaked, her throat rough from the recent asphyxiation. "Just give me a minute." One of the lykans parted from the pack, her fur a beautiful raven black. She was a smaller version of Lucien in wolf form, except for the streak of silver that ran from between her eyes to the tip of her black shiny nose. She whined as she approached Caia and stopped to nuzzle her face before licking her cheek.

"I'm okay." Caia stroked the lykan's head. "I'm okay, Irini. Really. Thanks for the help."

The bing of the elevator doors startled them all, and they spun to face the next enemy, Jaeden's hand braced in front of her, ready to use her telekinesis once more. A surge of pride ran through Caia. Jae was getting good at controlling her powers.

Her pulse slowed when Reuben stepped out, followed by Vanne and a couple of the Council members' families. Reuben's eyes narrowed as he took in the scene and then darkened with a menacing disquiet on Caia's near-prone form. He strode toward her, brushing past Jaeden rudely.

"What happened?" he asked softly, dropping to his haunches beside her, his eyes taking in her injuries.

"I'm fine." She shook him off, unnerved by his concern. "I just need a minute."

He nodded tautly and stood to face Jaeden. Caia couldn't see his expression, but Jaeden tensed—it couldn't be good.

"Where were you?" he said, his voice low with anger.

Jae's jaw dropped. "Where was I—"

"Hey!" Caia yelled weakly at him. "It's not her fault. I shoved her back into the elevator and stupidly took on Marita and the others by myself."

The vampyre rolled his eyes at her. "Acting the hero is going to get you killed."

Annoyed at his proprietary tone, Caia drew up all her energy and stretched onto all fours. She curled her lip at him. "Don't worry, vampyre, I'm not going to get myself killed and ruin all your plans."

"Caia—"

But she wasn't listening to him anymore. She pushed the change and a flow of beautiful, warm energy rushed through her body, soothing her aches. She gave a bark of jagged pain as a rib sealed back into place. She hadn't even known one had cracked. As her muzzle grew out from her nose and her head morphed into wolf, her ears kicking back with the shock of how fast it was, Caia felt a new tooth grow in where the other had come out. Her wolf eyes watered a little, but she was reassured by the fact that she wouldn't have to glamour a new tooth and that her burns and blisters would heal enough to leave her with only red marks. Her skin would be a little sensitive, but at least she wouldn't be in agony.

When she was sure her wolf had healed her as much as it could, Caia changed back, magikally clothing herself in well-worn jeans and a black T-shirt. Jaeden was by her side in an instant, helping her to her feet.

"You okay?" she asked anxiously.

Caia could curse Reuben for making the girl feel bad. "I'm good, thanks." She turned to her waiting comrades and then glanced at the containment center door. Lucien was right on the other side. Her heart flipped at the thought of seeing him. Goddess, it had felt like forever. "Let's just get everyone out."

Vanne strode by the lykans still standing around their kills. He threw the magiks a quick glance and seemed to shake his head in pity, muttering under his breath. Even from a distance, Caia could make out the words with her lykan ears. She wouldn't repeat them. They were kind of foul ... something about Marita and Hades ... with a lot of bad words thrown in.

He nearly ripped the containment center door off its hinges, and Caia rushed to follow him inside.

She was so distracted by the thought of finding Lucien, she was barely aware of Vanne's heartfelt curse before he ducked in front of her. She soon realized why: he was avoiding the huge lykan that flew at him. Instead it landed square on Caia's chest, sending her crashing into Jaeden who'd been right on her heels. Jaeden stumbled and fell to the floor, taking Caia and the lykan with her.

Caia ducked the lykan's ferocious wide jaws as it lunged for her face and then screamed as its teeth clamped around her shoulder and tore into her skin. She felt it rip through muscle and bone, and the nausea sent her head lolling back, black spots floating in front of her eyes.

The wolf's teeth were abruptly gone and its heavy weight collapsed fully on her. A warm, thick liquid soaked her stomach and ran down her hips and legs. She blinked, trying to clear her eyes.

"Cy? Cy, you alright?"

Was that Jaeden? She felt a tangle of limbs underneath her, and her vision cleared. Jaeden's blade was lodged deeply into the lykan's belly as it lay across her. It wasn't dead. It was whining and trying to move, snarling and snapping at Caia's face. She thanked the gods it couldn't reach. Before she could panic at the thought of getting out from under it without being torn into again, its weight was lifted off her.

Reuben. Her eyes widened in awe even as her shoulder

flamed with pain. Reuben held the wolf with one hand clamped around its thick neck, his lips drawn back in a matching snarl, his fangs the only thing she could see. And then he squeezed, and the most horrific crunching, squishing sound could be heard as he crushed its neck in his bare hand. The lykan's body went limp, and Reuben promptly let the dead beast drop to the ground.

Once the initial shock wore off, Caia tried to move so Jae could get out from under her.

"ARRRGGGH!" she screamed. Her shoulder felt like it was about to detach from her body.

"Ssh, ssh, Cy," Jae whispered in her ear. "Don't move. Oh Gaia, don't move. Your shoulder, crap—"

"Jaeden, please refrain from making her panic," Reuben snapped and moved around to the back of them. "I'm going to slide you gently from under Caia. Before I do so, are you hurt?"

"Like you give a crap."

"Jaeden!" he warned.

"No! I'm fine, all right, I'm fine. Just … help."

Tears streamed down Caia's cheeks as her shoulder throbbed with each movement underneath her, but she was proud of herself for not screaming out loud again. That was until Jaeden's feet slid out from under her, and Caia hit the ground with a jolt. The blinding, white pain induced an earth-shattering scream.

"CAIA!" The roar of rage came from Lucien.

"Oh gods," she whimpered. "Someone better go tell him I'm all right."

Jaeden's face hovered over her. It was ashen as she glanced from Caia's face to her wound. "Vanne's doing that. He fought the magik who runs the center. It wasn't much of a fight. He's got her unlocking the Council members and then they'll get Lucien and Ryder out."

The thought of Lucien finding her like this sent her heart thudding. "No, no, no. Help me up." She grabbed hold of Jaeden's collar, choking the girl down toward her. "He can't see me like this. I have to change."

Jae gently unpeeled her fingers and abruptly Caia's panic took over at the pinched look on her face. "What?"

"Cy, you can't change." Jae shook her head. "There's ..." She gestured vaguely to her shoulder with a look of horror. "There's too much damage—no, don't look!" She grabbed Caia's chin and turned it away.

Too much damage. All of a sudden, she was scared. As scared as she was the night the daemon had ripped her belly open. She felt her breathing pick up and was sure she was about to hyperventilate.

"Caia ..." Now Jaeden looked panicked. She was knocked out of the way by an irritated Reuben. He grasped Caia's face in his cold fingers.

"Caia, look at me." His black eyes took hold of hers, and she felt herself inextricably pulled into them. She actually felt her whole body diving languidly into those black pools and swimming right alongside him somewhere warm and sparkling. "Good, Caia. You're going to be fine. We just need to get you bandaged up before you can change."

She felt herself nodding, but the truth was, she didn't care about her shoulder anymore.

Swimming with Reuben was nice.

CHAPTER 10

THE FEAR THAT FEEDS ON LOVE

*A*n unshakable rage poured out of Lucien's pores like smoke. A pale-faced Ryder watched him warily as they listened for the next noise from outside their cell. The sound of a faint commotion had been going on for a while—they'd already heard a door crash open and the growl of a lykan. Then a girl screamed, and Lucien and Ryder had looked at each other in horrified surprise. *Was that Caia?* And then the female magik who guarded them shot past their cell, her face readied for battle. It had barely been two seconds before her body flew past the cell again, followed by a bristling Vanne.

The girl screamed again, and they heard Jaeden's voice. Ryder forgot himself and rushed toward the Plexiglas. Lucien grabbed him just in time, but he hadn't let go of his shirt, his fist clenched in anxiety around the material. A howl of agony shook his last vestige of control.

"CAIA!" he roared, and then it was Ryder who was pushing *him* back, having a difficult time of it too. Lucien didn't care; he had to get to her, no matter what. He shoved

Ryder off and strode to the cell door but the idiot was on him again. They started grappling.

"Stop it," a cool voice commanded, and they both whipped around to see Vanne. He clutched a terrified guard.

"What is going on?" Lucien spat.

"We're taking the Center back. Marita has flown the nest." His dead eyes sparked with hatred.

Lucien put aside enough of his worry to ask, "You're in on this?"

He nodded stiffly and pushed the magik against the Plexiglas. "Blair, free them."

As Blair worked, Vanne looked back up at Lucien and Ryder. "I've been working against Marita for a long time. Everything will be explained to you later."

"Caia?" Lucien asked anxiously.

Vanne nodded. "She'll be fine, but she's badly hurt."

The energy on the Plexiglas buzzed like a broken fluorescent light and then disappeared. Blair's fingers shook as she hurried to open the door with a swipe card. As soon as it sprang open, Lucien rushed past and turned to his right. A large crowd was gathered at the entryway surrounding something ... or someone.

"The Council and their families," Vanne explained the crowd as he strode past him, still holding on to the witch. "Now we need to rescue the children from the labs."

Lucien wasn't even listening. Ryder gripped his shoulder in comfort and the two of them took off after Vanne.

"Ladies and gentlemen, you are needed upstairs where you can bring that riot back under control. Penelope, we would be grateful for your help with Caia once you're done."

She nodded, throwing Caia a sympathetic look.

"Marita is gone, then?" one of the Council members asked.

Marita's husband—ex-husband?—nodded and ushered

them all quickly out of the door. The sight they left sent Lucien's heart plummeting to his stomach. His sister, in wolf form, sat rigidly, her eyes glued to Reuben who hovered over someone lying on the floor.

"Ryder!" Jaeden flew from her crouched position and launched herself into Ryder's arms. Lucien brushed past them as they kissed, and his nose told him what he had feared.

"What the fu—" He grabbed hold of the vampyre and dragged him out of the way. Reuben hissed at being manhandled but stood back, allowing him access.

Caia lay on the ground, her T-shirt and jeans soaked with blood—his nose told him it wasn't hers, thank the gods—but as his eyes swept the rest of her, his stomach flipped. Her shoulder had been turned into a chew toy. Bone and muscle clearly visible. Blood, her blood, spread on the floor around her. His eyes met hers. She smiled. She actually smiled. "Lucien."

He dropped to his knees and grabbed her hand in his. "Holy—" he choked. She was so pale. "I can't leave you alone for a second."

She made to shake her head but hissed in pain at the movement. "Nope. I guess you can't." And then she grinned at him again. "I missed you."

"I missed you too," he whispered hoarsely. And although she was wounded, he was so glad she was here, that nothing fatally bad had happened to her. He desperately wanted to know where she'd disappeared to. Why was Vanne working for them? What did Reuben have to do with it all? But instead, he croaked, "I love you."

"Love you too."

He whipped around to look at the vampyre. "What's happening? Can we get her up?"

Reuben nodded. "I had her under mesmerism. It stops her

from feeling the pain. I'll need to be the one to take her up to the infirmary so I can hold her mesmerized."

The thought of some other guy's arm around Caia sent his back up. "No," he growled.

"Lucien," Jaeden snapped, unlocking herself from Ryder's embrace. "Let him take her to the frickin' infirmary or I'll stab *you* next."

He raised an eyebrow at her. Had everybody completely forgotten he was Alpha? "What did you say?" he asked quietly, dangerously. Sudden realization dawned on her face, and Jaeden curled back into Ryder protectively.

His friend eased closer. "Come on," Ryder pleaded. "Just let the guy do this. If you carry her, her shoulder will hurt the whole way."

Lucien glanced back at Caia. She'd gotten even paler. "Please," she whispered weakly.

That was all it took. He nodded jerkily and let Reuben take the reins.

* * *

LUCIEN CONCENTRATED on watching the gentle rise and fall of Caia's chest. He sighed. He was never going to get used to this feeling. Even when she was right there in front of him, he worried about her. Her lids fluttered in her sleep, and he hoped to the gods she wasn't having nightmares. What she needed right now was a dreamless sleep to help heal the shoulder that had been ripped open.

At present, she was lying beside him in a huge bed in one of the suites a council member used while she stayed at the Center. Penelope Argyros. She was a kind woman and seemed fond of Caia. Vanne had brought the magik straight to the infirmary, and she'd used some herbs and magik to seal Caia's wound. She had then insisted they use her suite while the Council and Vanne brought the Center to order.

While Caia was being treated, Lucien questioned Vanne on what the hell was going on. He now knew all about Reuben—the slick bastard—and how Vanne and Saffron had been working for the vampyre all these years. Vanne had been placed as Marita's husband. He had done his duty. He hadn't loved Marita, but he'd respected and admired her. Then the years passed and he'd grown to dislike the secretive, pretentious, callous shrew she was turning into. After discovering what she'd been planning with the labs, and especially now that Marion was dead, Lucien could see hatred for the Head of the Coven blazing in Vanne's eyes.

The warlock had gone on to tell Lucien about persuading Alistair MacLachlan of the truth, how they'd had to wait thirty minutes before they believed it was really Vanne in their home telling them that Marita was experimenting upon lykan and vampyre children, and that she had imprisoned the Council. After that, it had been pretty easy to persuade them to rescue the Council and the kids. According to Caia, Vanne said the Council members' families didn't need persuading. They were waiting for them at the gymnasium when they arrived.

Lucien shook his head. This time last year, he'd thought his biggest worry was what Caia and Irini's return was going to do to his pack. With Caia being part Midnight, he hadn't known whether she would be dangerous to them all. A troublemaker? And then there was the thought of being tied to someone you didn't know for the rest of your life. Never in a million years would he have suspected that Caia's arrival would turn his entire world upside down, the Daylight and Midnight Covens now sharing the same purpose: to see the Head of the Daylight Coven destroyed. He sighed again.

Crap, all he ever did these days was cock his head and sigh wearily.

He brushed Caia's hair back her face and thanked the gods she was still here. Every day his gut twisted with panic that today might be the last day he ever saw her again.

"Stupid son of a bitch," he whispered. Why couldn't he have fallen in love with someone simple and uncomplicated? Someone like Rose—Rose who had joined his pack in the fight without question when she saw Phoebe fighting off a vampyre from the Center.

But it wasn't Rose who ran through his veins as if she were part of his blood.

"Why are you a stupid son of a bitch?" Caia mumbled. He smiled as her eyes fluttered open.

"Hey, you," he whispered back and leaned over to press a soft kiss on her lips. She smelled like Caia, damp earth of the wolf and the vanilla scent of a magik.

"My shoulder feels better." She twisted to have a look at it. She wore a nightdress, as the clothes she'd been wearing were so drenched in blood, one of the witches had insisted on incinerating them with her fire magik. Her shoulder was in one piece again, although the scar was still healing. "Hmm, nice ... dress."

She wrinkled her nose, and Lucien chuckled. Getting Caia into anything remotely feminine was like asking the moon to be the sun. In fact, this was probably only the third time he'd seen her in something that wasn't jeans or shorts.

"I like it," he purred, tugging at one of the straps.

She laughed and reached up for him, her lithe arms wrapping around his neck and pulling him down to her. He went more than willingly, cuddling her into him and breathing deeply of her, reassuring him she was okay.

"I was so worried about you," she whispered in his ear,

and he felt himself laughing. "What?" she asked, pulling back, a cute frown wrinkling the bridge of her nose.

"You were worried about me?" He shook her gently. "Of the two of us, who disappeared from whom? And who had her shoulder ripped open? Oh, and I heard about Marita's attack." His voice rose as he continued on. "Apparently you were set on fire and drowned from the inside out?" He knew his tone would annoy her and wasn't surprised when she wriggled out of his hold and eased herself into a sitting position. She was so easy to read. She hated being vulnerable to anyone, and it bothered her that she was with him.

"Lucien, do I have to remind you that this is a war? I'm going to get hurt now and then."

He shrugged and turned away. "I'm just saying it would be nice for once to be waking up in bed next to you for a reason other than you having just come under attack."

"We have ... you know ..." She blushed, and he struggled not to smile. "You know ... there have been times—" She stopped, watching his expression, her eyes narrowing as realization dawned on her. "You enjoy tormenting me, don't you?"

"I've just never met a lykan as shy about sex as you, that's all." He smiled and then gave a bark of laughter as her expression turned mulish.

"That's what every woman wants to hear. My boyfriend finds me amusing in bed ... not sexy ... amusing. Shy? Wow. Hot."

All this talk of sex ... He took a deep breath, trying to regain some control. But he leaned into her anyway, his lips inches from hers. "Your mate," he corrected her hoarsely. "Not boyfriend. *Mate*. And I find your shyness refreshing. I find it even more so when it completely goes out the window when you're in *my* bed."

He felt her breath shudder against his lips, and that was it.

His control snapped. Her hair slipped through his fingers as he clasped a hand behind her head and pressed her mouth to his gently. She groaned and kissed him back, and when he felt her tongue against his own, he growled, kissing her harder.

"Lucien," she whimpered against his lips, and he knew what she wanted. He held her face between his hands, gazing into huge eyes that were, at the moment, glazed with lust.

He trembled with indecision. And then an eruption of laughter from the other side of the door brought him back to reality.

"We can't." He shuddered and pulled back. "You need to rest that shoulder ... and we have company."

She gazed at the door, a moue of disappointment touching her lips. "I hear that." And then her eyes widened. "For Gaia's sake! I didn't even ask what happened. The Center?"

CHAPTER 11

TRIGGER

*J*aeden snuggled deeper into Ryder on the sofa, breathing him in deeply. She felt his arm tighten around her but his gaze never left the television. They were *Harry Potter and the Half-Blood Prince*, and the boy wizard was presently pissing off Jim Broadbent's character.

"Badly done, Harry," Magnus muttered, and Jae hid a snicker in Ryder's chest. He felt it and squeezed her. He was telling her to quit it. You did not make fun of Magnus when he was watching the *Harry Potter* movies.

"Do you think Caia is awake?" Rose asked from her spot on the other sofa next to Alexa.

"Ssh," Magnus hushed without looking at her. Jaeden, however, turned to look at her sharply, her gaze narrowing on the wolf. Jaeden knew from what Caia had told her, Rose was Lucien's ex-girlfriend. The lykan was watching the double doors to the bedroom and had been ever since Lucien had closed them behind himself and Caia. Jae did not like the possessive look in Rose's eyes when she watched Lucien … and she watched him *all* the time.

When the fighting had stopped, Rose made her way to the

infirmary to see Lucien. Jaeden had watched her face when she realized Lucien and Caia were no longer ignoring their mating. Hatred for an unconscious Caia seared in her eyes. But no one else seemed to notice, Jae mused. Hmm, didn't matter. She noticed. And she was going to be sure to keep an eye on Rose from now on.

She thought about the state of the Center outside of this suite. The Council had been amazing. They'd taken control in a matter of minutes, their combined power washing over the Center and stopping everyone in their tracks. They ordered everyone into one of the large reception halls and explained the truth about Marita and the labs downstairs. When Christian and Lucia, along with a couple of magiks, came out of the altar with the kids in question, the supernaturals could smell the truth in the air and see it on the faces of the traumatized children. Those supernaturals who wished to leave were asked to do so; those who trusted the Council could remain and help place protective spells around the Center to keep Marita out.

After the revelations about the labs, though, there were only a few who left. Unfortunately, the kids had to stay to answer the Council's questions so they could uncover exactly what had been done to them, especially since the lab techs had fled at the first sign of trouble. The children's families were being brought in, however, to be with them during the questioning.

As for the Pack Errante kids in Christian and Lucia's charge, Alfred promised to question them that night so they could return with the pack in the morning. Jaela was too young to be questioned. Thank goddess. Jaeden had been relieved to feel little Jaela in her arms. Jae had cried and blubbered over her family for a minute before the events of the last few days seemed to be forgotten. Thankfully, Jaela was young enough for this to become a distant memory.

A lump of anguish lodged in Jae's throat as she thought of Sunday, Ivan, and Kerianna. Unfortunately, she couldn't say the same for them. It was going to take them some time to get over what they'd endured. *Damn it*. She tensed, and Ryder turned to look at her sharply. She shook her head and rested it against his shoulder again. She was just so mad. They were too young! They shouldn't have had to go through what she had! And thank the gods it had only been a mild version of it.

The day they hunted Marita would be the day Jaeden took a turn tearing into her. The witch was going down! Because of her, they had traumatized kids on their hands. One of the MacLachlans had been killed alongside two of the Council's family members fighting with them. Word had also reached them that Desi, one of the Travelers who Caia had befriended, was injured fighting on their side. Jae's own brother had been wounded, but he'd changed and healed himself. It hadn't stopped Lucia fluttering around him and Jaela like an overcaffeinated mother hen.

Jae glanced at Alexa who watched TV, brooding. She'd had quite an eye-opener today. Alexa had a tough fight with another lykan, and Jae could see her wince every time she shifted in her seat. Over all, though, to their surprise and smug delight, their side had managed to take down a number of the coven who'd fought against them. According to Phoebe, two of them had been Michael Brown, the head of the Third Unit (Vampyre division) and Lyla Thomson, the head of the Second Unit (Lykan division). Ironically, Michael had fought by Caia's side just weeks before. They were powerful enemies to have, but thankfully the two of them, like good soldiers, stood down under the Council's orders.

The atmosphere in the Center was horrible, full of anxiety and fear and hostility. But the Council were competent and altogether more powerful than Marita, now that she didn't have any goons working for her. Well, except for the group of magiks who left the Center when she did. According to Alfred Doukas, she had perhaps ten magiks with her at the moment, but with the trace magik, it would be easy for her to find more followers. They had to move fast. At this very moment, they were trying to figure out her most likely hiding place and putting together a plan to capture her.

Jaeden rubbed at the tension headache in her temple. Ryder made a noise above her and then he was pulling her hand away from her head, replacing it with strong fingers that pressed soothingly against her forehead, making gentle circles. She sighed happily and relaxed into him.

"You'll have me drooling in a minute," she whispered so as not to disturb Magnus.

He leaned down, his lips brushing against her ear, sending a shiver of delight throughout her entire body. "I'd like to be doing more to you than that in a minute."

She grinned. There were lykans in the room. Lykan hearing. Magnus snorted. Yup, he'd heard them.

"Ryder," she admonished him lazily, but that didn't stop her hand from inching over his thigh.

He jumped under her touch and then growled, "Right." He grabbed her hand, pulling her up from her seat, his hazel gaze light with passion. Clearly he was intending to take her somewhere private to ravish her! *Hell yeah!* They had missed their wedding night, after all, and Ryder, the perpetual gentleman, hadn't wanted to make love to her until she was his mate for real. She'd been waiting for this night forever.

The door behind them cracked open, stopping them in their tracks. Caia appeared, her arm wrapped around Lucien's waist. In normal circumstances she was tiny next to the giant that was Lucien, but there was a strength to Caia that made you forget her stature. Now, however, after the beating she'd taken today, she looked fragile and so small. Jae felt a rush of protectiveness at the sight of her and tried to forget what it had been like to see Marita and the others torturing her.

"Hey, guys." She smiled brightly, and Jaeden grinned, happy to see her friend's eyes sparkling. Being with your mate tended to have that effect on you. It was kind of annoying, she grunted, determined to remember she was an independent woman.

"Lucien." Rose half stood and Jaeden frowned at her.

Lucien nodded gently but didn't leave Caia's side as he said, "Thanks for all your help today, Rose."

She smiled warmly at him, lighting up under his praise. "No problem. Of course. Anything to help."

Jaeden snorted and then bit back a cry of pain when Ryder pinched her. Instead she threw Caia and Lucien a sly smile. "You were in there awhile." She wriggled her eyebrows suggestively. Caia blushed, making Jaeden laugh. "Jeez, I was kidding … but if we're to go by those red, red cheeks of yours, clearly I was on the mark."

The grit of Cy's teeth told her she was probably bugging her, but the look on Rose's face was worth it. There was nothing wrong with hitting home to the delusional woman that Lucien was no longer on the market. And she knew Caia would never be underhanded or mean to Rose, so it was up to Jae to do that for her!

"Hey, I have a question, if you're feeling better, Caia?" Alexa asked.

Jaeden wasn't buying the tone. Something *not good* was about to come from Miss World's Bitch Division Crown Champion. Caia nodded, probably too weary to be on alert. Jaeden tensed, waiting.

"So." Alexa turned toward Cy. "How come you let Marita beat the living crap out of you?"

"Ale—" Lucien began, but Caia held up her hand to cut him off.

She frowned at the other female. "What do you mean?"

"Well." Alexa shrugged. "I wasn't there, but according to the good folks in this room who were, you turned Ethan's insides into kitchen décor last time you were faced by an all-powerful magik. Uh, I've heard stories that you took out four magiks in one go just a few weeks ago. All I'm saying is, how come you sucked ass *today*?"

Jaeden was right. "You're a bitch," she snapped.

Alexa exhaled. "Uh, hello, where have you been?"

"Jaeden's right." Ryder shook his head in disgust at her. "You always have something unpleasant to add to an already bad situation."

Ah, that was her man ... always a gentleman even when he traded insults. She patted his arm affectionately and then glanced up to see her Alpha's reaction. Clearly he was biting back a retort cuffed by Caia's nails digging into his arm.

"You're right, I don't know why I sucked ass today."

"Tut-tut," a new voice entered the room, and they turned to watch Reuben swagger in. "I was waiting on that answer with bated breath." He shook his head. "It was a letdown."

Ugh. Soulless fiend. Cheating, lying son of a bitch. A son of a bitch who'd used mesmerism on her to make her leave her own pack! Why was she the only one who saw how messed up that was? And to think she had defended him to Ryder.

"Did I mention you were right about this douche bag?" she huffed, turning to her mate.

He smiled sympathetically. "I heard."

"Still angry, Jaeden?" Reuben smiled too sweetly, holding a hand to his heart. "That's nice. I guess our friendship meant something after all."

Ryder snarled. Jae grinned but threw him a "down, boy" look.

"Anyhoo." Reuben smirked and looked back at Caia. "I can answer Alexa's question, no problem."

Caia perked up at his regard, and Jaeden sighed inwardly. Caia actually trusted this jerk, even after he'd lied through his abnormally elongated teeth the entire time Jae had known him. And he was *good*. He'd had her completely fooled. Did the others know about him? Did Lily and Styx know they were living it up with a twenty-four-hundred-year-old, second-generation vampyre who could snap them in half without even blinking? This guy had lived centuries doing gods know what, and now he wanted Caia to go off on some suicide mission to destroy trace magik and free them all! And the Caia was considering it.

Jae sighed. Some serious intervention was going to be necessary. And she really hoped Lucien would be the one to do it 'cause she had a wedding night to get to.

"We're waiting," Alexa told him shrilly.

Jae snickered. Alexa was finding the adjustment of not being center of attention when there were men in the room a little tough. After almost eighteen years of school with the girl and drooling humans following her around with their eyes, it was a nice change of pace.

Reuben shrugged. Goddess, his every movement bugged her. She stifled an irritated growl. "When Marita attacked Caia, the only person in danger was Caia herself." He smiled softly at Cy.

Alexa rolled her eyes. "Uh ... meaning?"

He threw her a distasteful look. "Uh ... meaning," he imitated, "that Caia, like, totally isn't, like, a self-absorbed bimbo. She only, like, totally mashes people into a pulp when someone else is in, like, total danger."

"I don't say *like* and *totally* that much, O-K!"

Jaeden felt a suspicious shudder from her mate. She scowled. "Are you laughing?"

He smirked. "It was funny."

"Hmm."

Yeah, it was ... but still ... Reuben equals bad. No laughing at his mocking a person no matter how much said person needed to be mocked.

"What are you saying?" Lucien batted away their bickering.

The vampyre turned slowly to look at him, his eyes narrowing. His expression had tightened imperceptibly. *Hmm, interesting. Does Reuben have a problem with Lucien?*

"I'm saying that if we rewind and think about the occasions when Caia's other powers have gotten the best of her ... you were involved."

That's true, Jaeden mused. Huh, that made sense. He was her mate, after all.

Alexa's eyes lit up. "Ooh, right, like when she blasted me against the classroom window for ..." She trailed off and then blushed.

Ooh. "For what?" Jae pushed.

"Um, nothing."

"Caia?"

Caia's eyes widened at having been put on the spot and then swung around to Alexa who was pleading with her eyes to not say anything. "Let's not get into it, but ... suffice to say Lucien's name came up."

Hmm, she'd find out from Caia later.

"See?" Reuben nodded. "A trigger."

Magnus, who had been leaning in closer and closer to the TV to hear *Harry Potter*, had given up and clicked it off with a frustrated press of the remote. He strode toward the group. "Reuben's right. Let's not forget it was only when Lucien was being tortured by Ethan that Caia splattered ... smooshed ... whatever it was she did to him."

Jaeden smiled at him. "And she only killed those magiks when Lucien was in danger in the forest."

"And I blew up a tree once," Caia muttered, but with lykan hearing they all whipped around, pinning her with amused glances. She blushed. "I was pissed off at him." She smiled adoringly up at Lucien. "I'm not anymore, sweetie."

Lucien looked like he wanted to ask what she'd been pissed off at him for, but Jaeden snickered. She couldn't help it. They looked at her. She gestured at Lucien pointedly. "*Sweetie.*"

Ryder chuckled and pulled her into his side. "Don't make the Alpha mad, baby."

Before she could retort with something flirtatious, Alexa was on her feet. "So … what? We can't expect Caia to save our asses unless Lucien's is under fire?"

Caia blushed again, but Reuben shook his head. "Not at all." He pinned Cy with his gaze. "We're going to train you."

"Uh, how about asking her?" Jae snapped.

Lucien growled and Jae bristled. Rose smirked, which made Jaeden want to tear out that pretty red hair or maybe throw her in a room with Alexa and hope the two of them took care of each other.

"Guys!" Caia stepped away from Lucien and gestured at them all. "I'm a big girl. I can speak for myself. And Reuben's right."

"Wha—"

"You can't—"

"Be ser—"

"Than—"

"Shut up!" Magnus demanded. "Let the girl speak."

Caia smiled gratefully at her uncle and then spoke directly to Reuben, "I want you to help me if you can."

"And you'll do what I asked?"

"I'm still thinking on it."

"You have one night to sleep on it."

"That's a little unfair."

"What are you talking about?" Lucien frowned, stepping between them. Ah, so Caia hadn't told Lucien yet about what Reuben wanted her to do. Yup … that wasn't going to go down well. There was no way Lucien would ever forgive her for killing Daylights.

"We'll talk in the morning," Reuben commanded, and she saw the way Lucien flinched. He was used to being the one who gave the orders. "Get some sleep. We'll get you all back to the pack tomorrow."

CHAPTER 12

"*W*hoa ... this place looks different," Caia said as she strolled into Marita and Vanne's suite. Before, it had combined their individual tastes (heavy on the wife's), but now all Marita's stuff was gone and in its place were sofas and mahogany tables, and a great big old library desk that looked like it cost more than Caia's once-upon-a-time, brand-new car. On the walls hung paintings of hunting scenes and birds rather than sumptuous Renaissance debauchery. The lamps with vine-leaf stands had been replaced with green banker's lamps. There was even an old-fashioned globe. Come to think of it, Caia had seen very similar décor once before elsewhere. Caia smiled at Alfred Doukas as he stood to greet her.

Alfred's study. Of course.

They had made Doukas Regent while Marita was AWOL. Caia had awoken to that news, as well as the request for her presence after breakfast. It had been difficult to pull herself out of Lucien's embrace, but at least her shoulder barely ached now.

"You know, there's still a few hours till after breakfast."

Lucien had grabbed her gently, trying to pull her back into bed.

Caia had rolled her eyes. "Aren't you tired out from last night?"

He grinned, eyeing her suggestively. "Hey, I wasn't the one who started it. I was going to leave you alone because of your shoulder, but nooo ... you needed your dose of *Lucien Love*."

Caia grunted. "Keep calling it that and I'm sure I'll be cured of needing a dose of *Lucien Love* ever again."

He frowned. "How's the shoulder?"

"Good. Ahhhh!" She squealed as he hauled her back into bed, rolling her over so she was pinned beneath him. She tried to shake him off, but he just laughed and peppered her face with kisses. The relief that he wasn't throwing things around in a fit of rage after she'd told him what Reuben wanted still amazed her. He actually understood why Reuben could be so ruthless.

"Two thousand years of death would do that to you."

He said he trusted Caia to make the right decision. The depth of his understanding floored her, and she took advantage of him being in the same room with a bed numerous times throughout the night.

"Lucien, stop." She giggled. "I have things to do. I have to check Desi and see if she's all right before I head up to see the Council."

"I know," he mumbled and then bit down gently on her ear as his hand slid up over her ribs. She gasped, falling into the deliciousness that was being with him and knowing he was safe ... and hers completely.

"Lucie—" She was cut off as he kissed her so deeply, she thought she might faint. She clutched him tightly, stroking his muscled back as he strained against her, clearly delighted by every gasp that escaped from her mouth when it wasn't being devoured by his lips.

"We really have—"

"We will, we will." He groaned and then kissed her harder. "Caia."

"Caia."

Oh dear goddess, she blinked and then blushed as she came back to the present, shaking the outstretched hand of Penelope Argyros, the magik whose suite they'd been using and whose bed she and Lucien had christened ... several times.

"Are you alright, dear?" she asked sweetly, a crinkle of concern between her brows.

"Oh, I'm fine. Now. Thank you, by the way." She gestured to her shoulder. Jeez, she had to start paying attention. Just because she had Lucien back did not mean she could forget that the Head of the Daylight Coven had fled and was probably gathering followers at that very moment to take back the Center. Then there was Reuben who was pressuring her into doing what he wanted because he'd helped rescue everyone and had offered to show her how to control her "superpower." Not to mention the complication she felt buzzing in the trace. A Midnight faerie had been spying in Paris and somehow got wind of what was happening at the Center. She warned Reuben, who in turn warned Nikolai, who was heading out to stop the faerie before she took it back to the Midnight Council.

When had her life gotten this complicated?

"Oh, I am pleased." Penelope nodded and then turned to gesture at the Council who circled the table at the other end of the room. Caia sighed. She'd had strategic meetings there before when she hadn't known Marita was a psychopath.

She wasn't going to lie—the Council intimidated her slightly. But this was no time to show that. They needed her help, and she had to prove she was as capable as she'd promised. Helping break them out of prison was a start, but technically that had been Vanne. She was, after all, being eaten by a werewolf at the time.

"Caia, do you remember the rest of the Council?"

"Of course." She nodded at them, glad to see them all in one piece. She smiled when she saw Vanne and Saffron, and they acknowledged the smile with a nod of their heads. They were both still grieving.

Marion.

Her absence, here, now, in this very room, was more gaping than ever. Caia missed her so much even her teeth ached with it. A fire erupted in the pit of her belly. Caia couldn't wait to find out what the plan was to bring Marita down.

"Caia, as you can see for yourself this morning, we, the Council, have brought the Center back under control." Alfred Doukas led her to the table, his hand on the small of her back, guiding her and giving her reassurance at the same time. "We're getting the word out to the rest of the coven about Marita, and things are progressing smoothly. We want to thank you for the part you played in rescuing us from the containment center—which, by the way, will be called *prison* from today onward." He rolled his eyes. Yeah, Caia had always thought it was a dumb name as well. "We brought you up here to thank you and to let you know that we know about everything ... Reuben and all that."

She blinked. Shocked. Surely ... they didn't know *everything*? Reuben wouldn't have allowed that, right?

"Vanne tells us that Reuben has a very particular gift against trace magik." Alfred was frowning, as were the others around the table. "As much as we'd love to know more, we are not Marita, and Reuben is free to go. Vanne tells us although Reuben isn't a very old vampyre, he is extremely apt at training and control. Apparently he has helped Vanne in the past, and with the loss of your mentor Marion, we think it only best that you do as Vanne has suggested and return home to the pack to train with Reuben. Not only will he serve as extra protection for the pack but it means we can get on with finding Marita and bringing her in."

OK ... so, one: Vanne and Saffron have lied to the Council about Reuben's age.

Two: They think he can train me in Marion's stead like it's nothing but an inconvenience she's not here to do it herself!

Three: They're politely asking me to stay out of their way.

Caia shook her head in shock. "I-I'm confused. I thought we had discussed before—"

"This is for the best, Caia," Vanne spoke, his eyes asking her to trust him. "Marita selfishly drew you into this war. You needed more time, more training. And I know we discussed the possibility of making you Head of the Coven to begin peace negotiations with the Midnights, but the Council is not in agreement on that account. You're still so young and untried and ... well, we don't all agree that peace negotiations are a credible solution at this point. So for now, no one expects anything from you.

"First, we're going to deal with Marita, and then if the time is right, we'll call on your help with the Midnights. And if you do hear anything in the trace that concerns you, you'll let us know."

They smiled at her like an adult would to a child. If she heard anything? Yeah, she was hearing something, all right. The Daylights wanted her out of their business until it was *convenient* for them, while the Midnights grew steadily more anxious and suspicious of Nikolai's motives. And Reuben! Hah, he was a peach! This was *his* doing! He'd told Vanne to convince the Council to let her go so she could concentrate all her time on killing innocent people in order to free them all from the trace!

She felt a twitch in her arm and held in a gasp. *My goddess.* She was so pissed off, she was starting to change.

Breathe, Caia, breathe.

She had to get out of there before she lost total control.

"Caia."

Startled, she whirled at the familiar voice and immediately felt the change recede. "Vil?" She rushed forward, hearing the scrape of chairs at her back as the Council tensed at the intruder.

Vil was out of breath, his pale eyes stark as he reached for her. "They told me to come get you."

Oh gods, oh gods ... what had happened now? She trembled, holding on to him. She didn't want to know. She didn't want any more bad things to happen.

Are you listening to yourself? You're in a freaking war, Caia. Bad things are going to happen. And people are going to come to you for help, so shake it off and be cool!

"Vil," she said calmly. "Who told you to come get me?"

He shook his head, blinking back tears. Oh gods, now she was near hyperventilating.

"Vil?" she demanded.

"Ella ... Mal ... they told me to come get you."

"Why?"

He shook his head again, his gaze so sympathetic, she thought she might die of panic. "Marita ... she attacked the house."

Someone brushed by her and she blinked, watching Vanne grip Vil's arm. "When? Did she get away? Did anyone get hurt?"

He nodded and his head dropped as he whispered, "A few hours ago. She and the magiks that were with her are gone. Six. Six members of the pack are dead."

A sob erupted out of her throat like a wail, and she felt someone holding on to her. It was Penelope. "W-w-who?" she choked.

He was crying now, wiping his nose. "I'm sorry, Caia. I'm so sorry. Laila felt something and I wouldn't let her go but she begged and begged me to take her to the house and when I finally gave in, it was too late."

"Who? Vil, who?"

"Mal's parents—Morgan. Natalia. The twins. And Yvana. Dimitri."

Oh gods, no. No. No, no ...

She felt the world fall away from her feet. Dana and Daniel were gone. Alexa and Malek's parents too. Yvana and Dimitri. No, no, no, no, no ...

"How?" Vanne asked.

Vil slumped, holding his hand out to Caia. "They just want you to come back."

A face appeared in front of her. Doukas, his eyes kind and sad. "Go get Lucien, Caia. And the others. We'll have a portal ready and waiting to take you straight home."

She nodded numbly and let someone escort her out. Saffron. She held Caia's elbow lightly, as if afraid the slightest touch would break her. Caia was thankful for her grip. The corridor kept tilting under her feet.

"I'm so sorry, Caia. This is too much grief for someone so young."

Caia shook her head. "I'll be fine," she whispered hoarsely, her heart aching. "But Lucien ... he'll blame himself."

And Jaeden. Oh goddess, Jaeden. Her dad.

"A good Alpha always does."

CHAPTER 13

BROKEN

It wasn't real. It didn't feel real, anyway. He could feel Caia's hand clasped tightly in his. That was real. His heart thudded. But everyone was so quiet as they waited for the portal to be opened that a sense of unreality washed over him. He heard sniffles and then looked at Jaeden who stood pale and shocked, frigid against anyone's touch. Ryder stood near her, watching her anxiously but keeping his distance.

If Lucien looked close enough, he could see the hurt her distance caused in his friend's eyes. Ryder had lost his mother. Jaeden wasn't the only one who'd lost a parent today. Alexa stood off to the side, her face mottled with anger, and he knew what she was thinking. She didn't believe her parents were gone. She thought this was all some nasty trick. But it wasn't. His pack members were dead.

And he hadn't been there to save them.

Dimitri. Yvana. Morgan. Natalia. Dana. Daniel. Hell, the twins were just starting out. At that thought, he glanced over at Irini and Aidan holding Sunday and Kerianna. Aidan kept glancing at his brother, unshed tears in his eyes for his mom.

And Christian and Lucia, Lucia holding tight to Jaela and Christian holding Ivan's little hand in his. His face was taut with grief, but he stood close to his wife and watched his daughter's face. At the forefront of the group stood Magnus, his eyes catching Lucien's every once in a while, seeming to match his, feeling for feeling. The grief oozed into him, replacing numbness with anger and pain so deep, it made him tremble.

He felt Caia squeeze his hand.

Someone gave them their condolences. Doukas, probably. And told them they would find Marita and make her pay for her crimes. Sure. Doukas was sending a couple of magiks with them for protection. They'd stay as long as Lucien wished. Why? Wasn't the damage already done? He was barely even aware of Reuben at his back or the fact that Saffron and Rose were with him. They were coming too? Then the portal was open and they were walking through. He was barely cognizant of the sickening mode of transportation.

The next thing he knew, they were on the other side of the bottom of the wooden steps that led up to his front porch. Lucien's heart tore at the sight before him. Laila and Vil stood off to the side, their faces pinched with sorrow. But it was Mal sitting on the stairs who brought reality crashing in, his legs wide so Finlay could sit on the stair below him, snuggled protectively into his big brother's leg. His large hand sat on Finlay's head, and the two boys looked up at the same time, their faces streaked with tears, their eyes puffy and red from crying. Mal's eyes met Lucien's, and he felt that look all the way to the bottom of his soul.

"They're gone," Mal choked out, fresh tears scoring his cheeks. "They're gone."

"No!" Alexa screamed and rushed up the stairs to her brothers. They caught hold of her jacket, tried to pull her back from the door, but she broke free and ran into the house. A heartbreaking howl hit them like a blast of sleet, and Mal and Finlay were on their feet, rushing inside to their sister.

Shaken, Lucien made a choked sound at the back of his throat and pushed past them all. He heard heavy footsteps behind him and knew Magnus was at his back. The smell of blood hit his nose on the first step and was overwhelming once they were inside the house. Morgan's body was the first they came across, his face and lips blue. Asphyxiation. There were cuts, large, bloody gashes and burns on his skin that hadn't healed because of his death. He'd been tortured before they killed him.

In the living room, he found Alexa wrapped in her brothers' arms, and they sobbed loudly into one another's shoulders. Lucien placed a comforting hand on Mal's arm, more sorry than he could ever tell them. Their mother lay at their feet. She'd been suffocated with air magik by the looks of it, but no signs of torture, which meant someone had gotten to the attackers before they could torture her.

Since Mal and Finlay were okay, Lucien could only assume the boys had heard the commotion and had changed into lykans and fought off Marita and the magiks. Finding Dana and Daniel in the kitchen furthered that belief. They, too, showed no signs of torture. Daniel's body lay curled over his sister protectively, and Lucien felt the prick of tears as he imagined the young wolf trying to comfort his sister while they could do nothing against death. His gaze stuck on their lifeless eyes. They were barely seventeen.

He gripped the back of a kitchen chair and the wood crumbled. The sharp, irritating pain of splinters set fire to his hands. Good. He deserved that and more. How could he have left his pack here, unprotected? How could he have left them to die? His family.

Dimitri, he flinched, feeling as if he'd been punched in the gut. The Elder had joined forces with Magnus to be a father to him since the death of his own. And now he was gone. Where was he?

"Fin and I were outside."

Lucien whirled at the dead voice and found Mal staring at him numbly, his face red and splotched. "You were running?"

Mal nodded. "I took him out. He was worried about Lex, so I took him out for a run to take his mind off it. We heard shouts and stuff crashing, so we rushed back." He shrugged, obviously trying not to cry, but no one would have mocked him for doing so. Lucien wanted to tell him to let it out, but he found he couldn't talk. "It was too late. D-Dana and Dan were already dying." He gestured weakly. "I chased off the magiks just as they started burning them. I chased them into the living room and scared … Marita … she looked a lot like Marion so I guess it was her, right? She was killing"—he choked on a sob—"killing Mom. I think she was going to make it slow but she had to finish it quick 'cause of me. She killed her. I could have stopped her—"

"No." Lucien strode toward him, gripping his shoulder and giving him a shake. "No. You couldn't have." Marita had obviously filled his mom's lungs with smoke and ash to suffocate her.

Mal shook his head. "Dad was already gone. They tore him apart."

Lucien felt him shudder and then Mal turned slightly, bending over to vomit all over the kitchen floor. "I-I'm s-s-sorry," he choked out, but Lucien shushed him, patting him gently on the back until he was done.

After a few minutes of unbearable silence, Lucien asked hoarsely, "Where are Dimitri and Yvana?"

The young wolf's head dropped as he wiped his mouth with the back of his hand. "Out front, to the side. You must've passed them when you came in. They were outside when Marita arrived. They're ... they're pretty messed up."

Lucien ushered him out of the kitchen and guided him back outside, taking care to shield him from the view of his father's body. He vaguely took in Lucia off to the side with Irini and Cera, who was holding her three kids as close as possible. With them stood Reuben, Saffron, and Rose, and altogether they hid the kids from the gruesome sight to Lucien's right.

He walked slowly toward the pack. Christian had his arms around Julia as she sobbed uncontrollably into his shoulder. Jaeden knelt on the ground, the knee of her jeans soaking up the blood of her father. Dimitri lay in front of her, his body mutilated, his face and lips blue. Just behind them was Yvana, her prone body in much the same condition as Dimitri's. Aidan and Ryder knelt beside her, quiet tears rolling down their cheeks.

And his own mother (Lucien thanked the gods she was all right) stood with her arm around Caia, the two of them between their dead pack members and their grieving families. Magnus hovered over Dimitri, his friend, his brother, his own silent tears coursing down his ruddy cheeks.

When Caia was taken from Lucien, he'd felt rage unlike anything he had ever known. At the massacre left in his home, the massacre of his people, his pack—the lykans he was supposed to protect—by that evil bitch ... it brought the rage back full force.

CHAPTER 14

EMOTIONAL BLACKMAIL AND ... JUST PLAIN OL' BLACKMAIL

There was no noise. It was as if the world had shushed ... or had she gone deaf? There were no smells. She could see the rain as it pelted the ground and plastered their clothes to their bodies; she could see the mud as it squelched underfoot; she could see the leaves rustle against one another as the wind rushed through Lucien's land in furious sympathy for their loss. But she couldn't smell the earth or hear the tears. She felt numb. Paralyzed. Sure that one gentle nudge would knock her over. It wasn't possible to feel this much pain, this much loss. And the anger, the rage, simmered beneath the surface like oil ready for the first strike of the match.

Six of the pack were gone. For the others who had survived, it had been a matter of chance. Julia had persuaded Imogen and Isaac to come back to her house to get some much-needed sleep. Ella was out shopping and checking on Lucien's store; Cera had gone with her. As for Draven and Kade, they'd taken the twins home as well, leaving Lucien's house under the protection of Dimitri, Yvana, Mal, Finlay, and their parents. Dana and Daniel would never have been there if they hadn't snuck out and back over to Lucien's, excited and desperate to welcome everyone back from the Center.

It should never have happened. She should've known Marita would target the pack. And now they were cremating innocent lykans in the woods behind the house. One of the magiks that had been sent by Alfred to protect them—Jason —was taking care of the mess their deaths had made in the human world. Memories and school files were being tampered with, Lucien's store, Yvana's café, all of their jobs were being erased as if they'd never been there. The house was emptied, all evidence of their existence wiped. Jason tampered with the memory of a realtor. For now, the house was part of some guy's inheritance. "He lived in Cincinnati and wanted the house put up for sale." The money from the sale would make its way back into the pack's accounts, but their lives here were over.

And Caia had sold her soul to the devil himself to keep them safe.

* * *

Twenty-four hours earlier

"Ryder's looking for you," Caia said softly as she made her way into her old bedroom. Jae lay curled up on her old comforter, a teddy bear Ella had given her when she'd first arrived squished tightly in her friend's hands. Her face was taut with grief, her usually lively blue eyes deadened as they turned upon Caia.

"I don't want to speak to him."

Caia nodded. It had only been thirty-six hours since they'd arrived back to the house to find their whole world ripped apart. Everyone was in unimaginable pain. Caia felt like she was sleepwalking. The sense of unreality was tormenting. And the guilt …

Everyone was angry, everyone felt guilty. However, Lucien was keeping them together. He didn't want vengeance; he wanted them all to take the time to grieve, to accept their new lives. For the most part, the pack seemed to have heard. It was a quiet and stoic grieving.

But not for Jaeden and Alexa, who weren't handling it well at all. There was more rage than sadness there, and Caia was hovering on a tightrope that threatened to throw her in with them. It had never occurred to her she would be the one battling the overwhelming need to punish. She'd always thought, with his volatile temper, she would be the one soothing Lucien. But after destroying pretty much everything in the house he could get his hands on, Lucien had cooled and put his efforts into helping the pack rather than taking vengeance—he was the one calming her. And he was almost succeeding.

It was just that every time she looked at Jaeden or Alexa or thought about Dimitri's death, she wanted revenge. Torturous and painful revenge.

She took a deep breath, trying to deal with her emotions. "Maybe you should talk to him. He lost his mom too. You should be comforting each other."

"I don't want his comfort!" Jaeden spat, causing Caia to flinch at the venom. "All he and Lucien have been spouting for the last twenty-four hours is how we have to accept this and come to terms with their deaths. Well, I don't want to! I want to find Marita and I want to rip her apart because that's what she's done to me!"

"I'm with her on this." Alexa appeared in the doorway. There were dark circles under her eyes, her mouth pinched, giving her the appearance of being older than her years. She brushed past Caia and sat down on the bed beside Jaeden. To

Caia's surprise, she reached for Jaeden's hand and they gripped onto one another. They looked up at her with twin expressions of fury. And she didn't know what to say, what to do to make it better.

"W-what can I do?" she asked softly.

"I have an idea."

The three of them snapped around to find Reuben standing in the doorway. For once there was no mocking in his eyes or lazy languor in his body language. He was dead serious, his eyes dark with sympathy.

"What idea?" Alexa asked urgently.

He slowly shut the door and wandered into the room to take a seat at Caia's old computer desk. "Lucien and Ryder are out making preparations for the funerals at the moment." Stalactites might as well have formed on the ceiling for how cold the room grew with that one sentence. Reuben ignored it. "I thought I would speak with you privately."

"What's the idea?" Alexa insisted.

The vampyre glanced up at Caia. "Caia already knows my plan."

"What plan?"

Jaeden shifted. "You mean the trace thing? How is that helping destroy Marita?"

"Because if Caia gets rid of the trace, then Marita no longer has that power over the Daylights. She can no longer gather people to her easily and she can no longer hunt down the people she wants destroyed. Once the trace is gone, we can hunt *her*."

A feeling of helplessness swept over Caia as she watched Jaeden's eyes glow with the news. Even Alexa, who was confused as to the actual technicalities of the discussion, looked animated.

"Explain?" Alexa asked.

Caia decided to answer instead. She couldn't help the flatness in her tone. "The trace magik was created by three members of the Daylight Coven and four of the Midnight. It's believed that killing the seven direct descendants of those first members will destroy the trace."

Alexa's eyes widened. "Seriously? How? How can we kill them?"

Caia's mouth dropped at the blasé question, shocked at her eagerness, but it was Jaeden who answered, "Only Caia can. They have to be killed simultaneously in the exact same manner."

"Then do it," Alexa demanded, her dark eyes flashing. "Fricking do it and we can get Marita!"

Jae nodded. "Caia, please," she begged.

Oh dear goddess. Do they know what they're asking of me? Of course not. All they could think about was their own loss, their own selfish need for justice.

And she couldn't hate them for it.

Reuben smirked at her.

Caia wanted to kill him. He was preying on their grief. And they were preying on her guilt and anger. "It's not that simple," she whispered. "These people are innocent."

"You don't know that, you haven't checked," Jaeden snapped.

"Jae," she entreated, "think about what you're asking me to do."

The lykan shuffled off the bed and strode around it to tower over her. "I'm asking you to avenge my father," she bit out, and with the words came the tears. "My father who loved you, who protected you as if you were his own."

When she heard Alexa's choked sob behind Jae, she wanted nothing more than to run from the room and keep on running. "I want to." She trembled. "I want to, but you can't ask me to kill people. That's not avenging your father.

They didn't hurt Dimitri or Morgan and Natalia. These are just *people*."

"They're magiks," Jae spat. "Magiks who started this stupid war in the first place!"

"No!" Caia hissed. "They just had the unfortunate luck of being their descendants."

"Caia, please," Alexa implored. "We'll come. We'll help. The last thing I said to my dad was that just because he wasn't brave enough to fight didn't mean I wasn't," she choked. "How could that be the last thing I said to him? I have to do something. Help me do this."

Caia shook her head, her ears filling with their grief-stricken pleas.

"Girls." Reuben stood slowly, quieting their demands. Caia trembled at the ruthless aspect of his face.

"What?" she whispered, her heart thudding in her chest.

"You're going to do this for them, Caia—no, don't shake your head. You're going to do this or the haven I promised for the pack and the assurance that I will manipulate every member of the pack's trace so that Marita can't find them will be null and void."

Bastard. Is he really ... that bastard!

Her chest tightened. Her fingers curled. Her teeth sharpened. "Are you blackmailing me?"

"Yes. Do it, and I'll protect the pack. Don't ... and I leave them here to rot."

There was no time for thought of repercussions. Caia lunged for him. Her claws unleashed as she swiped for him. A band of restraint enveloped her waist, and she struggled and twisted in Alexa and Jaeden's secure hold.

"Tut-tut, Caia." The vampyre smiled humorlessly at her. "You need to control that temper."

Her tongue had gone thick with humiliated rage. It took

her a moment to speak. "I was actually beginning to trust you, you son of a bitch!"

"I'm doing what needs to be done." He shrugged unapologetically. "I've never pretended to do anything else."

Remember, Caia, you can't hurt him. Take a deep breath. Control your animalistic urge to hunt and kill the wily fox.

She let her body relax, breathing deeply in an effort to cool her temper.

"Caia, please," Jae whispered, slowly letting go of her. "You have to do this for us."

"What if I can't?"

"At least try," Alexa snapped. "For the pack."

Gradually, as the implications of Reuben's threat settled in, along with Jae's and Alexa's beseeching, Caia nodded. "OK," she croaked. "I'll do it. Under one condition."

Alexa nodded. "Anything."

"It goes no further than this room that I was blackmailed into this."

Jaeden frowned. "Why?" She glanced anxiously at Reuben.

She thought of her mate and his reaction to her decision. There was a huge possibility he wouldn't speak to her ever again. Still ... she loved him, so ... "Lucien already feels terrible that he wasn't here to protect the pack. Telling him about Reuben's ultimatum will only make him feel worse."

Reuben smirked. "So gallant and self-sacrificing of you, Caia."

"Bite me, asshole."

Jaeden shook her head. "Seriously, Caia ... he might not understand like we do. He'll be mad at you."

"Then he'll be mad at me."

With that, Jaeden hugged her tight and whispered a thank-you into her ear.

* * *

CAIA TREMBLED and walked away from the cremation sight, glad Jason had cloaked the smell of her pack's burning bodies. She didn't think she'd be able to cope otherwise. So deaf to the world, she wasn't even aware of Alexa and Jaeden on either side of her until Lucien's hand clamped down on her shoulder, opening up her senses again.

"Jae, Alexa, can you give us a moment? And Jae, Ryder wants a word."

Jaeden grunted and walked away, her hand clasped in Alexa's. Caia watched them, thinking how sad it was that death had been the one to create a friendship between the two young women.

"Caia." Lucien sighed. She snuggled into his chest as his arm slid over her shoulders, drawing her into his heat. "How are you holding up?"

Not good. You see, I have to kill seven people in a few days or the pack will be under constant threat of attack from Marita. You want to help me kill the blackmailer instead?

She didn't say that. She mumbled incoherently and tightened her grip on him. "How are you?" she whispered.

He dropped a soft kiss on her head, and she heard the tears in his voice as he replied, "Ask me that question later."

They walked in silence, holding on to one another until they came out of the woods and rounded the house. Six cars were parked around the driveway as well as three moving vans. A lot of stuff had to be left or thrown away. Lucien kissed her again and moved unhurriedly toward one of the vans as if encumbered by a heavy weight. Ryder pressed keys into his hand and nodded toward the other moving vehicle. Magnus was supposed to be riding with Lucien in one of the vans.

Caia shook her head as if she were conversing with them. No. She would ride with Lucien, not Magnus. Part of her bargain with Reuben was a haven for the pack. Apparently, a twenty-four-hundred-year-old vampyre tended to collect real estate. He owned a large hotel in the middle of nowhere the next state over. It hadn't been in operation for ten years, but he'd paid a couple of magiks to clean it up for the pack. They could use it for as long as they needed (as long as Caia kept to the bargain). The drive was a good few hours. And it was quite possibly going to be the last few hours that Lucien respected her. She strode toward Magnus and her mate.

"Magnus, I'll drive with Lucien," she said quietly.

The Elder frowned. "No, honey, you don't have to—"

"I want to," she cut him off, giving Lucien a pointed look.

He smiled gratefully back at her. "Yeah, Magnus. You take Caia's place in Ella's car."

"If you're sure." He didn't waste time arguing. Ella's car was way more comfortable. He nodded and made his way over to it.

"Thanks." Lucien gazed lovingly down at her.

"Hey, Lucien." Rose appeared around the corner of the house, and Caia's stomach flipped. It was such an inappropriate time to be jealous, but she hated that Rose was here with them. Apparently it was thought she'd be safer with the pack for now, since Marita probably knew she had betrayed her. It was nice having her mate's ex-lover living with them. Really nice.

"Caia." She nodded at her but turned her bright smile back on Lucien. "I thought maybe I could save Magnus a numb butt and offer to ride with you instead."

I hate her.

"That's nice, but Caia's already offered."

"Oh, you don't have to, Caia," Rose tried to insist.

Caia glared at her. "No, I do."

Rose had the graciousness to look abashed at least. "Of course. I'll just ride in one of the cars."

As soon as she was out of earshot, Lucien sighed. "You know, you don't have to be jealous. You can be nice to her."

His tone was prickly. *Actually prickly.*

"I'm not jealous," she snapped. "And don't talk to me like that."

"I'm just saying, there's nothing between us anymore."

"Yeah, maybe for you but not for her, Lucien. Come on ... the way she looks at you—"

"Is her problem. Not ours. Can you please get in the van? Not the time for this, Caia," he admonished, and she immediately felt guilty.

She bit her lip. "You're right, I'm sorry." She shuffled around to the van's passenger side like a scolded child. She frowned as she caught Jaeden and Ryder out of the corner of her eye.

"I don't want to!" Jae snapped and pulled out of Ryder's grip before loping over to the car Alexa and Mal were going to be riding in. Ryder growled, staring after her with a look of pure frustration. He shook his head angrily and turned, jumping into the rented moving van he would be driving. Caia didn't know why Jaeden was pushing Ryder away, but if it didn't stop soon, she knew Ryder would blow a gasket.

Caia sighed again and looked around. There were only twenty-three members of the pack left, and they were all organizing themselves into the cars. With them were Vil, Laila, Reuben, and Rose. Jason and two other magiks Alfred had sent stood off to the side, and Caia held up her hand to them in a grateful wave. They nodded back in acknowledgment but stood stiff and vigilant as the pack geared themselves up to leave their home.

CHAPTER 15

THE ULTIMATUM

Jaeden always assumed grief would feel the same no matter who the person was you lost. With Sebastian's death had come a heartbreaking ache, a bitterness for how short his life had been, and an everlasting gratitude that someone had loved her enough to face death to save her.

Losing her dad was completely different. She just felt … so alone.

She could barely breathe for the crushing weight she carried on her chest every minute of the day. Her stomach churned constantly, and it was like a thick fog she couldn't make her way through had descended over her. Her dad had been her everything. They were more alike than anyone else in the family, and they'd understood one another better than anyone else ever could because of it. His presence in her life, no matter where she'd been, had offered a kind of comfort and protection she couldn't get anywhere else. Everything was always all right because, no matter what, she had her dad to run to … and somehow he always made it better.

And now he was gone. She was so alone and terrified because without him, a part of her no longer made sense.

She shifted uncomfortably in the back seat, her throat burning with the agony of repressed tears. Her head already ached like a bitch from her crying jags. Her gaze slid toward Alexa who sat in the passenger seat next to their designated driver, Reuben. Mal and Finlay shared the back seat with her. It was weird the person she felt closest to at the moment was Alexa, but out of everyone in the pack, she knew Alexa had been as close to her dad as Jae had been to Dimitri. And at least she still had her mom. Alexa had lost both her parents. So if anyone could understand the magnitude of her wrath, it was Alexa.

She glanced at Mal. He was so changed. He used to tease and flirt like life was one big joke. But he'd lost his parents, his best friend, and his on-again, off-again girlfriend all in one fell swoop.

Now he was quiet and intensely protective of his sister and little brother, hovering over them constantly these last few days. But despite his grief, he was just like Lucien and Ryder. They were determined to fix the pack, give them a fresh start. Where was the talk of vengeance? Of justice? Apparently there was to be none; in fact, Lucien had demanded it so! *The pack has seen too much loss,* he said, *it's time to move on.* How could they move on? Their family had been destroyed, targeted like deer on a hunt! And was he forgetting that his own mate was a part of the war? Caia wasn't getting out of it anytime soon ... Was he intending to abandon her?

Thank the gods for Caia.

Jaeden refused to feel guilty for manipulating her into doing what Reuben wanted. And funnily enough, she was no longer mad at the vampyre. She was glad he blackmailed

Caia. Together they'd gotten her to do something she never would've willingly done otherwise.

And if it changes Caia beyond repair? If it destroys her?

Jaeden shook her head. She couldn't think about that. She couldn't. Caia was a good person and asking her to do this was going to have its consequences ... but hadn't they all sacrificed something for this war? And it wasn't like she was intending to leave her on her own to do it. She and Alexa had every intention of going with her and giving her moral support.

Moral support for killing innocents.

Stop it. It has to be done. It's the only way to stop Marita.

Keep telling yourself that.

Arrggh! Jaeden shoved the thought out of her head and turned to stare at the passing scenery. She felt her pocket vibrate and shifted up so she could slip her cell phone free. It was a text message from Ryder. He was a couple of cars back on the road.

Stupid idiot, fiddling with his cell while driving.

We gotta talk when we get to the hotel.

There were no *xxx*'s at the end like there would usually be. He was pissed. Yeah, well, so was she! She didn't want him near her, comforting her, loving her. She didn't want to fall into that. If she felt this bad losing her dad, she couldn't imagine how bad it would feel to lose Ryder. Not to mention she might not make it out of this war, and she didn't want him to hurt any worse than he had to. Making him hate her would make it easier on him if she did die.

She sighed. She wouldn't text back. It would only distract him from the road. But if she could have, she would have said ...

There's nothing left to talk about.

No *xxx*'s.

* * *

THE DRIVE so far had been silent. Lucien hadn't expected it to be fun filled, of course, but Caia had been extremely quiet. He couldn't work out if it was just the magnitude of everything that had happened or if she was mad at him for rebuking her about Rose. He glanced quickly at her. She looked tired and as sad as he felt.

But he was actually proud of himself for putting aside his instincts for revenge and making a deal with Reuben to protect the pack. He was paying rent and protection costs to the vampyre to keep the pack off Marita's radar. That burned a little, considering he wanted to rip the creep apart for taking Caia and scaring the crap out of him, but the pack needed Reuben. They'd lost too many, and they were lucky to have the kids back. And if anything happened to the kids? Gods, he couldn't bear to think about it. This was the right decision. It stuck in his craw a little to retreat, but it was the right decision.

As for Caia … he would cross that bridge when they got to it. He knew the Council would come back to her, but for now he was glad they were allowing her to stay protected until Marita was found.

"You alright?" He couldn't help asking. He feared a discussion about Rose. There was nothing going on between them, and it annoyed him that Caia could even think about being jealous at a time like this.

"I don't know," she whispered.

He braced himself.

"Something's happening."

He stilled, alert. "What do you mean?"

"With the Midnights." She straightened in her seat. "I've been feeling stirrings all morning, but … the Council … I think I need to warn Reuben and Nikolai."

It was weird to think of Caia and Reuben working with this Nikolai guy. But Vanne had attested to his trustworthiness so Lucien guessed he could let it go.

"Warn them about what?"

She shook her head. "Where's my cell?" she hissed as she rummaged through her bag. She made a sound of triumph at finding it, and Lucien grew steadily more irritated at being on the outside of whatever was going on.

"Caia—"

She held up her hand, cutting him off, and pressed a button on her cell. "Reuben."

She had the vampyre on speed dial? Lucien leaned closer to her to pick up the vamp's end of the conversation.

"We need to get word to Nikolai."

"What's going on?"

"He's in trouble."

"He stopped that faerie from telling the Council about the mess at the Daylight Center. It's all fine."

Caia huffed. "No, it's not," she protested, clearly aggravated. "Between the two of us, who's the one with the trace? Jeez, arrogant ass—"

"Get on with it."

She exhaled in what Lucien sensed was growing exasperation. "The Council is going to have Nikolai deposed. They want to start sending out a task force against Daylights again. And if they do that—"

"They'll find out about Marita," Reuben finished and hissed, "Damn. Okay. Who exactly on the Council is doing this?"

She gulped, and Lucien reached over to soothe her. "All of them."

"Ah, I see. Well, there's nothing for it. We just get Nikolai out of there."

"What do you mean? The Midnights will start attacking again."

"They'll just have to. We can't deal with that and Marita."

Lucien watched with pleasure as Caia growled down the phone at Reuben. The vampyre didn't know her that well. "I'll deal with it. I'll just do what I was doing before. I'll send reports to Alfred and the Council."

"And what about our—"

"We'll talk later. Warn Nikolai to get his ass out of there."

She hung up, trembling.

"And what about our—" She'd cut Reuben off for a reason. Something was going on Lucien wasn't aware of. He'd felt it every time he'd spoken with her in the last day. She had a guilty look in her eye. And it had something to do with the vampyre.

"What's going on?"

"I thought you would've guessed from that conversation."

"I'm not talking about Nikolai and the Council. I'm talking about you and Reuben."

She guffawed. "What are you talking about? You're not suggesting that Reuben and I are ..."

He bristled at the implication. "No. But it's funny that was your first thought. Something I should know about?"

"No," she snapped, and he almost flinched at the resentment in her voice. "And need I remind you that you reprimanded me like a child for being jealous about Rose. It's not an appropriate time, remember?"

Damn her for throwing that in his face. "That's not what I was saying."

"That's exactly what you were saying."

"No, that's what you said. I was just asking what's going on. Because you're clearly hiding something from me."

Surprised by the sudden silence that descended over the cab of the van, Lucien looked sharply at his mate. She was staring straight ahead, her hands twisting and untwisting the hem of her overlong T-shirt. His heart skipped a beat. Something *was* going on. And he knew he wasn't going to like it.

* * *

FIVE MINUTES LATER, Lucien was struggling to contain his anger and disbelief.

"Please tell me you're joking," he managed hoarsely.

She shook her head, her eyes wide and pleading with him.

What? Is she expecting me to accept this? To understand?

"How the Hades can you even think about doing this?" he bellowed, not caring that it caused her to skitter back in her seat.

"Because I have to. You said before you trusted me to make the right decision."

"Because I thought you would know that killing innocent people is the *wrong* decision!" he spat. "You don't *have* to do this! How can you … Caia, these are innocent people! You can't kill innocent people! How can you even—"

"You don't know they're innocent!"

He threw her a disgusted look. "Is that your argument? Jeez, Caia … do you even know if they're innocent? Have you checked out the Midnights' trace?"

"I haven't had a chance yet."

Lucien drew a deep breath. This was Caia. There had to be a reason she would even consider doing this, some reason he didn't know about. His Caia would never—*could* never—hurt anyone, unless it was absolutely necessary.

"Why?" he managed quietly, calmly. "Why? There must be a reason."

"There is. Lucien, Marita will only get more powerful with the trace. If I can get rid of the trace, then she'll be a much easier target."

Okay, that was not a good enough reason.

"Is this about the pack? About revenge? Because I already told you the pack is not getting involved in a vendetta. We have to move on."

"And you can. But I can't. I'm a part of this, and while I am, I might as well get some justice out of it."

His fingers turned white on the wheel. "Caia, you have to give me another reason. There has to be another reason. You wouldn't do this. You couldn't." He glanced at her, and he saw her mouth tremble. There was more. There had to be more.

"No. I just want this to be over."

"So you're going to kill the Septum? Seven innocent people?"

"Seven against thousands. Do the math, Lucien."

An overwhelming ache flooded through him, his stomach churning, his heart palpitating. After the last horrendous days, Lucien hadn't known he could feel any worse. "If what you're telling me is true, then we have a serious problem."

"I have to do this."

"No. You don't." He took a shuddering breath and momentarily squeezed his eyes shut. He opened them just in time to see he was hovering a little too close to the car in front. He eased off the accelerator, wishing he could do the same with his relationship with Caia. "If you do this, and I let you, my word with the pack will be worth nothing. And after all they've been through, they need a strong leader. They need me more than anyone else needs me right now. I owe them this."

He knew she understood at the sound of her harsh indrawn breath. "You'll kick me out?"

He pounded his fist against the wheel. "Damn it, Caia!" he roared, shooting her a venomous look. "Don't do this!"

Her eyes widened with shock. "You're kicking me out?"

"No! You are not doing this!"

147

"I am doing this," she persisted. "And you're kicking me out?"

Panic overwhelmed him. He fought to breathe. "You're not doing this."

"I am."

A wave of nausea rushed over him but he maintained control, staring straight ahead. How could his life change so much in the matter of five minutes?

He hardened his heart against her. Fine, if she wanted to play hardball, he'd play it right back. *There is no way she'll walk away from the pack*, he told himself. *No way.* An ultimatum was the only way to stop her.

"Then I'm kicking you out."

CHAPTER 16

BANISHED

"Y̵ou can't be serious," Ryder responded in a hushed tone, his body language betraying his shock.

Jaeden sneered, throwing Lucien a look of disgust. "Oh, he's serious, all right."

Caia stood in the dining hall of the hotel Reuben had given to the pack as part of their bargain. The last hour of the drive with Lucien had been one of the worst of her life. The silence had been brittle and furious, and dislike for one another had resonated in every corner of the van. How could he do this to her? How could she do this to him?

Lucien gathered everyone in the dining room as soon as they arrived and updated them on Caia and Reuben's plan to take out the Septum. The pack stared at them in disbelief. She hugged herself, trying to stop the trembling.

"Caia, tell him you're not going to do it." Magnus turned on her gruffly, his kind eyes bright with worry. "You can't do this."

She shrugged wearily, hating to see the disappointment on his face. "I'm sorry, but I have to."

"For the love of …," Ella whispered. "Please don't do this

149

to us."

"She's not doing anything," Jaeden snapped and brushed away from them all to stand by Caia's side. Caia felt the heat from the lykan as if a warm blanket had been placed around her. She smiled gratefully at her, momentarily forgetting she was part of the reason this was happening. If Lucien knew she was being blackmailed into this, he wouldn't be kicking her out of the pack. She felt like she'd been kicked in the gut.

Lucien is kicking me out of the pack!

He stood across the room glaring at her, Rose and all his pack gathered around him protectively. Only Laila and Vil stood close to her uncertainly, and now Jaeden. Oh, and now Alexa.

"Yeah," Lex snapped at them. "Lucien's the one kicking her out. Kicking her out for doing something that, as our Pack Alpha, he should be doing!"

"Alexa," Mal warned, shaking his head. "Lucien's doing what's right."

"How can you say that?" she cried. "Our parents are dead, and he's not doing anything about it! But he's going to kick out the one person who will?"

"Enough!" Lucien growled and strode into the center of the group. His silver eyes blazed into Caia's. "My word is law. I said there would be no acts of vengeance. This war is no longer ours. If Caia breaks the law ... then she's out of the pack." He might as well have taken a knife and shoved it right through her heart. She couldn't hate him for protecting the people they both loved.

The pack chattered in confusion and hurt, completely certain that Caia wasn't doing the right thing but uncertain that Lucien was. Caia shook her head and moved to meet him.

"Don't," she said sternly, and they all quieted. "Lucien is right. I have to do this, and I don't expect any of you to understand." She struggled to hold back the tears. "It's for the best. I would've been pulled back into the war no matter what happened, and I don't want to drag you back in with me." A sound to the right drew her attention. Reuben was there waiting for her. "You'll be protected here."

She turned and looked Lucien straight in the eye. With that look, he begged her one last time not to do this. But she shook her head slightly, and his face mottled with uncontrolled anger. "Will you keep Laila and Vil here with you? Please?"

He nodded, and she thought he might not trust himself to speak.

"I'm leaving with Reuben. Now."

"Caia, we're coming with you." Alexa and Jaeden rushed over.

Lucien opened his mouth to speak, but Caia beat him to it. "No, you're not."

"But Caia—"

"Do you want me to do this?" she hissed, feeling so angry at them. Stupidly she'd hoped their conscience would make an appearance, and they'd tell her no. Not that it would matter because Reuben would still take away his protection if she didn't do it.

Jaeden blanched but Alexa nodded enthusiastically. "Of course we do."

"Then stay here."

"Bu—"

Jaeden grabbed Alexa's arm. "Be quiet, Lex. We'll stay," she agreed, and Caia could see a shimmer of guilt in her eyes. She wasn't so comfortable with blackmail after all. Too late.

Caia turned away from them and gave Vil and Laila a reassuring smile. "You'll be fine here," she promised and strode toward Reuben who stood at the doorway, waiting for her.

"Caia, wait!" Magnus ambled after her. He grabbed her arm and spun her around. She'd never seen him look so mad before. "Why?"

Impetuously, she pulled him in to hug him close so she could whisper in his ear where the others couldn't hear. "I can't explain. I wish I could. But I can't. I'm still me, I promise." She choked on tears, and he squeezed her tight.

"I love you," he told her softly.

That was it. She had to get out of there before her control broke. "I have to go," she mumbled and pushed away from him, hurrying from the room. Through the glass-fronted doors, she caught sight of Saffron waiting by Reuben's car in the driveway. She crossed the foyer and felt Reuben at her back.

"I hate you," she told him quietly.

After a moment of silence came his sad reply, "I know."

Caia flinched at the sound of Lucien's almighty roar from the dining room. It was followed by a horrendous crash. A shower of tinkling ensued.

Reuben sighed as he held the front door open for her. "There go my windows."

* * *

JAEDEN HAD NEVER FELT this guilty in her life. She still couldn't believe Lucien had actually thrown Caia out of the pack. And everyone had let him! Ryder had let him! She wanted to beat the crap out of him for that.

She ambled wearily along the corridors of the hotel. The place was surprisingly big and nice. Everywhere was hardwood flooring and bright lighting. Faux flowers added a little romance here and there, and the paintings and décor were modern and airy, giving the whole place a sense of openness. The bedrooms were huge as well. She'd taken one next door to Alexa and was studiously avoiding Ryder, who, for the moment, was thankfully preoccupied with making sure Lucien was alright. Their Alpha had cut himself up pretty good when he threw chairs through windows and smashed, crushed, and basically destroyed everything in his path after Caia left.

If it hadn't been for Laila and Vil, who managed to magik them up some new windows, they would all be freezing their asses off. So ... who gave a damn if Lucien was hurt? He'd thrown Caia out.

You're angry at yourself, not Lucien.

Like hell!

Dad would be so mad at you.

She growled and stomped through the halls. She was looking for Lucien's room. She wanted to give him a piece of her mind.

"There you are."

She tensed at the voice and turned slightly to see her mate walking toward her determinedly. "Ryder." She nodded at him as if they were strangers instead of mates.

He grunted at her. "Jaeden. Nice to see you. It's been awhile."

"I'm not in the mood for your pathetic wit."

He pushed her up against the wall, his eyes sparking with irritation. "I'm not in the mood for your childish behavior but still I'm going to put up with it because you're my mate ... or have you forgotten that?"

The feel of him close to her, his scent, his heat nudged at her heart, adamant to start it beating again. And she so wanted to just let go, to fall into his arms and tell him everything and make him persuade Lucien to retrieve Caia. But she wouldn't. Instead she pictured the gory sight of her father's body.

She wanted revenge more.

"I haven't forgotten," she replied quietly. "Although I'm trying."

Ryder flinched, and she refused to feel bad for the hurt that flickered in his gaze. "What the hell does that mean?" he growled, pushing his face aggressively closer.

She shrugged, pretending indifference. "I don't want it. I don't want … you," she lied, struggling to forget her amazing first time with him that night at the Center. She'd never felt closer to anyone in her entire life.

He exhaled slowly and took a step back. "You're grieving. And you're angry. Confused. You need time."

"I do need time," she agreed with her dead eyes. "But I don't need you."

And with that, she brushed past him, ignoring his shocked countenance, and continued on through the hotel in search of Lucien, determined her heart wasn't breaking.

After all … she didn't have a heart left to break.

* * *

"Lucien." Rose sighed, gazing up at him from the sofa in the bedroom suite he'd chosen for himself. "Talk to me."

He didn't want to talk to anybody. He was afraid of the damage he would do, afraid he would take the frustration over Caia's departure out on one of the pack. He had managed to shake off Ryder—who was pelting him with questions—and retreat to his room. Then Rose had shown up. She didn't deserve his attitude.

"I appreciate your concern, Rose, but—"

"But why don't you stick your damn nose in someone else's business."

They turned to see Jaeden striding into the room, the door slamming shut behind her. Lucien frowned as she glared at Rose.

"Jaeden," he warned.

She sneered and he flinched at the disrespect. Jae had never dared to look or speak to him in any manner but that which she owed her Alpha. "Don't," she bit out and then turned back on Rose. "Get out."

Rose's mouth fell open momentarily before she remembered herself. Her eyes narrowed dangerously. "You don't tell me what to do."

"Jaeden, don't speak to Rose like that."

"Don't speak to Rose like that?" She guffawed and sliced him another disdainful look. "Pity you can't show the kind of concern you reserve for your ex-girlfriend for your *actual* mate. Or has Caia already been forgotten and I'm interrupting the reawakening of a beautiful relationship here?"

Her remark stung, and Lucien felt a sense of shame. Not about Rose. There was nothing going on with Rose. He loved Caia. Which was exactly why he felt sick to his stomach for kicking her out of the pack. His plan had backfired.

"Rose, can you give us a minute?" He nodded to the door.

By the tensing of her shoulders, he knew Rose was annoyed at being dismissed, but if he didn't have this out with Jaeden now, they would be at each other's throats for days … weeks, even.

When Rose was gone, Lucien turned his full attention to Jaeden, reminding himself she was going through an unimaginably difficult time and to be patient with her. "If you've come to shout at me about Caia, you can stop. I already feel as bad as I'm going to feel."

Jae curled her lip. "I somehow doubt that. I mean, you have Rose hanging out with you already."

He sighed, running his hands through his hair. "Jaeden, Rose is none of your business."

She smirked derisively. "Is that why you kicked Caia out? To be with Rose?"

"For goddess' sake, Jaeden, no!" he yelled, dropping into a seat, glaring at her the whole time. "I love Caia."

"Oh yeah, sure, I really got that, you know ... when you humiliated her and kicked her out of the only family she's ever known."

Sharp streaks of guilt spiked him all over. "Don't. Do you think I wanted to? But this pack has been through enough, and Caia is going to do something unforgivable. We need out of this, and Reuben has promised us safety."

A tense silence fell between them before she finally nodded and lowered herself into the seat across from him. Her eyes were limpid pools, and he saw a reflection of his own guilt in them. "And what about Caia's safety?"

"You think I don't care?" he hissed. "You think I just threw her out of here like it was nothing? She is my mate, Jaeden. It goes against everything I am to throw her to the proverbial wolves like that ... but she's made this insane decision and her reasons are not good enough for me to back her up."

He couldn't understand. He needed to understand. He needed to run.

"I don't think her decision is insane."

Lucien shook his head. "Jaeden, we're not going to kill innocent people to further our means. I don't know why Caia feels she has to do it. There's no good reason—"

"Oh, for the love of the gods, Lucien!" Jaeden snapped out of her seat. "This is Caia! She always has a good reason!"

What did she want from him? What did she want him to say? That what Caia was doing was okay? Because it wasn't. It would never sit right with him.

"Jaeden, I don't want to argue. In fact, I want to go for a run. So you can stay here bitching at the wall or you can come with me."

She screwed up her face at him like a child and took a moment. Finally, she exhaled with a huff, "Fine. I'll come running with you. But I want you to know that I think she's doing the right thing."

He shrugged numbly, refusing to look at her, feeling little more than a young boy lost.

"Dear Gaia," she gasped. "You think she's going to change her mind. You only kicked her out 'cause you don't believe she'll go through with it."

Ten points for wolf girl. Of course he didn't believe Caia capable of killing innocent people. The only thing holding him together was that hope. And he wasn't letting go.

He nodded in reply. "I kicked her out hoping that would stop her. It hasn't, but … I have Reuben's phone number. I'll check in with him to make sure she's alright. And then—"

"And then what? Be there when she changes her mind?" She shook her head sadly. "Jeez, Lucien … even if she does miraculously decide not to take out the Septum, do you honestly think she will ever forgive you for letting go of her so easily?"

Her question caused his throat to close, and he felt the unbearable need to swipe at something with his claws outstretched. Finally, he pinned her with his own penetrating look.

Fight fire with fire.

"You really think if you keep pushing Ryder away, he'll still be there when you realize what an idiot you're being?" He shouldn't have enjoyed the way she paled, but the animosity between them egged him on. "Yeah, I didn't think so," he whispered with a smirk.

"You're a jerk."

"Misery loves company, sweetheart." He shrugged, speaking the truth.

She gave a pathetic half growl before jumping toward him with an animation she hadn't shown in a while. "OK, so … you didn't actually mean to kick Caia out, right?"

"Right …"

"Then let's go get her. All of us. Let's do this together."

He shook his head. "I told you, I'm not dragging the pack back into this. Plus … for the hundredth time, I don't agree with what she's doing."

"But you love her?"

"Yes."

"And you want to protect her?"

"Of course."

"So let's just you and I go. We'll go get her. Keep her safe."

He sighed, running his hands through his hair in frustration. Why was Jae doing this? She was making him feel bad … it was like kicking a puppy, for Gaia's sake. "I can't. I can't leave the pack alone again." He cursed, feeling his anger at his mate building. "And Caia knows that! No. She made her choice. I have to make mine."

He watched her shoulders slump, the dim light in her eyes dying. There was more to this for Jae than she was letting on, but getting it out of her would mean nothing short of torturing her. He could only hope she came around on her own.

After a few minutes of silence, he shrugged. "You still up for that run?"

"Do I get to bite and hit you?" She snapped up from her chair and crossed the room to the exit.

He sighed and followed her out the door. "Will you ease up on the verbal assaults if I say yes?"

"But they hurt more."

"True. But I'm sure you'll find more satisfaction taking your frustration out on my hide rather than coming up with new caustic witticisms to scar my soul."

"Well there, see … that's where you're wrong."

CHAPTER 17

A LAIR, A GIRL, AND A "HELL, NO!"

*I*ncense flooded her nostrils and clogged the back of her throat. She fought hard not to cough, not wanting to offend Reuben. But the place really did smell bad.

Reuben grinned back at her. "The incense covers the odor."

Caia frowned as they walked down the dark, narrow hall and approached the doorway covered with a beaded curtain. "What odor?" she whispered to Saffron who glided beside her.

Saffron glowered at Reuben's back. "You'll see."

Curious as to the dark look Saffron had thrown Reuben (who as far as Caia could gather was technically her boss), she followed the vamp through the red-beaded curtain and came to an abrupt halt at what she found on the other side.

Saffron nudged around her. "Caia," she prompted.

But Caia was in shock. They stood in a cramped living room where old, worn-out sofas and beanbags took up most of the space. A TV flickered in the corner where a couple of people sat watching it hypnotically. Soda and beer cans littered the floor, and spilled chips and cookies feathered with mold kept them company.

The mess wasn't what shocked Caia. It was the humans— three, to be exact. And the three vampyres who were sucking blood out of the humans' necks and wrists. More shocking were the moans of pleasure escaping, invisible *oh*'s and *ah*'s from the mouths of the humans. And the odor was the coppery headiness of blood mixed with sex.

Caia made a face. *Lovely.*

Caia realized two people in front of the TV were also human. One of them turned and noticed them, his eyes flaring wildly at the sight of the intruders. He scrambled to his feet, his eyes wide with panic as he rushed to the female vampyre on the couch sucking on some guy's wrist.

"H-heey, D-Dee … w-w-we got compaanyy," he stuttered, moving cautiously closer to the vampyres.

Caia was totally confused. When Reuben told her they were going someplace safe to hang out while she looked into the Septum's trace, Caia didn't think he meant a vampyre lair … where there were actual bad vampyres. And she was guessing the vampyres hadn't been expecting old Reuben to drop by. Boy, was he going to crack some heads!

The vampyre she assumed was Dee looked up languidly from her feeding and smiled, thick blood made extra slippery from saliva trailing down her chin.

Again. Lovely.

"Reuben," she sighed happily.

"Dee." He nodded, giving her a slight smile hello.

What? Was he freaking kidding? There were vampyres, feeding on humans! *Hello!*

"Reuben," Caia said sternly and then stopped as Saffron's hand wrapped around her wrist in warning.

"Caia." Reuben turned back to her, grinning at the look of concern on her face. "This is Dee, Andreas, and Charles. This is their lair. They've kindly allowed us the use of one of their private rooms at the back so we can get down to business."

"By business, you—"

"Just follow," Saffron insisted, and Caia was dragged through the room, past the bloodsucking, through a tiny 1980s kitchen, down another corridor and into a back bedroom that was much larger than she would've guessed. It was also empty other than a heart-shaped double bed. *Oh my.*

"What the Hades is going on?" she hissed as Saffron closed the door behind the three of them.

Reuben scowled at her. "Dee knows we're here on a mission, but she doesn't know what ... *you* nearly blurting it out was very intelligent, thank you."

How dare he?

"Me?" she huffed incredulously. "I'm mucking up the mission? You brought us into a den of iniquity! I thought you *hunted* rogue vampyres, not partied with them!"

He looked to Saffron for backup. The faerie shrugged. "You'll find no help from this quarter, Reuben. You know I hate these places."

"These places?" Caia snapped. "What is this place?"

He sighed and shrugged. "It's not illegal, Caia. It's a place where willing humans act as donors. They're addicts. The act of taking someone's blood can be quite pleasurable to a human."

"Is that before or after they die?"

A growl erupted from the back of his throat. "They don't die. They're donors. They're well taken care of."

Caia didn't care if they were well taken care of or if they were willing. It was just ... wrong! It was like a twisted version of a drug house. An ugly thought occurred to her. "You don't ... do you?"

Reuben looked affronted by the suggestion. "No. I do not feed on humans. I never have. But this is the last place

161

anyone would think to look for us. We're safe here while you gather the information you need from the trace."

Safe? Somehow she didn't think so.

"So you trust the vampyres with the human blood decorating their teeth and gums, do you?"

With another sound of annoyance, Reuben crossed the room and lowered himself onto the bed. His dark gaze blazed with command. "I trust Dee to not tell anyone we're here. I've known her a long time. She does favors for me, and I allow this lair to remain open for business. It's not pretty, but it's the way of the world, little girl. So quit squalling and take this." He thrust the paper with the names of the Septum out to her. "Sit down and get started."

Disgruntled, Caia nonetheless did what he asked and settled into an armchair. Reuben and Saffron made themselves comfortable on the bed, and Caia looked up to see them both drift off to sleep. It had been a long drive, and while Caia slept in the back of the car, Reuben and Saffron had remained vigilant up front. They made only one pit stop where Saffron ran into a diner to grab burgers for her and Caia. They ate hungrily while Reuben drank what she presumed was blood out of a flask.

The silence was only penetrated by the soft sounds of their breathing, and Caia looked nervously down at the piece of paper that had gotten her kicked out of her pack. It was still hard to believe Lucien had thrown her out. She'd thought there was literally nothing that could come between them. She didn't think there was anything she wouldn't do for him and had thought the feeling was mutual. But he'd done it to protect the pack, and that she could understand— that she respected. The way he was with the pack was one of the reasons she loved him so damn much.

But, and though she knew it was irrational, she was cut to the quick. The hurt was as deep a gash as the loss of her pack, as the loss of her friends, Marion, Sebastian. And she was afraid the hurt her mate had caused might not be the kind of scar that disappeared after the change.

Wow. She really was on her own now. But she'd been here before, and she could do this. She could do this alone.

At that, she spread open the paper and began investigating the trace. To her absolute relief, the first two were Midnights, one of whom was a member of the Council who had propagated the idea of a witch hunt against Nikolai. The other Midnight wasn't nearly as prominent within the coven; however, he was equally a racist and believed in the rightness of the war. She let loose a long stream of relieved air. This was good. This was really good. No guilt for killing the bad guys, huh?

She straightened in her seat and touched the third name. Eliza Emerett. With a whoosh Caia was pulled into the girl's trace, her essence dousing her in floods just as Laila's had.

She felt sick to her stomach when she realized why.

Eliza Emerett was an eleven-year-old Midnight. An eleven-year-old innocent girl with no real understanding of the war. The only world she knew was that of her parents, the farm they owned in England, her horses Star and Pooka, the cat, Lightning, and the two dogs, Bob and Fred. And let's not forget her imaginary friend, Nicky, who hung out by the old oak tree down by the stream.

The trace devoured her, refusing to let go, and Caia struggled, pulling and twisting to be released, the nausea of her find overwhelming.

She jerked back and felt her head slam against the wall behind the armchair. Reuben shot up from his half sleep and stared at her in concern. Saffron was slower to wake, but Caia waited for her to do so.

And then she pinned them both with a look that would fry their asses to the bed.

"You bastard," she whispered.

He groaned, scrubbing his face before swinging his legs over the side of the bed. He leaned toward her, studying her face quietly. Finally, just when she thought she might change into a lykan and attack him, he nodded at the paper. "What happened? What did you find?"

She glared at him. "You really don't know?"

"I really don't know."

"Eliza Emerett." She stabbed the name on the paper with her finger.

"What about her?"

Was he deliberately being a jackass or did he honestly not have a clue what she was talking about?

She stood and he watched her warily as she approached him. *Yeah, he better be wary.* "She's eleven, Reuben." She threw the paper at him. "She's an eleven-year-old Midnight. Her biggest fear is when her old dog, Fred, is going to bite the bullet!"

Saffron groaned and buried her head in her knees. Reuben swore and snapped up off the bed, crumpling the paper in his hand. "Nikolai," he hissed.

Caia stopped, watching the tension ripple through the vampyre's body. "You really didn't know?"

"No!" He whirled on her.

"Wow." She relaxed a little, seeing how upset the news made him. "You're not so evil after all."

He chortled but the sound was anything but happy. "Don't kid yourself, Caia." He sneered at her and held up the crumpled paper. "*This* wouldn't stop *me*. Nikolai knows that. He seems to have forgotten, however, that we aren't dealing with me. We're dealing with *you*. And I know even threatening the pack couldn't get you to kill a little girl." He slammed a fist into the wall with a rare show of loss of control. "We are so screwed!" he spat, ignoring the crumbling plaster.

Caia looked at Saffron whose face was blank. "Well … at least he knows when he's hitting a brick wall. I mean, metaphorically speaking. You know … I'm the brick wall. I won't budge on the killing of a little girl and he gets that. You get what I—"

Saffron threw her a look of disdain. "You're prattling. Shut up."

She stepped back against the wall and let herself slide to the floor. "Where do we go from here?"

"Hades?" the faerie suggested dryly.

Caia made a face. "Not helpful."

They stayed in tense silence for a while, avoiding eye contact. Finally, Reuben cursed again under his breath. "Why is this going wrong? This isn't the way it should be going. That damn Prophet …"

Something niggled at Caia.

Reuben? The Prophet? Yes! That was it!

Caia's head jerked up. "The Prophet!" She leapt to her feet in one fluid movement. "That's it."

Reuben frowned. "What's it?"

She smiled slowly. "We need to talk to the Prophet."

When they weren't getting giddy with excitement like she was, Caia almost slammed their heads together. Then she realized she hadn't actually explained what she was so excited about. It *had* been a long week.

"Okay," she said hurriedly. "My original plan was to get the Council to take away Marita as Head of the Coven and have the gods replace me. That way I'd be in control of the trace and begin peace negotiations—I know, I know, how terribly naive. But what if we find the Prophet and ask him if he thinks the gods will take away the trace if I *do* become Head of both covens?"

They stared at her blankly for a moment before Reuben asked, "And why would the gods take away the trace?"

She threw up her hands in half-assed exasperation. "Because! The trace exists for one reason only—a weapon for each leader of each coven. If I'm the Head of both covens, then the purpose of its existence no longer endures! Surely the two traces would cancel each other out. The gods wouldn't see a reason for us to have it anymore."

The vamp and faerie stared at her for what seemed forever and then they looked to one another. Slowly but surely, a mirror-image grin spread on their faces. Reuben turned back to Caia, his eyes glittering with respect. "That's brilliant, Caia."

"You think so?" she whispered, feeling the first glimpse of relief and warmth shimmer within her chest since the loss of the pack.

"I more than think so." He shrugged into his coat. "Right, we have to find the Prophet."

CHAPTER 18

THE PROPHET

The last few weeks had been excruciating to say the least. Patience, she discovered, was not one of her virtues. But at least she didn't have to stay in that horrible place with Dee and her band of merry bloodsuckers anymore. Caia never would've thought she'd be so grateful to be invited by Nikolai to stay at his safe house. *His* safe house wasn't a basement apartment full of blood and empty kitchen cabinets. Yes, the fridge in his safe house was filled with bags of animal blood belonging to Reuben (courtesy of a butcher—she wasn't going to ask when he'd had time to visit a butcher, as she was realizing there wasn't any point interrogating the most mysterious person she'd ever met), but the safe house was a modest-size beach cabin with no neighbors for miles. It was plush and luxurious inside, and Caia could lose herself in the sound of the surf while they anxiously waited for the Prophet to get back to them.

After leaving Dee's lair, Caia had tracked down the Prophet in the trace. The old guy was in Greece, putting up his feet while the Midnights figured out just who was in charge now that Nikolai was AWOL. Tracking him was the easy part; it was getting a hold of him that was proving to be problematic. Caia wasn't confident enough in her communication spell to travel somewhere she'd never been before, and she didn't have Vil because, well, he was with the pack. Saffron could transform into a bird and fly there, but that would take days they didn't have.

In the end, it was Nikolai who came to the rescue. Reuben called and asked him if he'd ever been to the Prophet's place in Greece, and surprise, surprise, the Midnight had. Nikolai told Reuben to bring Caia and Saffron to his beach house, and he'd get the Prophet to come back with him to speak with Caia. And that was exactly what he did.

Caia hadn't known what she'd been expecting. Okay. So she did know. She'd been expecting some withered old man with a long, white beard, wearing ancient Greek dress and banging around the place with a staff. Pretty much Gandalf, except Greek. The Prophet hadn't been anything like that. He had been old … like, seventy old, but with a full head of pepper-gray hair and a trim physique. He walked like a man years younger, a handsome older man in white linen trousers and shirt. The dude was less Gandalf and more Sean Connery.

He'd been a charmer, all right. He'd approached Caia with a careful smile, his light eyes drinking her in from head to foot. Almost tentatively, the Prophet had taken her hand between the palms of both of his and shook it gently.

"So this is Caia Ribeiro." He'd smiled, shaking his head in wonder. "You're just what I imagined."

That had amused her. "You're the only one who pictured me like me. I think people were imagining … taller and, well … just taller."

He chuckled warmly and nodded. "I've waited a long time to meet you."

"So I've heard."

"And now you wish to speak with me?"

Caia gestured to Nikolai's sofas, and the Prophet followed her to the seating area. He laughed a little at the way Reuben, Saffron, and Nikolai trailed them, barely giving them room to breathe.

"Nice to see you, Kirios." The Prophet grinned at Reuben.

The vampyre narrowed his eyes on him. "Your last bout of information regarding the Septum turned into crap. That's why you're here."

"Jeez, Reuben, are you always so rude?" Caia admonished and turned politely back to the Prophet. "Ignore him."

"Ignore him?" Reuben spluttered. "Old man, you sent us on a twenty-year goose chase."

The old man shrugged lazily but his eyes turned serious. "And yet here I am speaking with Caia. And she has something very important to ask me. Something that will matter. So ... maybe the goose chase wasn't really a goose chase after all."

Saffron had taken that moment to roll her eyes. "Oh, please, don't give us that 'everything happens for a reason' crap."

Their disrespect toward the Cassandrian made Caia uncomfortable, and she gritted her teeth, waiting for him to decide their insults weren't worth it and just ... poof! Leave them with no words of wisdom or plan.

But he didn't do any of that. Instead he pinned Saffron with an implacable look and said in a voice that sent shivers down Caia's spine, "You're a child of the gods and you don't believe in fate? If you don't believe in fate, then what have we been doing for the last seven hundred years, Saffron?"

She grumbled under her breath and tossed her hair. "I believe in fate," she finally said and then twitched a little before throwing herself into an armchair. "Sorry. I'm just very anxious and very tired."

The Prophet nodded, dismissing Saffron's childish outburst. And then he turned his attention back to Caia. "My dear, I already know what you wish to ask. You wish to ask me, if you were to become the Head of the Daylight Coven, as Head of both covens, could we ask the gods to take away the trace."

Caia gaped at him. "Did Nikolai tell you?"

"No," the Prophet and Nikolai replied in unison.

The Prophet tapped his fingers to his head, smiling kindly as he told her, "Visions, my dear. The gods see all and they communicate through me."

Excitement buzzed through them in that moment, all three leaning in toward the old man. "So?" she asked. "Will they? Will they take it away?"

Disappointingly, the Prophet merely shrugged. "They're still deliberating."

"What do you mean they're still deliberating? What's there to deliberate?"

He let out a gust of laughter, leaving them all bemused, which was pretty much how the entire meeting had gone so far. "My dear girl, we are the gods' only source of entertainment. They'll drag this out a little."

"And by a little, you mean?"

"A few days, a few weeks—"

"Not months." Caia gasped. "Please don't say months."

"I don't know. But as soon as I do, I will return with the answer."

And then he was gone.

"Whoa." Reuben shook his head. "That guy has had some serious work done. Last time I saw him, he was wheezing and banging around with a stick."

Nikolai nodded. "He really let himself go during Devlyn's reign. My Regency did a world of wonders for him."

Caia stared at them like they were crazy. Sometimes they were so inappropriately blasé.

* * *

SHE'D BEEN WAITING for a couple of weeks now, slowly going mad as she wandered from room to room. She'd spent her time going for runs on the beach as a human during the day and as a wolf at night. Other than Reuben's "helpful" training regimen every day, where he tried to get her to focus the unknown energy that made her so special—and they were getting there, slowly but surely—he and Nikolai weren't much company. When Nikolai wasn't complaining about furniture and accessories he was losing to Caia's training (she was successfully turning items to ash by choice), he and Reuben could sit still for hours, staring at nothing and speaking to no one. It was creepy.

As for Saffron, the faerie came and went as she pleased, and Caia had never envied anyone more for their abilities than during those weeks cooped up in the beach cabin with only a vampyre and a magik for company. With no one to talk to, she found herself dwelling on the pack a lot. At night it was hard not to cry herself to sleep thinking about their loss.

For her, the biggest hurt was the loss of Dimitri. It wasn't just that he'd looked out for her or cared for her; it was more how much his loss was hurting the people closest to her—Jaeden, to be exact. Her friend had already suffered through so much. Caia ached for her. And she ached wondering if she would ever have the pack back, admitting only to herself how lonely she was without them, lonely without Lucien to fall asleep with at night.

On top of that was her trace. It had been tingling all over the place, telling her the Midnights were reorganizing. Two magiks were out in front for leadership—Jack Straton, an Australian, and a Russian woman called Orina Beketov. Caia had been praying for Straton to make the grade since he wanted to find Nikolai first (a task she knew was impossible and would keep them occupied forever) before taking on the Daylights. Beketov wanted to begin where they'd left off, starting with a major attack against the New York Krôls, one of America's largest vampyre covens.

The worst day for Caia came when the trace told her Orina had won the votes. She was the new Regent of the Midnight Coven, and the woman was as vicious as they came. Her plans for the attack were set in motion, ready to take off in one month's time. Of course, Caia had wanted to go straight to the Center to let them know so they could prepare themselves and warn the Krôls.

But Nikolai and Reuben wouldn't let her, and by wouldn't let her, she meant Nikolai had put a spell around her that stopped her from using her communication spell. And she couldn't find a way around it. Unfortunately, she still had so much to learn.

* * *

IT HAD BEEN a week since she'd learned of the Midnights' plan for attack. For once they were all together—Saffron, Nikolai, Reuben, and her—sitting around the kitchen, actually participating in conversation.

"No, it's definitely a different guy who's the voice of Kermit the Frog. It has been for years," Reuben insisted as he sipped from a mug of warm blood.

Nikolai frowned. "No. We get *Sesame Street* in Russia too. You can't fool me ... Kermit has sounded the same for decades."

Caia tried to hide her snort in her toast.

Reuben groaned. "Yeah, because they found a guy who sounds exactly like him."

The Russian looked pensive for a moment. "So … how long are we talking?"

"I dunno … Jim Henson died in 1990."

Nikolai shook his head, looking disturbed. "No, that's not right. I've seen *Muppet Christmas Carol*. That was definitely the original Kermit."

"Oh." Caia grinned, remembering watching that movie during the lonely Christmas holidays she spent with Irini. Obviously they didn't believe in Christmas and all that stuff, but most supernaturals celebrated it to fit in with the humans. "I love that movie."

Saffron leaned back in her chair. "Were you even an egg when that movie came out?"

"It was 1992." Reuben nodded. "Caia was just about to hatch."

"No," Nikolai insisted. "Then that can't be right. You said Henson died in 1990, da?"

"Yeah, and Steve Whitmire took over for him. He's the voice of Kermit the Frog in the *Muppet Christmas Carol*."

This seemed to upset Nikolai, and Caia shared an amused look with Saffron. He shook his head again. "I could have sworn Kermit has always been Kermit. What I want to know is how he sounds so much like the other man?"

Caia grunted into her juice this time. "What I want to know is how Reuben knows so much about this stuff?"

The vampyre scowled at her. "Photographic memory."

"And the Jim Henson Company was one of the institutions you felt necessary to study up on?" Saffron asked, deadpan.

Caia choked on a bite of toast.

"Isn't anyone going to rescue Caia from the toast?" a familiar voice intruded. Caia was suddenly whacked on the back (hard) by Nikolai, and the toast dislodged itself. She looked up to see the Prophet standing over the table.

"Better?" he asked softly.

She winced at the sting Nikolai's hand had left but thanked him nonetheless before turning back on the Prophet. She gazed up at him. "Please tell me you have news."

He grinned back at her. "Finally, I have news."

"Well?" Saffron snapped.

The Prophet's grin grew wider. "Looks like the apocalypse is coming, children. The gods will take away the trace if Caia succeeds in becoming the Head of both covens."

Relief swept through her like a tidal wave, and for the first time in weeks, she felt as alive as a surfer crashing under it.

"Ahhhh haa haaaa!" Caia jumped up happily and threw her arms around the old guy. He hugged her back tight, laughing at her excitement. After a moment, he drew back from her, his expression serious.

"Now all you have to do is convince the Daylights of your plan and start your witch hunt for Marita."

She was sobered by the thought. To do this, to free them all from the trace, she was still going to have to kill someone. Yes, it was the evil bitch who'd murdered members of her pack, tortured innocent children, and inevitably caused the death of her mentor, Marion. Hmm, when she thought about it like that, maybe taking her out wouldn't be so difficult after all.

"The hard part is explaining all this to the Council." Saffron sighed.

Reuben shook his head. "Not necessarily. Vanne will believe us."

"Maybe." Nikolai nodded. "But if you don't mind, for now I'll stay here. I don't want to be imprisoned just for being of Midnight blood."

"Fair enough." Reuben patted him on the shoulder. He looked up at the Prophet. "Thank you. Again."

The Prophet smiled. "It's always a pleasure, Kirios."

And then he was gone.

Caia stared a moment at the spot where he'd been standing before spinning around to face the weird trio that had become her trustworthy companions (which wasn't saying much). "OK. So … the Center it is, then."

Reuben nodded in agreement. He didn't smile but there was a new light in his dark eyes. "The Center it is."

CHAPTER 19

BLOOD OATH

*T*he atmosphere at the Center was different from before. There had always been this tension, this sense of everyone being wound tight, but also a sense of security, of feeling powerful and protected at the same time. The stressful tension, however, had unfortunately been replaced by a heightened sense of expectation, and the worst of it was, it was kind of like that butterfly-in-the-belly feeling when one was unsure of a situation. Moreover, Caia discerned a new uneasiness among the Center's inhabitants —a paranoid awareness of one's own surroundings, as if awaiting imminent attack.

Reuben had called Vanne, and after explaining what Caia needed to discuss, Vanne had granted them entry to the Center. Caia hadn't been expecting a reception, but on the other side of the portal stood Vanne, Alfred Doukas, and Penelope Argyros, and they were surrounded by other magiks acting as bodyguards. The Center was electrified with the news of Caia's return, and she could feel the stares heating the back of her neck as she was taken through corridors she'd never walked before. Disappearing behind the group were the cold magnolia walls and tough tiled floors she'd thought made up most of the Center's décor and appearing before them were plush carpeted corridors and mahogany-paneled walls.

Finally, they came to what looked like a waiting room with eight-foot grand double doors beyond it. Caia stopped apprehensively. Something didn't seem right. No one had spoken since they were greeted at the portal, and ... what *was* this place?

Penelope spun in her kitten heels, smiling gently at Caia, and she felt a little better. It seemed Alfred and Penelope genuinely liked her, so maybe convincing the Council wouldn't be so difficult after all.

"Caia." Penelope nodded to the waiting room. "If you would like to take a seat while Saffron and Reuben follow me. We'll be back for you in a few minutes."

Caia looked to Reuben, and she noted the look of realization on his face as he shared a glance with Saffron. They knew what was happening. Why the hell didn't she?

"What's going on?" she asked warily.

"You'll understand in a moment," Alfred assured her.

Saffron scowled at him. "Mr. Doukas, can you not tell her? It could come as a shock."

What could come as a shock? Holy Artemis, what on Gaia's green earth was going on here? *Do not hyperventilate.* "Yeah." She bobbed her head. "Tell me."

Doukas shook his head after throwing Saffron a reproving look. "It's not the way it's done, Caia. I'm afraid you'll just have to wait. Reuben, Saffron ... please follow us."

It was only then that Caia noticed the insignificant-looking side door on the adjacent wall to the double doors. Just as they were all about to disappear through it (and no, she couldn't get a look beyond them to see what the Hades was on the other side), she threw up a hand. "Uh, Saffron, tell them about the Krôls."

The faerie nodded and bent to speak with Penelope as they disappeared through the door; Caia gathered she was imparting the pivotal information.

It felt like forever, sitting there, waiting, gradually growing so anxious, she was sure she was going to upchuck all over the waiting-room floor. Nothing had ever seemed to take as long as this wait did.

Dear goddess, she was actually going mad from the wait. Her eyes bored into the double doors, wishing (and not for the first time) if she had superpowers, why couldn't they include X-ray vision? Seriously, what was going on behind those damn doors, and why was it so damn quiet out here?

Her heart jolted at a loud creaking and her eyes widened as the double doors slowly opened out toward her. She stood on trembling legs and gaped as a tall, young magik she recognized as a member of the Council stared at her pensively. His name was Derren. He was the magik who had gone under-cover to discover the labs.

"Caia Ribeiro," his voice echoed behind and beyond him. "Please enter the Court of the Council."

The what of the what?

There was no time to ask; he was already spinning on his heel. Caia hurried to follow, only seeing a high, dark wooden wall carved with images of warfare. As she drew past the doors, however, her heart nearly exploded in her chest. At either side were stairs leading up into a room with the highest ceiling she'd ever seen, a ceiling so grand it could've been painted by Michelangelo himself.

But the heart thudding had more to do with the faces she could see peering down at her from above the stairs. Derren waited at the top of the set to her left. Tentatively, Caia climbed them and as she did so, she saw over the carved wooden wall. The stairs led up to a massive circular room. In the center was a round platform ringed by rows of benches that rose away from the floor at a steep gradient. The rows were filled with inquisitive Daylights peering at her in a mixture of anxiety and excitement. At the farthest end of the hall, in the front row benches, sat the Council, waiting expectantly. Reuben and Saffron were seated with them beside Vanne.

"Follow me," Derren demanded, and Caia crossed the platform, surprised her legs didn't buckle. The hush that filled the hall was crippling, all eyes burning into her. Was the entire Center here? She felt her cheeks heat under their watchful eyes. The funny thing was, she thought she might be able to cope better if she were in wolf form.

Instead she straightened her spine and followed Derren until he stopped in the center of the room.

Am I on trial?

She really wanted to ask but was frightened of messing up this ceremony—or whatever it was.

Once Derren was seated with the others, an elegant man stood. Caia recognized him as the guy who hadn't seemed to like her much when she'd first met with the Council to tell them about the underground labs. He should be fun.

Like Derren, his voice boomed around the entire court. "Caia Ribeiro, allow me to introduce myself." His dark stare wasn't at all friendly. "I am Benedict De Jong, a member of the Council. We have just spent the last thirty minutes—"

Thirty minutes? That was all?

"—listening to a young man with no affiliation to the Center tell us of your plan to kill Marita and ask us to make you Head of the Daylight Coven to gain control of both Midnight and Daylight trace, all with the intent to perform a rite soliciting the aid of the gods to remove the trace from the supernatural world, thus freeing its inhabitants."

It sounded really cool when he said it.

"Is this or is this not true?"

Caia nodded. "Yes, sir, it is." She almost flinched when she realized her voice was just as loud. There must have been a speaker spell of some kind on the room.

A rumble of murmurings followed before De Jong gestured for them to be quiet.

"Such a request would have been completely dismissed if not for the support given by not only Saffron, one of our most trusted and experienced shapeshifters, but also Vanne, who has helped lead this coven in war for decades. These are supernaturals who have sacrificed many things for the cause, and now they are risking their good name for you. Why? Why should we believe you, a girl of Midnight blood, a girl who has been thrown out of her own pack, who has aided and abetted the escape of a young female Midnight imprisoned at this Center, who trusts the words of a Midnight Prophet, and who hides out in the home of the former Regent of the Midnight Coven?"

Caia had to stop her mouth from dropping open. She glanced up at Reuben who gave a barely perceptible shrug. The son of a bitch had told them everything and hadn't even had the decency to warn her first. She stiffened and met De Jong's gaze. He was making it sound like she was a traitor.

"If Reuben has revealed all of this to you, then he must have explained the circumstances."

"Yes." Benedict smirked. "Nikolai Petrovsky is a double agent. The Prophet is neither Midnight nor Daylight at heart, and Laila is—"

"The purest soul I've ever met," Caia interrupted, squaring her shoulders and blasting him with a ferocious look.

Gasps echoed around the room.

Benedict curled his lip into a sneer. "A Midnight ... pure?

180

Please do not tell me you still believe this nonsense that there are 'good' Midnights."

She wanted to punch the arrogant bastard. She sneered right back at him. "It isn't nonsense. There *are* good Midnights. Many of them."

More gasps. Great.

The warlock glared at her. "I rather doubt it."

"Between the two of us, last I checked I was the one who has the trace, so you can stand up there with your 99 percent certainty of *doubting* it. But I stand up here 100 percent *knowing* there are Midnights out there who don't believe in the war." She turned, letting her voice carry to the spectators on the benches. She glimpsed the familiar faces of Desi and Ophelia and the other Center friends she'd made. "The trace has kept this war alive far longer than it ever should have!" She spun slowly back to face Benedict, determined. "Let me go after Marita. If I kill her, make me the Head of this coven, and I will free us from the trace. It is the first step to ending this war. I don't just believe that," she stated assuredly, "I know it. I know it with every fiber of my being."

The magik clenched his jaw. "Your word is not enough. Neither is the word of three other supernaturals—"

"Then let us see." Penelope stood, looking up into the crowd. "Are there any others who would back Caia?" She smiled softly. "Outside of the Council, that is."

Benedict glared at the interruption. "That is pointless. She would need at least twenty others of significant background."

Caia wondered if that was a jab at the Travelers. People were kind of snobby about them since they couldn't really do powerful spells, but they could use a communication spell to take them anywhere in the world, regardless of whether they'd ever been there before.

Penelope shrugged. "She is afforded the right of demonstration."

The Council looked to the crowd expectantly, and Caia wanted to die. It was like being in high school with humans all over again, waiting to see if anyone would sit with her at lunch or ask to be her lab partner when they were told to pair up. No one ever did.

The sound of wood creaking lifted her gaze off Benedict as Reuben, Saffron, and Vanne made their way toward her in the center of the room. They smiled reassuringly, Vanne squeezing her shoulder as they took their places behind her. The next person was a surprise because Caia hadn't realized she was at the Center: Phoebe MacLachlan. The statuesque beauty strode across the room self-assuredly, her expression as serious as always.

Caia smiled gratefully at her, and Phoebe nodded before turning to the Council. "My vote of confidence in Caia is shared by all members of my pack, including its Alpha, Alistair MacLachlan. That is approximately fifty other lykans, Mr. De Jong."

The magik paled slightly. "Well …"

But before he could argue, the noise of people standing from their seats drowned him out. Caia watched in amazement as Desi and Ophelia led eight other Travelers to her side. Michael Brown, the Head of the Second Unit of vampyres, descended the stairs with most of his unit in tow. He smirked at Lyla, the Head of the Third Unit of lykans, as she came along the aisle to meet him, lykans trailing at her back. Others crossed the room, all faces Caia recognized as the people she'd conversed with during her studies here at the Center. Altogether at least sixty people stood at her back.

De Jong stared in utter shock.

Penelope smiled. "I think this is proof enough that Caia is trusted among many here at the Center and that many are looking for the promise of change. Which means the Council will take this to a vote. Excuse us while we convene in the chambers below."

Silently they made their way downstairs.

"Well done, Caia." Reuben grinned and drew her into a surprising hug. He pulled back and stroked her cheek affectionately. "Not just a pretty face."

She rolled her eyes at him and turned to speak with Phoebe, thanking her for her support. The lykan stood vigilantly by her side as Caia spoke with everyone who'd taken to the platform in favor of her plan. It was overwhelming and unbelievable and yet ... undeniably wonderful.

As Desi and Ophelia giggled and hugged her, a moving realization hit. It would appear she wasn't quite so alone after all.

* * *

THE CROWD DISPERSED, everyone reluctantly finding their seats among the rows again as the Council reentered the hall. Their combined power intrigued Caia, their energy announcing their arrival before she even saw them. Alfred nodded kindly at her as he resumed his seat, and she took hope in the fact that Penelope seemed pleased with herself. Benedict stood up for the Council once more, his expression revealing little.

"Ms. Ribeiro, the Council has voted. The outcome, although not unanimous—"

Yeah, I'll bet.

"—is in your favor."

An outburst of hoots and claps came from the Travelers, and Caia was afraid to grin and look over in case it changed the Council's mind.

"HOWEVER!" Benedict shouted over the noise, causing silence to descend. "You must agree to a blood oath, promising to give up the trace to the gods, as you say is your intention, and not keep it for your own gain."

She began to speak, to promise that of course she would, when Alfred interrupted quickly. "Caia, you should be made aware of what a blood oath entails first ... before agreeing to anything." He shot Benedict a look of rebuke.

Benedict sneered. "Of course. Ms. Ribeiro, a blood oath is made between yourself and the person you have sworn the promise to. In most cases, this is merely one person. In this instance, you will swear the blood oath to the nine members of this Council."

OK, that didn't sound so bad.

"The blood oath acts as a binding spell. If you break your oath to the person you swore it to, then part of your power transfers to that person." He smiled wickedly. "Usually, it is not that detrimental to a person. But for you, Ms. Ribeiro, well ... if you break your oath to the Council, then each of us will acquire some of your energy."

Okaay ... she could see where he was going with this.

"Losing energy to nine people under a blood oath would mean the loss of all your magikal power, Ms. Ribeiro."

A tense silence filled the air. De Jong smirked as if this were some form of torture for her. In fact, everyone seemed to be on tenterhooks waiting for her reply. Only her friends sat confidently in their seats because ... they knew her. This wasn't a problem.

She smiled slowly. "Mr. De Jong, I have no hesitation in agreeing to a blood oath, because I have every intention of giving up the trace."

He lost the smirk as most of the Council relaxed, relieved at her answer. Chatter bounced off the walls while Caia stood there. Finally, Penelope stood. "If you will follow us, Caia, we will begin the ceremony for the blood oath immediately."

CHAPTER 20

*J*aeden held out her hand toward the plate as it hovered in the air, kept under tight control with her telekinesis. With a wave of satisfaction, she flicked her wrist, sending the china careening into the nearest tree. She smiled humorlessly as the shattered remnants found company with the other pieces of china she'd obliterated. Glancing down at the box filled with more expensive dinnerware, she tried not to feel impotent that this was her only act of revenge on Reuben.

Wow. Destroying his china pattern. What a kick to the cajones.

After weeks of berating herself and the vampyre, Jaeden had finally dashed into the huge kitchen to look for something to train with in the woods. Instead, she'd stumbled across some expensive china Reuben had locked in a closet at the back of the kitchen. She didn't know for certain if the stuff was his, but she decided to use it for target practice on the off chance that it might be. Now she was far into the woods, away from the rest of the pack, doing just that.

Ah, away from the rest of the pack, she mused. No change there, then. For the week Caia had been gone, Jaeden had avoided almost everyone. The only person she really spoke to was Alexa, and thus Mal and Finlay since they never left their sister's side. It was beginning to drive Lex nuts, and Jae's company was always a welcome relief from her brothers. But as the weeks turned, so did Jaeden's heart.

The immediate rage she'd felt over her father's death had calmed enough for her to begin to feel all kinds of guilty for what she had done to Caia. She couldn't comprehend how she could've let Caia be kicked out of the pack. And all she wanted to do now was find her and fix it. But how could she fix it when she couldn't even fix herself and her relationships with the pack? She hadn't spoken to her mother and ignored her when Julia tried to approach.

As for her relationship with Ryder, it was pretty much over. Her heart flipped in her chest at the thought. Their meeting in the hall the day Caia left wasn't to be their last. For two weeks Ryder cornered her whenever he got the chance, and all she did was insult and offend him ... oh gods, she had said some horrible things. She'd told him she didn't love him anymore. And Hades, that wasn't true. She loved him so much, she was terrified of losing him too. So pushing him away ... that had been a smart plan. *Not.* Now he could barely look at her.

And Lucien was trying his best to keep the pack together, insisting on weekly runs and meals together. At first those occasions had been blunted by grief and Jaeden's animosity, but she'd gradually been relegated to an outsider through her own means, the pack easing into casual conversations with one another, easing into playing and enjoying the euphoria and release of the pack runs. Except for Alexa and herself, the pack grieved as one and were the better for it.

Jaeden didn't miss that Vil and Laila's soothing presence helped. Especially little Laila; she had a gift for creating peace among them. Their other gifts had also come in handy when members of the pack went food shopping in the nearest town—Laila used her magik to glamour them so no one would question the strangers who kept popping into town.

Their other guest, Rose, was a different matter. As Jaeden's guilt over what she'd done to Caia grew unbearable, her misdirected anger at Rose grew as well. She snapped and snarled at the lykan any chance she got. Part of her knew it was psychological crap, but the other part of her knew, as she watched Rose with Lucien, that the female wolf was biding her time with their Alpha, awaiting the moment when he threw away Caia's memory for good and made Rose his partner.

Dear goddess, it was all her fault.

The box of dishes shook, and she clenched her fists, bringing her emotions back under control. It was all too late anyway. What was done was done, and there was nothing she could do about it. She didn't have the energy to do anything about it.

Frustrated as all Hades at herself, Jaeden ripped off her clothes. Once naked, she crouched on to all fours, luxuriating in the soft mud that seeped between her fingers and toes and cushioned the weight on her knees. She pushed the change, wincing in relief at the piercing of each hair through her skin, eyes burning as her ears transformed, her face shifting. Her jaw cracked as it elongated, her teeth filling her mouth rapidly. The echoing snap of her bones as her spine, legs, and arms morphed sent a premature howl from between lips still formed from the median change. Jaeden gasped in satisfaction at the stinging pain of her claws lengthening and concentrated on slowing the process to prolong the happy liberation the change wrought.

Finally, she lay in wolf form, panting into the forest floor. She wondered if she would be happier as a wolf. And then she saw a rabbit dash from between the trees, its frightened eye catching sight of her before it tore off into the camouflage of the woods. A real wolf would see the rabbit and lick its lips at the thought of the hunt and kill, but a lykan like her still had "aw, a bunny" thoughts running through her head. *Probably wouldn't be happier as just as a wolf, then.*

Ignoring the frightened lump of fur, Jae got up and ran in the opposite direction. Her mind cleared with the run, her muscles unknotted, her soul forgotten along with the time. She ran for hours, the fading light suggesting she head back and change into her clothes for dinner. With a huff through her snout, she raced back through the trees and skidded to a stop when she came to her clothes and the broken china. The change back was faster, and the cold night air made her hurry back into her clothes. She was just pulling her T-shirt over her head when a familiar voice sucked the breath out of her body.

"You were gone awhile."

Jaeden finished dressing and spun to find Ryder leaning against the tree she'd used as target practice. He gave the broken plates a pointed look but didn't say anything.

She gulped as he crossed his arms over his chest, his biceps rippling as he moved. Oh goddess, he looked good in those jeans and white T-shirt. *Smells good too*, she thought longingly as she caught his scent in the breeze.

"No hello?" he asked, straightening. His eyes were narrowed and challenging. Full of dislike.

She shrugged defensively. "What do you want?"

He laughed, low and grim. "What do I want, she asks. That's funny."

Her stomach churned, not liking his tone at all. They hadn't spoken in weeks, and before when they had, she'd still had all that anger keeping her nice and detached. Now she was just a vulnerable mess. An easy target.

"What's funny?" she asked quietly, trying to infuse some belligerence into her voice.

He moved slowly toward her, and she felt herself back up unconsciously. "You. Asking me what I want? Not really something that's crossed your mind these last few weeks."

Jaeden didn't reply. There was nothing she could say. She had abandoned him when he needed her most.

"What?" he mocked. "No witty comeback, no insult to cut me to the quick?"

"Ry—"

"How about telling me you don't love me anymore … 'cause I gotta tell you, I really enjoyed that the first time around."

"I—"

"No. Forget about me for a minute. Why don't we talk about the fact that you haven't spoken to your mother since her husband died—"

She growled, "My father!"

Ryder glared at her and smacked a hand off his forehead. "Oh, stupid me, I forgot Jaeden was the only one to lose someone that day!"

She groaned, feeling frustrated tears burn her throat and eyes. "Ryder, please don—"

"Ryder, don't what?" he spat. "Finally give you hell for all your bullshit?"

Jaeden squirmed, wishing the ground would swallow her whole. Her mate had finally snapped, and he wanted to have it out, here and now. She didn't think she could handle it. So she did what she'd been good at lately and walked past him toward the hotel. A frightening snarl ripped from the back of his throat and his hand shot out, gripping her by the T-shirt and propelling her back with force into a tree. He loomed over in the darkness, his amber eyes bright with fury as he pinned her there.

"You're not going anywhere until I'm finished," he cursed. "I lost my mother. Julia lost her husband. Mal and Fin lost their parents. And Draven and Kade lost their kids, for Gaia's sake." His hot breath rushed over her face, and she couldn't help but tremble under the heat of his anger. "I am sorry about Dimitri. I know how close you were, but that does not give you the right to treat the people who still care about you like dirt."

"I ne—"

"I'm not done!" he roared, and she flinched back, truly scared of him now. This was a Ryder she'd never encountered before. "This might be the last real conversation you and I ever have, and I want you to know exactly what I think about you."

Oh goddess, no, please no, let it end, let it end, please let me be deaf, please let me be deaf.

Ryder took that moment to take a deep breath, clearly trying to control himself. He stilled, and his eyes washed over her face as if he were tallying up her features. "I never thought you would ever be this selfish. I never thought you would ever be this cruel or hateful. And I never thought there would come a day, and so soon into our mating, that I would say I couldn't trust you—" He broke off, the words catching in his throat.

Jaeden's lips trembled. She had lost him. She had really done it now. This wasn't how the mating was supposed to be. How could she and Caia mess it up this badly?

Ryder sighed wearily and dropped his arms from the cage he'd made around her, taking a step back. "Talk to your mother, Jaeden. She needs you."

The tears spilled down her cheeks and through the blur she saw him pause, watching the show of emotion with surprised alert. When he didn't make a move toward her, Jae was humiliated by the unexpected and uncontrolled sob that burst from deep within her chest. Still, he made no move toward her, but he wasn't leaving. And she took comfort in the way he clenched his fists as if stopping himself from going to her.

After a moment, she pulled in a shuddering breath. "And you?" she managed. "Do you, Ryder?"

He hissed and then replied, "Do I what?"

"Still need me?"

Instead of replying, he turned away. "Just talk to your mom."

Panic floored her and she tripped a few steps toward him. "Ryder, wait."

"No," he threw over his shoulder as he walked away from her.

Just say it! There's nothing left to lose.

"I'm sorry!" she cried. "I'm sorry. I'm so sorry—" She began to cry for real, all the tears she'd kept locked up since her father's death. She slid to the ground, burying her shame-faced head in her hands, trying unsuccessfully to control the rib-cracking sobs taking over her body.

Then like the relief of sun after days of relentless rain, warm, familiar arms encircled her, drawing her into an equally strong and familiar chest. Ryder tightened his hold on her, stroking her hair and rocking her as she let it all out. At the feel of him, eventually Jaeden's cries eased. As his scent flooded her senses, she shuddered for another reason. She wanted him. She wanted him to make it all go away.

Slowly, Jae lifted her head to look at him, his face inches above her. She winced inwardly at the uncertain look in his eyes as he gazed down at her. Panicking at the thought of never being able to erase that look, Jaeden scrambled to cradle his face in her hands.

"Ryder," she gasped, pulling herself even closer. "I am so sorry. I didn't mean any of it, I swear. I was just so angry, I—"

"We were all angry, Jaeden," he said through clenched teeth, but his eyes betrayed his desire as they drew down to her mouth.

Jae took heart in that. "Ryder." She locked onto his gaze, resolute. "I love you. I never stopped loving you ... I was just so—"

"Just so what?" he demanded, shaking her by the shoulders. "What, Jaeden? What was so damn important that it was worth putting me through the worst weeks of my life?"

Explain it, Jae, explain. It's your only shot at keeping him.

"My dad knew me so well," she whispered against his lips. "Losing him was like losing a part of my own soul."

"Jae—"

"Let me finish, please." She looked up into his eyes. Gods, he looked so determined to not forgive her. "But with you, it's like you *are* my soul. You're such a huge part of me that I don't think I'll survive losing you. I thought if I could keep all the people I cared about at a distance, it might not hurt so much if anything were to happen to them. The thought of losing you, Ryder ... I won't come back from that. I love you so much it terrifies me—"

Her words were cut off as he crushed her mouth beneath his own, his kiss demanding and punishing, taking everything she had. And she gave it to him, kissing him back with as much abandon and need. Ryder pressed her backward, sending her crashing onto her back on the damp ground. She barely noticed they were outside while he continued to kiss her as if this were their last moment on earth. His large body pressed upon hers, brushing across her deliciously as he braced his arms on either side of her head. Jaeden growled into his mouth, sliding her hands into his hair and bringing him down on top of her with one hard tug. That seemed to sever any control he might have had.

She sizzled with fragile excitement as he pulled away

from their kiss long enough to tug his T-shirt over his head. He then relieved Jae of her shirt and bra. The feel of his rough hands on her overheated skin drove her to the edge, and Jaeden reached for him again, whispering love words against his skin as her hands did some roaming of their own, her lips pressing hot kisses to his throat and jaw. Ryder groaned under her assault, and she felt him undoing the buttons on her jeans. Desire for her mate flooded from the pit of her belly, flushing her skin to the roots of her hair.

"Ryder," she panted.

They had only consummated their mating once, and part of the frustration and animosity between them these last few weeks had been their need. They still wanted each other, even when they were struggling.

Naked beneath him, Jaeden urged Ryder's jeans off and then enveloped him in her embrace, her legs wrapped around his waist.

"I love you," he whispered as he gazed down at her. "Do you love me?"

That he even had to ask. A tear escaped, aching for having hurt him so badly, and she pressed a sweet kiss against his lips. "I will always love you. Never doubt it, no matter what stupid thing I say or do."

He groaned and made love to her, a slow, gentle love that caught fire and grew frenzied, as if they were both afraid the other would disappear.

* * *

AS THEY STROVE to catch their breath, Ryder pulled her closer into the warmth of his body, gazing up through the trees to the sky that had darkened to midnight blue above them. He smelled of Jaeden and now she smelled of him. As soon as they walked into the hotel, the pack would know what they'd been up to, but he didn't care. He was glad to have her back.

And he did have her back, that he was sure of. Life with Jaeden was always going to be interesting, but he'd never doubted she loved him, no matter what she said. They were mates, blessed by the gods themselves. She'd been right before. He was as much a part of her as she was of him. He knew she was angry, and he knew exactly what she'd been doing when she pushed him away like that. Ever the strategist, he'd decided to back off for a while, let her cool down on her own. That morning at breakfast, he'd seen the vulnerability in her eyes for the first time—the guilt, the realization of what she'd been doing to them all. It was the best time to bombard her, make her think she was going to lose him.

Worked like a charm.

And he wasn't even going to feel bad about manipulating her because his mate was tucked up nice and safe in his arms, just where she should be.

"I have to tell you something," she whispered hoarsely, and Ryder stilled. The sound of guilt gilded her words.

"What did you do?" he groaned, peering down at her.

OF ALL THE things in the world, he had not been expecting her admission that she'd helped blackmail Caia into killing the Septum.

"For Gaia's sake, Jaeden!" he snapped, pulling out of their embrace and shoving himself back into his jeans. "I can't believe this!"

She started dressing herself, her body shaking, her lips trembling. He tried not to feel bad but he couldn't believe she'd been keeping this to herself for weeks.

"That little bloodsucking fiend blackmailed Caia into

killing the Septum, and Lucien thinks she just left! He kicked her out of the pack, Jaeden!"

"I know!" she cried. "I wasn't thinking. It was just another one of the many selfish things I did this last month, alright?"

"Lucien is going to kill you!" he swore, shoving his hand through his hair. "I'm going to have to fight my best friend because he's going to want to kill you."

"Ryder." She stamped her foot, a bit of the old Jae creeping back into her voice. "I feel terrible about this—you don't have to make me feel any worse."

Holy mother of ... Lucien would go ballistic. Ryder sighed and grabbed hold of her hand, tugging her toward the house. "Let's get this over with."

CHAPTER 21

FAITH

The dining hall looks good, Lucien mused, gazing around as he ate the roast chicken Lucia and Cera had prepared. Ella roped him and some of the others into appropriating dressing screens from the bedrooms and placing them across the dining hall as a temporary wall. Shortening the length of the room had instantly made it cozier, and they'd arranged the tables into one massive table they could all fit around. Then they had taken fabrics—throws, curtains, bits of muslin—and dressed the windows. With some candles to soften the lighting, Lucien had to admit, despite himself, that Ella had been right. The place was starting to feel more homely.

It would be even more homely if his mate were at his side instead of Rose. His gaze dropped to the redhead and then lifted almost instantly. He and Rose had had a difficult conversation today. She'd found him in his suite with a photo of Caia and himself from Irini and Aidan's mating ceremony. Magnus had made a big deal of Lucien putting his arm around Caia, and she'd blushed like an idiot as he drew her into his side for the photo to be taken. Only hours later he'd kissed her for the first time on the back porch and had been relieved when she'd kissed him back.

He'd kept the photo in his wallet ever since and showed it to Caia once they had gotten together, teasing her about how she looked at him in it, gazing up at him shyly. He'd been thrilled to see a look akin to love in her eyes as she stared at him.

Since kicking Caia out of the pack, Lucien gazed at that picture every day, trying to make sense of what had happened.

"Whatcha looking at?" Rose grinned as she strode into his bedroom without knocking. He really should reprimand her for that, but she was smiling so endearingly, he couldn't. When Lucien didn't answer her question, her gaze fell to the photo as she rounded the sofa, and her smile instantly dropped.

"Lucien, what are you doing?" she moaned.

Frowning, he tucked the photo back into his wallet. "What do you mean?"

"You." She gestured to his wallet. "Mooning over her when she's betrayed you."

His jaw clenched. "You don't know that."

"I know she left to do something you specifically told her not to. That's not how a pack works."

"It's complicated."

"That's the problem." She smiled sadly, coming around to sit beside him. "It's too complicated."

He shrugged.

After a minute of silence, he felt Rose tense before she cleared her throat. "It's been awhile now. Weeks, actually."

Yeah, he was painfully aware of that.

"Lucien, I wanted to give you time. But I can't wait anymore. Love doesn't have to be complicated."

Uh-oh.

He glanced up at her, and suddenly, she was pressed against him, her hand running up his thigh. "Love can be easy and good. Like with us." And then she kissed him. Not just a sweet peck on the lips. Rose grabbed his head hard and kissed him, tongue and all, with as much passion as she could summon. Like an idiot, he now thought, he'd been totally surprised by her attack, and it had taken him a minute to pry her off. He did, though, and stood from the sofa to put some distance between them.

"What?" she whispered.

"That can't happen ever again." He gestured stupidly at the spot where he'd just been sitting.

Rose gazed up at him, hurt. "Why not? You kissed me back."

"No!" he argued vehemently, fearing what such a sentence would do to his relationship with Caia if it ever got back to her. "No, I didn't. I was surprised."

"Surprised?" She snapped up off the seat. "Lucien, how can you be surprised? It's obvious I'm in love with you. Everyone knows it."

"Rose. I care about you, I do. But I love Caia. She is my mate."

"She has a funny way of showing it."

"Our problems are between us," he warned. "I don't want anyone bad-mouthing her."

"I'm not bad-mouthing her—I just don't get it. I don't get your relationship with her."

"You don't have to get it." He ran a hand through his hair, trying to brace himself for her reaction to his next suggestion. "Maybe we should try to contact the Center and see if it's safe for you to go home. Or maybe see if you can stay at the Center."

Rose shook her head, looking frightened. "I don't want to. I feel like part of a family here. I'm sorry I've made you uncomfortable, Lucien, I really am. I promise I won't cross the line again. I just had to tell you how I felt—"

"Yeah, but it could be a problem—"

"It won't. Jeez, Lucien, the female members of the pack who aren't related to you are all half in love with you anyway. I'll get over this ... but not if I lose your friendship."

He sighed. "You never have to worry about that."

So here they were, having dinner with the pack, and he hoped he wasn't delusional about their circumstances. Rose believed they could make it work as just friends, and he really didn't want to kick out one more female he cared about.

As he mused over this, Lucien felt a change in the air and was taken aback to see Jaeden and Ryder walk into the dining hall smelling of one another and holding hands. Lucien knew Ryder was heading out to find Jae and try to talk some sense into her, but Jae had been so adamant of late, he hadn't thought his friend would succeed. His fault for not trusting the strength of a mating ... probably because his own was going *so* well.

Lucien smiled at Ryder as they crossed the room toward the pack.

"You guys alright?" He grinned cheekily.

It was good to see Ryder smile back at him. His friend was generally a lighthearted person. It was tough seeing what the last few weeks had done to him. To them all.

Although, he had to admit that their time together as a pack at the hotel had helped them get through it. Draven and Kade's suffering was different, having lost their children, but Draven's brother, Isaac, and his wife, Imogen, were proving inseparable companions, having lost Sebastian last year, and subsequently understanding the hell they were going through. Lucien especially thought their nieces, Seana and Sunday, helped Draven and Kade. Nothing could ease the pain of losing those closest to them, but Lucien reckoned it would've been harder for them all if they hadn't had this time together.

The only exceptions had been Alexa and Jaeden. Alexa wasn't budging, but Lucien noticed the difference in Jae as she stood with her mate.

Ryder nudged Jaeden toward him. "Jaeden has something to tell you." He looked at her sternly. Lucien watched in bemusement as Jae glowered at her mate.

"You don't have to shove me forward like an errant child," she huffed.

"Jaeden," Ryder warned.

The look in his eyes abruptly caused Lucien to tense. Ryder was serious, which meant this was serious. He scowled. "What's going on?"

The trembling of Jae's lip sent his heart into overdrive. Okay, if Jae was afraid to tell him, then this was *really serious.* "Lucien." And then she looked up at the pack gathered around the table. "Everybody. I did something. Reuben—"

"NO!" Alexa cried shrilly, leaping to her feet, knocking her chair to the floor with a loud clatter. "Don't you dare!"

What the Hades was going on?

Lucien stood slowly, emitting mega Alpha vibes. Alexa faltered. "I want to know exactly what you've done and why Alexa doesn't want me to know about it."

Jaeden nodded quickly and leaned back into Ryder for support. "Caia didn't leave by choice."

Her words turned to a panic that gripped his chest, and he grabbed hold of the back of his chair, curling his fingers around it. He had a very, very bad feeling about this.

Alexa was yelling again, her face mottled with fury. "NO! Jaeden! You st—"

"YOU!" Lucien roared, interrupting her. "Shut up!"

The tension in the room intensified, seizing the entire

pack. Only Magnus had the courage to speak up. "Jaeden, get to the point," he bit out.

"Reuben blackmailed Caia into killing the Septum."

The air rushed out of Lucien's lungs as emotion took hold of him—that under the skin, brain-buzzing, won't let go of your body kind of rage. "Explain." His lykan overpowered his vocal cords. The hush continued among his pack.

Jaeden was trembling again, but distractedly, he admired the way she stood her ground and met his eyes. "Reuben told Caia he wouldn't give us refuge and mask our trace unless she killed the Septum, and Alexa and I didn't stop him. In fact, we encouraged him."

Oh gods. He dropped back into his chair and groaned into his hands. He felt his mother's hand on his shoulder, trying to offer comfort. But no one could give him that. He'd kicked his mate out of his pack when all she'd been trying to do was protect them ... protect them when he should have been!

He roared, seeing only red as he stood and threw his chair across the room. It shattered against the wall. "Where is she?" he demanded, spinning back on Jae who had paled considerably.

"I don't know," she whispered. "Lucien, I am so sorry. I feel terrible. Caia promised me not to tell you the truth, and I was just so angry, I wanted revenge and I couldn't see past i—"

"Enough!" he ordered. He didn't want to hear her excuses. Hers or Alexa's. Gaia, he could barely look at the two of them. "You had weeks to tell me this—"

Ryder stepped forward, looking wary but determined. "She's telling you now. Caia was the one who didn't tell you, man."

"Because she knew I would stop her, and the pack would be without protection!"

"I'm just saying—"

"Save it! I don't want your excuses for your mate's behavior. Alexa and Jaeden are now under house arrest. No runs, no dining with the pack. They'll be locked in their rooms and their meals will be brought to them."

Jaeden nodded but Ryder scowled. "For how long?"

"For as long as I need them out of my sight," Lucien spat. He cursed, trying to think. Having no idea where Caia could be wasn't giving him much to act on. But he wanted her back with the pack, even if it meant they didn't have Reuben's protection. She was his pack, and he should've been protecting *her* all along.

He ripped his cell phone out of his pocket and searched his contacts for Reuben. His whole body trembled as he pressed the call button.

"We're sorry, this number is not in service."

Lucien paled. The son of a bitch had disconnected his phone! The pack looked around at one another grimly, having heard the misdial message with their lykan hearing.

"Lucien." Magnus stood as the pack stared at their Alpha, apprehensively awaiting the next explosion. "You couldn't have known."

That wasn't an excuse. There wasn't an excuse. He had acted like a faithless fool.

He curled his lip in self-directed derision. "I should have. I should have trusted that Caia doesn't have the soul to kill seven innocent people unless under extreme duress. Like a true Alpha, she did it to protect her pack … while I let that slimy bastard walk out of here with her without a fight."

"Lucien—" Rose spoke up but he shook her off with a glare. He didn't want anyone's reassurances. He didn't deserve them.

For a while, Lucien just stood there, numb, shock taking over his system. Finally, when it felt like the entire room might crack under the tension, he glanced over at Vil who was watching him carefully. "Can you find her?"

Vil shook his head sadly. "I've been trying these last few minutes. Something's blocking me. I can only try places she might be."

Jaeden coughed. "Can I make a suggestion?"

He shot her the filthiest look in his repertoire. "What?" he snapped, and she flinched at his temper.

"Well," she managed with a shaky breath, "it's been weeks. I reckon Caia's dealt with the Septum and is now at the Center, since she has nowhere left to—" She broke off awkwardly.

"Nowhere left to go, right?" Lucien hissed, approaching her slowly. She backed up into Ryder. "Whose fault is that?"

"Hey!" Ryder pushed Jae behind him and held up a cautioning hand to Lucien. "Back off, man. She said she was sorry. You've dealt out your punishment ... now back *off*."

He wanted to kick Ryder's ass. He wanted to punch him and throw him and smash him against something. The feeling was overwhelming, until Ryder's familiar eyes locked with his and he remembered who it was in front of him—his best friend, his brother. Lucien shuddered, trying to gain some control.

"Shall I go to the Center?" Vil asked tentatively.

Lucien exhaled and turned back to the magik. "Yes, please, Vil. Tell her what has happened. Tell her ... just bring her back to me. Please."

"Of course." The magik pressed a soft kiss to Laila's lips and then disappeared at the table.

"Lucien, are you going to be okay, man?" Ryder asked quietly.

"No."

There was a possibility Caia would never forgive him for

this. That she would never trust him, just as he hadn't shown her enough trust.

He glared at Alexa who was still spitting mad at Jaeden. "You," he growled. "The pack is going to love you and Jaeden. House arrest means work for everybody." His gaze slid to Magnus. "You have first shift, Magnus. You will escort Alexa to her room and guard her door. Aidan"—he turned to his brother-in-law—"you will have the unfortunate task of guarding outside her window."

"Lucien, is this really necessary?" His mother piped up. His only reply was a withering look that made her clamp her mouth shut.

"Mom, you will relieve Magnus of his duty in eight hours. Ryder, you will relieve your brother of his in eight hours. As for Jaeden"—he glared at her again—"since your and Alexa's rooms are next to one another, I suppose the one guard outside will do."

"I know you hate me right now, but can I ask a favor?" Jaeden asked softly.

The only reply she got was a long, drawn-out snarl.

"I know. I just … I would really like to have some time with my mom."

Lucien groaned inwardly. How could he say no to that? Julia was grieving for her mate and at a loss on how to deal with her daughter. Now Jaeden wanted to speak to her mom … he would be an ogre if he said no. He gave a quick nod and ignored the grateful smile she threw him before Jaeden and her mother ambled out of the room together. Magnus trailed behind them, his hand cuffed tightly around Alexa's upper arm. As always, Mal and Finlay weren't far behind their big sister.

As the pack slowly filtered out, leaving Lucien in the dining hall with his best friend, a wave of anxious nausea rushed over him. For a guy who hadn't been afraid of anything before, he was suddenly terrified of a tiny blond who had the power to hurt him more than anybody else on this planet.

"She'll forgive you," Ryder assured him softly.

"I don't even forgive myself, Ryder. How can I expect her to?"

CHAPTER 22

EXPECT THE UNEXPECTED

Once more Caia glanced down at the palm of her right hand where it was temporarily scarred by a faint silver annulet. The scar was a reminder of her blood oath to the Council, every inch representative of that vow and the consequences that would follow should she break it. It was her hand that was scarred, for the hand was often a symbol used to represent a pledge of sincerity and justice.

If Caia made good on her oath, the scar would disappear immediately; if not, all her powers would transfer to the Council, leaving her with the annulet as a reminder of her deception. Not that she had any intention of keeping the trace.

A loud grunt shook her from her thoughts, and she looked up to see one of Michael Brown's unit members pulling a magik up off the mat. Caia sighed, watching the team that had been put together to hunt down Marita train in their private gymnasium. First she had to find and kill Marita before she could even contemplate performing the rite that would ask the gods to give her the Daylight trace.

"Caia." Lyla hurried over, sweat glistening on her forehead suggesting she'd been working out for longer than she should've been. "Come take over for Phoebe." She gestured to the lykan who was scowling at one of the vampyres and shaking her head at whatever he was suggesting. "She's killing me. I could use some light relief." She winked, and Caia snorted. Lyla was only teasing her, but what she said was true. Compared to these people, she *was* relief when it came to sparring. They trounced her good. She was covered in bruises. Caia inwardly groaned at the thought of fighting Lyla, who was only marginally less aggressive than Phoebe.

"I, uh—"

"She can't," a familiar voice interrupted, and Caia smiled at the sound. Saffron. The faerie had come to save her. *Thank you, Hemera.*

Lyla raised an eyebrow—the kind of eyebrow raise that suggested interest—as she gazed over Caia's shoulder. Ah … so Reuben was with Saffron. Caia turned and rolled her eyes. She was right. Jeez, the females at the Center were really wound up about Reuben. Desi and Ophelia had been blah-blah-blahing about him for the last few days. What was so special about him? Ha, she wondered if they'd be so into him if they knew how old he was.

"Hi, guys." She gave them a wide-eyed, "thank you for rescuing me" look that Lyla couldn't see.

"Hey, Reuben." Lyla ran her tongue along her upper teeth. "How's it going?"

"Better for seeing you, Lyla, better for seeing you." He smirked.

Ugh, gag me.

"Oh, please," Saffron grunted, not as polite as Caia to keep the thought to herself.

Reuben ignored her and threw Lyla another flirtatious grin. "If you don't mind, we need to steal the little one away for a while."

Uh, what? "Uh, the little one—"

"Of course," Lyla cut off her protest. "She's all yours." *As am I*, her eyes conveyed.

Caia sighed. She'd never understand her sex. With a nod of acknowledgment to Lyla, Caia ushered Saffron and Reuben out of the gymnasium.

"What do you want to talk to me about?"

But Saffron was still stuck on Reuben's behavior with the lykan. "Do you have to be so disgustingly juvenile with the women here?" she huffed as they got into an elevator.

He grinned wickedly at her. "Jealous, Saffron?"

"Guys—"

"Jealous! Puhlease, our day in the sun has been over for a long time, *Kirios*. I just don't want to have to listen to you have verbal sex with everything that has breasts. I am stuck here beside you for now while we see this through, so please refrain from the mundane, and try to engage in some intellectual conversation with these people, rather than trying to decide which one's pants you want to get into as if you were choosing between chocolate or vanilla ice cream!"

Caia hid the face she made. *Jealous much was right.* Apparently even seven hundred years of Reuben's presence hadn't put Saffron off. If Caia had to guess, the faerie was perhaps just a wee bit in love with her vampyre friend. Saffron's diatribe had apparently struck Reuben dumb. Under the growing silence, Caia looked up to see him staring at Saffron with an inscrutable expression on his face. As for the faerie, she stared straight ahead, her beautiful face pinched with tension as if she knew she had revealed more than she'd meant to.

Caia felt bad. She knew what it was like to care about someone and not know if they felt that way about you. And Reuben flirted with everyone. Come on, he'd even flirted with Caia.

The elevator doors binged open, and she realized they were on her floor.

"Guys, you wanted to talk to me about something, remember?"

Saffron sniffed. "Of course. Let's go to your suite."

And so she walked behind them to her bedroom suite, not speaking or intruding upon their private business, even though she was impatient to know what they wanted. Just as they neared her door, Reuben leaned over to Saffron and hissed, "We'll talk about this later."

Saffron shrugged and then spun around, holding her hand out to Caia. "Key."

"I am quite capable of opening my own door, thank you." Caia nudged her aside and swiped the key card and the door popped open. It was the same room she'd stayed in before Marita had gone bat-shit crazy. Her eyes took in the magnificent panoramic view of Paris. She sighed, wishing life were as uncomplicatedly beautiful as the city.

When the door swung shut behind them, Caia spun around. "OK, what's going on? Why the secrecy?"

Reuben exhaled and shared an anxious look with Saffron. "Maybe you should sit."

Wow, there were just never enough of these heart-pounding, nauseating, "what now?" moments in her life.

"Okaaay." She slowly lowered herself onto a sofa.

With that, the vampyre stepped back, gesturing Saffron forward. The faerie gave a militant nod and then took a step toward her. "Caia, we have something that we haven't told you. We kept it back from you—for a good reason—with the intention of telling you once you killed the Septum. That's all changed now, of course. You see …" She trailed off, a strange look entering her eyes. "Marita has always had a weakness. The biggest threat to her, if you like. And that was Marion. Marion knew Marita better than anyone, could anticipate her moves better than anyone, knew the family's past haunts and private hideouts. We had every intention of telling you this when the trace was gone, but, well ..."

Caia's pulse raced and she clasped a hand over the throb in her wrist. That didn't do much for the visible throb in her neck. "Tell me what?"

The faerie's answer was to vanish.

Reuben hadn't even moved. He just stood there like he'd been expecting it. Caia clenched her jaw. "What's going on?"

He didn't say a word, just stared at her, waiting. Then Caia felt the telltale buzz of energy and Saffron was back in the room, smiling. A second later, another slight figure appeared beside her.

Caia's jaw dropped as she took in the familiar mass of fire-red hair and fey features.

"Marion?" she gasped and got to her feet on trembling legs, tears filling her widened eyes. Was it really her? Was she really here ... alive?

The witch's own familiar violet eyes watered up, and then she rushed at Caia, her strong arms encircling her in a tight hug. Caia held on for dear life, breathing in the familiar scent of her friend and mentor, clutching her as if afraid she would disappear at any minute.

"It's really me, sweetheart, it's really me." Marion stroked her hair, murmuring reassurances. The overwhelming relief took over, and Caia's body shook with hard sobs. Marion merely held on tighter.

* * *

"HOW ARE YOU ALIVE?" she asked sometime later.

Marion smiled smugly, a familiar expression that served to lighten the weight on Caia's chest. "I was never really dead."

Drawing Caia back down onto the sofa, the four of them sat as Caia was told the tale of their deception.

"You see," Saffron said, "I'd already contacted Reuben, telling him Marion was very ill from having traveled with too many children. That's when he came up with his plan to deceive Marita. He masked Marion's trace, making Marita think her sister was dead. If she thinks Marion is out of the picture, she won't hesitate to go to the places that Marion knew about."

Clever, Caia thought. Pity that along with it, they'd caused her, Magnus, and Vanne untold heartbreak.

Marion must've seen the anger in Caia's eyes because she patted her hand. "I know it was ruthless and deceitful, but we couldn't risk anyone finding out I'm alive. This is the best weapon we have against her."

Caia gazed at her in admiration, taking solace in Marion's seemingly unending strength and determination. "I am sorry about Marita, Marion."

She frowned and looked away. "I am sorry that I was a fool not to have seen it sooner."

"Apologies aside," Reuben muttered, eyeing the witch carefully, "Marion claims to know where Marita is."

A mixture of excitement and apprehension rushed through Caia at the thought, and she gripped Marion's hands harder than she meant to. "Really? Where?"

"In a small village in Scotland. She has a safe house there, a derelict inn. Only myself, Marita, and my mother knew of it. Not even Vanne knows of its existence."

Caia's heart was going overtime. "So we're going there? We're going after Marita?"

Reuben nodded grimly. "That's the plan."

"But what about Vanne and the Council? I have to tell them I'm going after Marita. The oath." She held up her hand, palm out, so they could see the annulet.

Marion frowned at it. "I can't believe they made you take a blood oath."

"I don't mind."

"I mind." She scowled. "It was unnecessary. Bloody idiots running this place like ..." Her voice trailed off as Reuben spoke again.

"Caia, I must remind you that no one can know about Marion's existence. Marita will be checking the trace for anything and everything, and we can't tell them about this safe house because she'll find out we know and leave."

Of course, dumbass, Caia silently berated. She took a minute, tracing the texture of the carpet with her foot. "OK. How about I just tell them I have a lead that I can't discuss because I don't want Marita to uncover it in the trace, and that I'll only be taking you and Saffron with me as backup, to ensure Marita doesn't find out."

"I don't see how they can argue with that," Marion agreed.

Finally, Reuben nodded. "It's our only chance. I think—"

Caia felt an unexpected prickle of energy, as did Reuben who stopped talking. Caia's eyes widened as Vil appeared behind the vampyre. Reuben was out of his chair in a blur, and when he stilled, it was with Vil clutched by the throat, Vil's pale eyes wide with fear and shock.

"Reuben!" Caia hissed, launching herself at him, tugging poor Vil out of his stone-hard arms. "Let. Him. Go."

He growled at her but finally let up, and Vil stumbled toward Caia, happily letting her place herself between him and the vampyre.

"It's just Vil," she snapped. Reuben grunted, shouldering past her to take his seat again. Vil hastily jumped out of his path. "What's going on?" she demanded. But Vil was staring at Marion like he'd seen a ghost ... which technically, he had.

It took a good few minutes to calm him down and explain it all to him, and all the while, Reuben grumbled that he had to add another layer to Vil's trace to mask his knowledge of Marion's existence.

"You can't tell anyone about me," Marion insisted sternly.

Vil nodded. "I promise, Marion."

"You better," Reuben warned. "Or I will take care of the problem."

"Reuben," Caia warned.

He ignored her and continued to unsettle Vil with his glare.

"Vil, what are you doing here?"

The magik tried unsuccessfully to ignore the evil looks Reuben was shooting him. "I ... uh ... I'm here because Lucien is looking for you."

She gripped his arm, her features a mask of anxiety. "Why, what's wrong?"

"Oh, nothing. I mean, well, something. I mean, Lucien knows all about"—his eyes flicked with reluctance to the vampyre—"Reuben's blackmail. He wants you to come home to the pack."

So he's sorry now, Caia thought numbly. "I can't," she whispered, and then glanced up at Vil's sound of confusion. "I didn't kill the Septum. I couldn't," she explained. "But I made a blood oath to the Council that if they give me the Daylight trace once Marita's dead, then I will ask the gods to take both the Midnight and Daylight trace back, freeing us all from it. I have to leave now to kill Marita." She couldn't keep the despair out of her voice.

Reuben groaned. "Hades, save me from emotional women. Fine," he snapped. "It can wait a little while longer. Go tell the Council about your lead and then we'll get back to the pack to assure them you're okay. Saffron, take Marion to your place for now. I'll contact you when we need you. Vil." He grinned swiftly at the magik, showing his fangs.

"You're leaving now. Go back to the pack and tell your Alpha that Caia will return shortly."

Vil immediately disappeared. Caia threw Reuben a disparaging look. "I don't know why people are so afraid of you."

His answer was a smug cocking of his eyebrow.

Someone really needed to put that guy in his place. She shared a look with the witch, and Caia knew Marion was thinking the same thing.

She felt a rush of pure happiness that the magik was back in her life.

CHAPTER 23

FENCES

"*I*'ve never done a communication spell with another person holding on to me before," Caia snapped at Reuben as they stood facing each other in her suite, both mirror images of each other with their impatient sneers and defiant arms akimbo. "Are you really sure it's necessary?"

Reuben shook his head, his expression that of someone who felt they were dealing with a person of little intelligence. "No, it isn't necessary. However, I think it's time you tried it, and you *can* since you've been to the hotel before."

"If I kill you, this will be all your fault."

"Caia, you won't kill me," he reassured her. "We really must work on your confidence if you're to have any hope of taking on Marita and winning."

"As much as I enjoy your pep talks, can we maybe get going?"

"Hey, I wasn't the one stalling."

Caia took a deep breath. Sometimes it felt like she was dealing with an obnoxious teenager. Bracing herself, she held a tentative hand out toward the vampyre and he gripped her tightly, her hand mostly disappearing in his large one. Butterflies erupted in her belly at the thought of seeing Lucien again after all these weeks and the bad terms they'd left one another on.

The Council hadn't been too pleased with her decision to go after Marita with only Reuben and Saffron for help, but they soon realized the method in the madness, considering how difficult it'd been so far to track her with her using the trace to escape all the time. Thus, they were letting Caia go, although she was unnerved by Benedict De Jong's goodbye, the smug asshole waving her off as if sure it would be the last time he ever laid eyes on her. Goddess, she hoped he was wrong.

"Caia, let's go." Reuben squeezed her hand. At his insistence, she closed her eyes and tightened her energy around them both, visualizing the front entrance of the hotel.

An immediate lethargy crashed over her body, and she felt a tug on her hand suggesting Reuben was holding her up. Taking a deep breath, Caia opened her eyes and forced her legs to straighten, demanding strength rush back into them.

She and Reuben stood in the empty foyer of the hotel, Reuben grinning at her.

"If you say I told you so, I will kill you," she snapped.

"Caia!"

She jerked around at the sound of her name and only caught a brief glimpse of Magnus running through the dining hall door before she was crushed in his arms like a little girl. She held on tight, breathing in the scent of her favorite lykan. "Uncle Magnus." She grinned and pressed a kiss to his cheek, watching as he glowed under her affection.

"We missed you." He pressed her back, glowering at Reuben. "*You* have some explaining to do."

Caia could see trouble brewing. "Where is Lucien?"

"In his room." Magnus continued to glare at the vampyre. "He wants to kill this one."

"Oh, he can't do that," she rushed, her hands fluttering nervously. "I need to explain to him before he sees Reuben ..." She trailed off and huffed at the blank expression on the vamp's face. He wasn't concerned in the least.

"Magnus," she growled between clenched teeth, realizing she was the only one anxious about the situation, "can you take Reuben into the dining hall while I find Lucien? And please promise you won't let anybody try to fight him. I know he doesn't look like much." She smiled sweetly at the scowl Reuben threw her. "But he can snap any one of us like a twig in under a second."

Magnus huffed but agreed. He gave Caia directions to Lucien's room, and she watched silently as they disappeared into the dining hall. She exhaled, brushing her hair off her face. Seeing a mirror hanging on the wall by the entrance, she rushed over to it and gave herself a quick once-over. She wanted to look cool and aloof but instead she looked short and tired. Grunting, she turned away and headed up the stairs.

As she neared Lucien's room, she could taste his scent in the air and her ears perked up, hoping to catch sound of him. What she did hear made her heart stop, and she paused outside his bedroom door, her fingernails making crescents in her skin as she balled her hands into tight fists.

"So you're just going to forgive her?" Rose snapped on the other side of the door.

What the Hades was Rose doing in his bedroom? Caia felt an overwhelming desire to scratch the female's eyes out and while she was at it, throw a good kick to where it would hurt Lucien the most!

"Rose," he said, quiet but determined, "we've been over this."

"I know, but I'm still your friend, Lucien. I'm concerned. You can't just forgive her for leaving you, for lying to you—"

Is that how he saw it?

"She's going to hurt you again and again because this war means more to her than you or the pack."

Bitch!

"You don't know what you're talking about," Lucien growled.

Yes! Thank you!

"I'm not trying to piss you off, Lucien. I'm trying to save you some heartache."

At the dawning silence, Caia had had enough. She pushed open the door with enough force to send it slamming back against the wall and had to stop herself from flinching under the crash it made.

She hadn't really meant to make *that* dramatic an entrance.

Lucien gazed at her wide-eyed, and as he noticed her pointed glances between him and Rose—Rose who was stroking his cheek affectionately—he flushed, realizing how it looked. "Caia ..."

She shook her head. All this time she'd been in turmoil, and he'd been letting the redhead cozy up to him in his bedroom suite. She glared at Rose and wasn't surprised to see hatred in the lykan's eyes. Jealousy was a powerful emotion. She should know.

Caia huffed, drawing her arms across her chest. "Looks like I wasn't too greatly missed, huh? Jeez, Lucien, you work fast." She seethed.

If she hadn't been so angry, she would've been amused by how flustered and panicky he got, pushing Rose away from him. "It's not how it looks."

"It looks like Rose has been trying to replace me. It looks like she's in your bedroom ... *alone* ... *with you*."

He made to move toward her, but Rose pushed him back, turning on Caia in an instant. "You're the one who walked out, so don't accuse him of things you know nothing about."

How dare this ... this ... this *person* speak to her like she had business being involved in her and Lucien's ... well ... business!

Caia walked slowly toward her, her eyes spitting fire. "For starters, I was kicked out. And as for you, what goes on between me and *my* mate has nothing to do with you, so I suggest you get out before I lose my temper."

The air around Caia crackled and sparked, and she felt the urgency of her power pleading for release as it tingled excitedly in her fingertips. Rose's eyes widened, and she looked up at Lucien for help. His lips pinched and he pinned her with a threatening look. Taking the hint, the lykan fled the room, dodging Caia, clearly afraid of her.

When she was gone and the door was closed firmly behind her, Lucien crossed the room to Caia but stopped so there was enough *obvious* distance between them. "That really wasn't what it looked like."

Caia shrugged as if it didn't matter when they both knew it did. "Whatever. You wanted to see me, so I'm here."

"Caia, don't." He shook his head angrily. "You must know how bad I feel about kicking you out. But you should've told me about Reuben. I'm supposed to protect my pack, and I didn't know one of them was being blackmailed!"

"In order to protect the rest of you," she argued.

"Yeah, but you are the pack, Caia! What is the point of preaching about looking out for one another and me protecting you all when I couldn't even protect my own mate?"

Caia exhaled wearily. "I did what I had to do."

"Is that our relationship from now on? Doing what we have to do to the detriment of our mating?"

"I had to lie, and you didn't trust me ... that's *not* the mating, Lucien, that's us!"

He shook his head as if he could dispel the accusation. "No! I only said I was kicking you out because I thought you would see how crazy you were being and change your mind."

Suddenly, all the resentment she hadn't even known had been there bubbled up to the surface. Caia grabbed a cushion off the sofa and threw it at him with all her might. It bounced off his chest, and he stared at her, incredulous.

"Didn't you even stop to think? Didn't you wonder why I was so adamant about killing the Septum? Me? Killing innocent people?" She gestured wildly. "Did that make sense to you?"

"No!" he yelled back like a child. "I knew something was up, but what the hell was I supposed to do? Run after you and leave my pack to deal with six deaths all by themselves?"

She grimaced and shifted away from him. "No," she mumbled and picked at the thread on a throw over the sofa.

After a minute of silence, Lucien dropped down onto a chair. "So you didn't kill the Septum." It wasn't a question. Clearly, Vil had told Lucien the little she had explained and hopefully left out the rest.

"I couldn't. There was a little girl ... anyway, we worked out something else."

"Worked out what?"

"I can't tell you."

His jaw clenched. "Can't or won't?"

Ignoring his look of betrayal, she sighed. "Can't."

He glared at her. "I can't believe you're being like this. Fine. Keep your secrets. But tell me one thing ... are you going after Marita?"

That much she could be honest about. "Somebody has to do it."

Lucien launched to his feet. "But why does it have to be my mate?"

Caia chuckled humorlessly. "Oh gods, Lucien, I don't know. But if I don't do this, things are going to get really bad. And it's not like I'm going into this alone. I have Saffron and Reuben."

He stiffened and his face turned a mottled red. "Is he here? Has he actually dared to come here?"

Yes, Reuben had acted ruthlessly, but Caia couldn't handle a disagreement between him and Lucien right now. "It is his hotel."

With a bellowing curse, Lucien blew past her and out the door. She heard him running along the corridor at an insane speed. Oh dear goddess! He was going to attack the vampyre who couldn't die! Swearing under her breath, Caia took off after him, scaling the stair railings to try to catch up with him.

As it was, when she barreled into the dining room, Reuben towered over Lucien, his large hand wrapped around Lucien's thick neck. The flashing glints of red in his eyes told her he was mesmerizing Lucien, keeping him still as he choked the life from him, Lucien's face turning a terrible purple as they all stood struck dumb by the sight of their Alpha on his knees.

Caia felt a rush of sickness. "Reuben … STOP IT!" she screamed, but he merely tightened his hold. Suddenly, Magnus leapt at the vampyre only to be backhanded as if he were a fly.

"REUBEN!" she screamed again as Ella followed Magnus's footsteps. Lucien's eyes were closing and terror took hold of her energy; her energy took hold of her, sneering at her hopelessness and flowing out in a stream toward the vampyre. To her utter surprise, it hit and Reuben was blasted across the room with enough intensity to send him crashing through the windows and outside into the cold. For a moment, she was stunned that her magik had actually worked on Reuben, and fleetingly she wondered if he'd been lying all along about being impervious to it.

But somehow … she didn't think so. A trickle of sweat slid down the side of his face.

Hacking coughs shook Caia from her thoughts, and she rushed to Lucien who was being helped up by Draven. Her hands fluttered over him, checking to make sure he was all right, and she breathed a sigh of relief as his normal color returned. He appeared dazed and pushed her hands away as if she were irritating him.

"Well, that was a surprise."

Caia looked up to see Reuben clambering back inside through the window he'd just been thrown out of. He brushed off pieces of glass and grinned unrepentantly. "Looks like I'm not impervious to you, Caia. Although, I have to say that a blast like that would have killed a lesser man. My feelings are hurt."

Her jaw dropped at his audacity, and her lykan colored her words as she replied through a mouth longing to fill with her sharp wolf teeth, "You ever touch one of my pack again and I will send you back where you came from, you son of a bitch."

He quirked an eyebrow. "I'll heed that warning. Since, apparently, you might actually be able to do it."

Draven looked bewildered by the man. "You don't seem that bothered."

Reuben shrugged. "I'm not. I'm impressed. I've been waiting a long time for someone like Caia."

Lucien growled and made a move toward the vampyre, but Caia pressed him back, scolding him. She was rewarded with one of his frostiest looks before he straightened his massive shoulders and thundered out of the room, Magnus and Ella following in his wake.

Caia felt tears of frustration prickle in her eyes. "You were going to kill him."

"No." The vampyre shook his head. "I know killing Lucien would mean losing you, and I need you too much. I was merely teaching him a lesson. He attacked unfairly."

"You blackmailed his mate."

"But it all turned out okay in the end."

"He doesn't know that! He thinks I'm punishing him for kicking me out of the pack."

Reuben threw her a condescending look before taking out a flask of blood from his inner coat pocket. He went to take a swig and noticed her watching. "You depleted my energy."

Caia threw her hands in the air, wondering why she even bothered trying to get answers from the guy. "I'm going to find Jaeden. *You* … stay away from my pack."

"I don't know if they're your pack again just yet, sweetheart," he taunted, and laughed when her only answer was a rude gesture.

CHAPTER 24

THE GREEN-EYED MONSTER

*R*ose's heart pounded in her chest as she stood in the middle of the woods, some fifteen minutes from the hotel. She'd rushed out of a pack meeting where Caia had told them all about the Septum and the little girl, Eliza Emerett, she couldn't kill. Caia seemed to go off into a world of her own as she described the little eleven-year-old Midnight and where she lived. Rose smirked. She doubted Caia had meant to be so detailed in her maudlin retelling of why she couldn't possibly go through with such a wicked plan. But that was all Caia was telling them, and Rose was more than a little suspicious.

Clutching the cell phone, she prayed the number she had for Marita was still in use. Surely if it was, and she saw who was calling, Marita could look into the trace and see Rose was sincere in her intentions. All she had to do was fight through the fog Reuben had put over her trace to hide her from Marita, but she would be careful to keep where they were staying still masked. It would be better if she held all the cards.

Rose was reeling from Lucien's betrayal, and yet she

couldn't blame him. It wasn't his fault. He was under that she-witch's spell. They all were! And Caia was going to bring the pack to disaster. Lucien and his pack were good people, nothing like the ambitious, deceitful pack she'd grown up in where your best friend would stab you in the back if it meant climbing the next rung on the hierarchical ladder. She had to save them from Caia, from themselves, and then she and Lucien could finally be happy together. Marita wasn't a bad person! It dumbfounded her how all these people could believe a woman who had successfully led the Daylight Coven against the Midnights could just become a monster. This was a witch hunt started by a *being* that needed to be stopped. And if Rose helped Marita stop Caia, she was sure she could negotiate a pardon for the pack.

Trembling with excitement, Rose dialed the number. It rang for a while, but finally the tone clicked.

"Rose," Marita's familiar stern voice.

Relief washed through her. "Oh, thank goddess, Marita. Do you know why I'm calling?"

"Hmm, yes, I'm reading the trace. Very interesting. What *is* interesting is I don't know where you are."

Rose paused. "I can't tell you that just yet."

"I see." She was silent for a moment. "Fine. I appreciate you calling, however. And this information I'm reading in the trace about this Septum and this little girl. It's all true?"

"Yes," Rose gushed. "Caia's planning on destroying the trace."

Marita hissed, "That little bitch."

Rose waited, her ears lifting under her hair every time she heard a noise. No one could know she was doing this. They wouldn't understand right now.

"I want you to keep pretending you're on their side, Rose. Contact me if you discover anything else of importance."

"Of course."

"And Rose ..."

"Yes?"

"I won't forget your loyalty."

CHAPTER 25

LAST MISTAKE

*C*aia *was dancing with Lucien, her cheek pressed against his shoulder as they swayed gently to the music. A soft breeze played with the hem of her dress and tickled through her hair as she sighed contentedly. It was a perfect night. The dark sky sewn bright with stars as colorful as fireflies, the air temperate and free, the sound of the surf crashing on shore as rhythmic as a lullaby.*

"I love you," she whispered and felt him squeeze her close.

"I love you too."

Caia pulled back to gaze up at him, smiling at the relief of it all being over, that they could finally be together in peace.

"Caia," he breathed ... and the sound was followed by a sickening wet whisper of metal through flesh. Lucien's eyes widened in surprise, his mouth falling open in shock. Blood poured out in its wake. He collapsed to his knees and Caia reached for him with a soundless scream, helpless to do anything as the sword that had torn through his heart twisted full circle. Lucien's eyes emptied, his expression going slack as he disappeared, leaving only a body that tumbled into the sand, a gory photograph of what had once been the real man.

"NOOOOOO!!!!!!!!!" Caia screamed, falling beside his body, stunned out of action as she glanced around for the killer. There was no one there. A sob broke from deep in her heart and she cried over her mate's corpse.

The cold solidity of it vanished, and Caia fell face-first into the sand. Propping herself up, spitting the beach out of her mouth, her hands searched the ground for Lucien. He was gone. Looking around she realized she was no longer on the beach. She was in a room that seemed familiar. A child's room filled with toys and books. Familiar toys and books. A scream rent the air, and terror exploded through her. Mama! she cried inwardly, hugging her small knees to her chest, shuffling back against the headboard of the bed she now sat on. Growls and howls reached her ears from the outside, and she jumped at the crescendo of items crashing on the ground floor of the house.

"ELIZA!" she heard her father scream, and she scrambled forward on the bed, hearing his footsteps pounding down the hall. Her bedroom door burst open and her father stood there, pale and grief-stricken. He clutched his chest, and it was then she noticed the swamp of thick blood soaking his entire upper body.

"Run," he ordered hoarsely, and then collapsed.

Instinct took hold. She must always listen to Daddy! Shutting out the sight of him dying on her floor, she turned to the tall window beside her bed and hitched it up with all her might. Rucking up her nightgown, her whole body trembling, she climbed through it and fumbled for purchase on the wall creeper that allowed her mother's ivy to decorate the wall outside. A blast of power shot past her shoulder, sending shards of glass in every direction. She felt little cuts slice through her skin like bee stings but it only made her move faster. She swung herself fully onto the creeper and scuttled down it. Thank goddess, she was on the first floor.

"GET HER!" an unfamiliar voice screamed as her bare feet touched grass. She turned and stared out over the garden. Beyond

the garden was her father's land and beyond that, a lake, and
beyond that, woods. If she could get to the woods, she could hide.

CAIA JERKED AWAKE, sucking in a rush of air in her panic.
Eliza. The little girl from the Septum! The little girl may not
have recognized the voice that screamed "Get her!" but Caia
would know it anywhere. Marita was going after Eliza
Emerett, and it was all her fault.

She jumped out of the bed she'd been given in the hotel
and hurried into her clothing. She had to save Eliza, and
there was no time to wait. Drawing on her energy, she used a
communication spell to take her to Vil and Laila's room,
praying she wouldn't interrupt *anything*. It was daytime, after
all. She snorted at herself. Like that would stop them. Thankfully she didn't, but her energy shook the two magiks awake
from a nap.

"Caia, wha—"

"No time to explain." She rushed to Vil, throwing his
jeans at him. "Put these on and take me to Eliza Emerett's
home. Specifically the gardens!"

Caia had never adored anyone more in that moment as he
pulled on his jeans and gripped her arm without a word of
question. She could have kissed him!

The travel was rocky, probably because Vil was still half-
asleep, so they got there feeling a little woozy. The sounds of
growls and shrieks met their ears instantly, and Vil paled as
he realized what she'd gotten them into. Perusing their
surroundings, her heart thumped as she saw the little white
figure in the dark a few hundred yards ahead of them.

"There, Vil, take me to her!" She pointed and they were
gone again, back within seconds.

"Oomph!" Vil grunted, and Caia shook herself together in
time to see Vil wrap his arms around Eliza who had ran

straight into them. She struggled and cried, and he fought to hold on to her.

A howl shot through the night, and Caia looked up to see six lykans crossing through the gardens toward them. Oh bloody Hades!

"Vil, this is Eliza Emerett, and those are Marita's lykans. Take her back to the pack. Now!"

His eyes widened as he struggled to hold the hysterical girl. "What about you?"

"Never mind me. Go! That's an order!"

Stunned and unhappy, he gripped Eliza and then vanished.

Heart thudding in her chest, Caia turned to face the lykans and sought the warm heat of her lykan energy. She was a wolf in seconds—a wolf that was ready to destroy those who'd killed Eliza's parents and were hell-bent on spilling the little girl's innocent blood.

She drew back her muzzle as they approached, snarling and posturing, thick saliva dripping over her jaws. With a harsh howl of her own, she propelled herself forward, launching at the nearest lykan, her claws slashing its fur. The lykan whined but managed to swipe at her, making contact and tugging her body close so they were locked in a fight, jaws nipping, bodies tumbling as each tried to gain an advantage over the other.

Finally, Caia managed to protract her claws into the lykan's belly and pull upward. The lykan howled and went limp. Dragging herself out from under its injured form, Caia found herself outflanked by five other lykans. Marita and an unfamiliar magik stood at their backs, smiling smugly.

"Oh, dear Caia. You are in a pickle now, aren't you?"

"Not quite."

Caia jerked her head around at the voice. Vil and Jaeden

stood before them, Jae's hand outstretched, face fierce with concentration.

A baffled yell.

Caia watched with pleasure as Marita and the magik were blasted a good hundred yards away from them.

A sharp, piercing pain ripped through Caia's side and she yelped at the attack, shaking off the wolf to turn around and face it. In her peripheral, she witnessed Jaeden using her telekinesis on the wolves and was stunned. Magik wasn't supposed to work on lykans! What the Hades …

But the thought drifted away as she was forced to spar with the bigger lykan, the wound in her side slowing her down. Just as she was about to dive on the other beast, a blur of fur beat her to it, the two wolves tumbling and rolling. She watched in amazement before a crunching noise unsettled her stomach and only one of the wolves got up. His silver eyes glared at her. Lucien. Oh thank goddess.

His warning growl told her to whirl around. She did, just in time to see another lykan leap at her. Falling under him, his huge jaws descending toward her, Caia gave a hopeless swat that barely stirred him. A massive weight collided with them and the wolf was thrown off her. A familiar brown wolf, his muzzle peeled back in a fierce growl, stood over her, his head bent low, telling the lykan she was under his protection. Ryder! She'd never been happier to see two people in all her life.

Rolling up onto her fours, Caia quickly took in Lucien and Ryder dealing quite nicely with the remaining lykans. Vil was nowhere to be seen, however, and she hoped to Gaia he'd returned to the pack.

Her heart jolted at the sight of Jaeden pinned to the ground by a magik, Marita and her companion grinning evilly down at her. This time Caia took control of the icy vapor that was her magik energy and used it to move her through the change instantaneously, clothing her naked form before it could be chilled by the crisp night air of the English countryside. She sent out a shock of water, forcing the pressurized liquid into the mouth of Marita's companion, flooding his chest cavity. Panic suffused his features and he dropped to the ground, clawing at his throat and gasping silently.

Marita looked up sharply, forgetting Jaeden and clearly feeling no compunction to save her companion. Caia held on tight to the water suffocating the magik, even as she trembled with fear at Marita's stoic face. They took quiet steps toward one another as if there wasn't a miniature battle going on behind Caia's back.

"I'm going to kill you slowly," Marita murmured, knowing Caia would hear her.

Before Caia could respond, the air shimmered with energy, and Marion and Saffron appeared behind Marita, causing Caia's eyes to widen and her grip on the other magik to loosen. She was pretty sure he was unconscious anyway.

Marita paused, her body tensing with the unexpected, her eyes telling Caia she couldn't believe it.

"The only person who will be dying today, sister … is you," Marion bit out.

Marita's eyes widened in disbelief and she spun to face her sister. "It can't be … you were dead. I felt it in the trace."

Marion smirked. "You really aren't very good with that trace, Marita. I think it's best we give it to Caia after all."

With a shriek of unchecked ire, Marita sent an animalistic stream of fire rushing at her sister, its body hissing and diving in attack. Marion easily deflected it with a mere swipe of her hand. "Is that all?"

Marita's retort was a wall of fire that encircled her sister from head to foot. Heart pounding, skin hot from the roaring flames, Caia envisioned a waterfall that appeared over Marion's head, obliterating the flames. Unfortunately, it doused Marion as well, and she threw Caia a bemused look, a look they shared in just enough time for Marita to use magik to suspend Jae in the air. When Jaeden screamed, Caia couldn't work out why, until she realized Marita was scoring burn marks into her with invisible flames.

An untold fury took possession of Caia, refusing to let Jae experience one more second of torture after having survived it at the hands of Caia's uncle, Ethan. She thrust out her hands and a tidal wave the likes of which she'd never conjured before towered over Marita like a python readying to strike. Caia gave a jerk of her head, parting a curtain in the wave so as it descended toward Marita, it bypassed Jaeden. A yell was muffled into a gurgle as the wave crashed to the ground, whooshing across the grass and taking a bedraggled and spluttering Marita with it. Her magik let go of Jaeden, and the lykan tumbled to the ground.

"My goddess, Caia," Marion's voice broke through and she looked up to see the magik smiling at her in wonder. "That was very cool."

Brace yourself, because there's going to be more! she thought as she strode toward Marita, who was pulling herself out of the water with a stream of curses. She straightened in time to see Caia heading determinedly for her, and her eyes widened.

Then they narrowed in hatred before she disappeared altogether.

"NO!" Caia screamed in frustration. She wasn't getting away from her that easily! This had to end! It had to end now! And Caia no longer cared how.

She made the decision to travel somewhere she'd never been before ... a feat that could only be performed by a Traveler, a magik with Vil's particular gifts. Marion had told Caia that Marita was probably staying at a specific inn, a condemned building in a small village in central Scotland.

Take me there, she whispered to her energy, squeezing her eyes shut and drawing on every ounce of magik that belonged to her. The travel seemed to take forever, moving through a black tunnel at warp speed, flashes of colored lights exploding in her eyes as a sickening pain bubbled under her skin.

With a thud, she collapsed on gritty ground, pebbles poking her legs and arms as she heaved forward, the contents of her stomach decorating what looked like a short driveway. She shuddered and convulsed, her flesh and insides so raw, it was as if a butcher had taken a meat hammer to her. When at last she stilled, lying prone on the stone driveway, Caia looked up through her hair to see a Gothic-style inn perched on a small hill.

Breathing deeply, she pulled herself to her feet, swaying a little, and gave her surroundings a fleeting look. A road along the side of the inn led to a residential area; below the hill was what appeared to be a main road with another road branching off, leading to houses that were stacked behind a tall wooden fence some yards down from the inn itself. It was pitch-dark, and there was not another soul around.

Thank goddess Eliza's family lived in England or Caia might not have survived a longer distance. She examined the inn carefully. It was old, its windows and doors boarded up with DANGEROUS KEEP OUT sprayed across the main door in red. She almost snorted. These people had no idea just how dangerous the contents of the inn were.

The thought of what she had to do next made her want to throw up again, but Caia braced herself. It was now or never.

With another forceful push of her energy, she transported herself to the inn's interior. A sharp pain exploded in her upper thigh and she bit back a yelp, but her efforts were in vain as she tumbled against the obstacle that had thrust into her leg and undone her, sending her crashing to the floor with a muffled *oomph*. Damn table.

See, this was why traveling was for the professionals.

Flipping herself over, Caia lay on her back panting and let her eyes drink in her surroundings. The inside of the inn was like a palace, every inch decorated exactly to Marita's Renaissance-inspired taste.

She wanted to burn it to the ground!

The sound of shuffling to her left seized hold of her heart, and she stiffened. A painful heat gripped her entire length and pinned her to the floor. She struggled against the magikal hold but there was no budging; every time she tried to pierce it with her own magik, she got nowhere. As five faces popped into view above her, Caia realized why. Five magiks, one of whom was Marita, had combined their powers to trap her. She sneered at that, feeling a little smug that it had taken five of them to best her.

But best you they have, you idiot.

Frantically, she struggled again as the import of the situation sunk in. She was going to die here. She was going to die right here in this spot any minute now.

"Caia," Marita snapped, "stop struggling. The least you can do is die with a little dignity."

Caia tried to speak, to curse the evil witch for all eternity, but nothing came out.

Marita snickered. "Cat got your tongue, Caia? I can't believe you and my sister deceived me so well. After I kill you, I'm going to have to leave this place, and then I'm going to have to hunt down my deceitful, wicked shrew of a sister and kill her too."

At the thought of Marita hurting Marion, Caia's struggles intensified.

"Tut-tut, Caia, you're only wasting your energy. I like the

fact that my killing Marion distresses you so. In fact, I'm not going to stop there. I'm going to kill everyone you care about. Your pack. That little Midnight bitch and her boyfriend Traveler. As for your best friend, Jaeden, well ... I'm going to give her a taste of what your Uncle Ethan gave her before I cut her open to see how she acquired telekinesis. It's the damnedest thing, you know. Oh, you don't like that at all, do you?"

A flicker of white heat licked across Caia's calves, and she pleaded inwardly for Marita to make her madder.

"It was Rose who told me where to find Eliza—"

Oh my gods! I will kill her! If I get out of here, I will rip that tramp apart!

"—she thinks I'll grant Lucien and the pack a pardon and she can live happily ever after with your mate." She snorted. "Delusional fool. I'll let her live, but I'm going to kill the pack slowly. Mutilate them like I did the others ... Dimitri and Yvana—"

The white heat stroked up toward her stomach.

"—Dana and Daniel. Morgan and Natalia. I didn't get to finish them off properly. But when I get to Irini and Ella and all those others you love ... I'll make sure to take my time—"

It gripped her stomach and crawled up through her chest, her throat closing under its blaring fire.

"—and then Lucien. Oh, I'll leave him till last. I'm going to make his torture last for months. First, I'll play with that beautiful exterior, give him a few scars he'll never forget. And then I'll take his insides out bit by bit while he's still conscious and—"

"ARRGGGGGGGGGGGGHHHHHHHHHHHHH!" The horrendous scream that ripped out of Caia was beyond her control, the white light blinding her as it exploded out of every cell in her body. Caia was no longer Caia but one with the greatest stream of energy she'd ever known.

And all it wanted was the destruction of Marita and her people.

It seemed forever that she ceased to exist.

But then ... the bright white faded and a hush fell. Her eyes slid closed of their own accord, silence pillowing her in her sleep.

CHAPTER 26

SOLIDARITY

The beeping noise was annoying. It pulled her from her sleep and forced her into consciousness. Caia groaned, her head pounding so hard, she was afraid to open her eyes. That was ... if she *could* open them. Her lids felt as if they'd been hot-glued shut. As for her mouth ... she made a smacking sound with her lips, her mouth as dry as Irini's Victoria sponge cake. The irritating beeping got louder. What the ...

"Miss ...," a lilting voice said softly above her.

Slowly, she peeled her lids open and then grunted at the harsh, stinging stream of light. She tried again, and as her eyes focused, she saw a woman standing over her. A nurse. Caia's heart kicked. Oh crap, where was she?

"It's nice to see you awake." The nurse smiled softly, her accent thick and sure ... and very Scottish? Oh my goddess! Caia twisted her head—a heart monitor was the source of the beeping. She glanced down to see herself tucked into a hospital bed, a tube plugged into her hand.

"Where am I?" she croaked.

The nurse frowned. "You don't remember?"

"No."

The woman's eyes widened. "You're no from hereabouts from the sound of that accent, are you? You dinnae remember what happened to you, at all?"

Yeah, that's what she was telling her. She shook her head impatiently.

"You're in the Western General ... in Edinburgh. You were found in the rubble of an explosion in a village a little west of here twenty-four hours ago. Do you remember how you got there?"

Marita! Caia sucked in a breath, the events of the night before whooshing into her body like a gust of wind. The inn ... she'd gone after Marita to the inn and ... had she killed her? Had she been successful?

"Were there any other survivors?" she whispered frantically.

The nurse frowned again, shaking her head. "No, honey, you were the only person found in the debris. It was just a load of ash and rubble, they said. Why? Were you wi' somebody? Can you tell me your name?"

Caia had to get out of there. She had to get back to the pack, and she had to get someone to come deal with all the people who'd been at the site of the inn, because clearly she'd made quite a mess. Glancing around, she was relieved to find herself in a private room.

"Can I speak with the doctor?" she asked.

The nurse pinched her lips. "I'll have a wee look and see if I can find him for you. The police are waiting to question you, so I'll hurry along, eh?"

As soon as the door closed behind the woman, Caia ripped out the tube in her hand and pulled off the leads for the heart monitor, silencing it with her magik. Hurriedly, she used magik to clothe herself in jeans and a T-shirt. She swayed badly, clutching a plastic chair in the corner to push herself upright. This was no time to be lacking energy.

Her nerve endings shaking, Caia took a deep breath and pictured the dining hall in the hotel.

Everything was black, her aching body pressed against something cold. Then noise exploded all around her.

"Caia—"

"Oh my goddess—"

"Caia! You're back!"

She felt hands tugging at her and realized she'd landed prone on the hardwood floor of the dining hall. Someone gripped her under the arms and turned her gently, and she looked up into the concerned silver eyes of her mate.

"Lucien." She reached for him, and he hauled her into his arms, his entire body shaking with emotion as they embraced.

"I thought you were dead," he choked and squeezed her tighter. She was vaguely aware of weeping, and people patting and stroking her back as she lay comforted in her mate's arms.

Eventually, Lucien pulled back a little. "Can you stand?" he asked hoarsely, his eyes washing over her face as if afraid to look away.

She nodded. There was still a lot to do, and she didn't have time to play the invalid. Slowly but surely, Lucien helped her to her feet. She stood to face a wearied and worried pack, including Marion, Saffron, and Reuben. Caia was heartened to see Ryder, Jaeden, and Vil all in good shape —she guessed they'd taken care of Marita's lykans. As her eyes took them all in, a frown formed between her brows. Wait a minute…

"Where's Eliza?" she asked, panicked.

Marion waved away the question. "She's at the Center."

"But she's a Midnight." Oh goddess, what if the Council locked her up?

However, Marion shook her head. "Eliza's fine. She's being well cared for. Penelope has taken her under her protection. She *was* surprised to see me alive, though."

Caia grunted but relaxed marginally at the news Penelope was the one watching over Eliza. Of all the Council, she seemed the most ready to believe that Midnights might be all right after all.

"Caia, what happened?" Jaeden asked abruptly. "Marion took Saffron and Vil to that inn, and when they got there, there was nothing left of it. Just rubble and debris, and the ash from Marita and her magiks' bodies."

Marita and her magiks' bodies! Relief flooded through Caia's entire being. "I did it?" she asked, near breathless. "I killed her?"

Reuben grinned. "Looks like."

She frowned, remembering the disgusting mess she'd made of Ethan when she'd used that same strange energy burst on him. "Why was there ash?" she whispered and looked directly at Marion, seeking answers. "Last time with Ethan ... there was ... you know ..."

The witch matched her expression. "Interesting. Did you feel any different this time around, when you did whatever the Hades it is you do?"

As she forced herself to relive the moment pinned beneath Marita and the other magiks' power, she realized her fear of Marita and her evil had been even greater than that of her uncle. Perhaps because now she fully comprehended the impact a person that powerful and ruthless could have on their world.

"I felt *more*," she whispered.

"Then perhaps the energy this time was more powerful.

Not to mention you've come along in your magik since then."

Nodding, Caia decided not to let it worry her. Knowing Marita was out of the picture should relieve her, take the pressure off, not add to it. She leaned into Lucien and he pulled her into his side, kissing the top of her head. "I did it."

"You did it," he murmured.

"What happened to you?" Jaeden persisted.

"I was taken to a hospital by humans." She threw a worried look at Marion. "We need to get back any blood tests and mess with the memories of all the people who dealt with me and the scene of the incident."

Marion nodded militantly. "Of course. Which hospital?"

"Edinburgh." Caia shook her head trying to remember the name the nurse had given her, but in all the chaos, she couldn't. "I dunno which one."

Reuben shrugged. "That's easy. You obviously used your magik there."

"Yes."

"I can sense each magiks' different energy." He tapped his nose. "I'll just follow this. I'll need Marion and Saffron's help."

"Of course." Marion nodded and then smiled sadly at Caia.

I killed her sister.

"I'm sorry, Marion," she whispered.

The witch shook her head, her lips pinched. She came forward, drawing Caia into a delicate hug. "Don't be. You did what I couldn't."

Pulling back, Marion glanced at Reuben and Saffron over her shoulder. "Let's make this quick." She held a hand out to Reuben, and he clutched it tightly as if offering her comfort.

Caia sighed. He could be sweet when he wanted to be.

With a little buzz in the air, all three of them vanished.

A tense silence fell among the pack, a heightened sense of expectation leaping from member to member. They wanted to know where they went from here. But as Caia's eyes drifted over them and stopped on Rose, who stood off to the side from the rest of them, they would have to wait and see until after her showdown. The lykan flinched under Caia's regard and she immediately saw the guilt there.

A snarl ripped from deep within her, and Caia shot out her hand, sending Rose flying back into the wall with a crack of her head. She lifted her with her magik and pinned her there.

"Caia, what the hell!" Lucien gripped her arm tightly and tried to pull her back. The pack broke apart as if unsure what to do. The children cried out, frightened by the unexpected attack. The only one who appeared calm was Jaeden who took a step toward Caia.

"What did she do?" she asked with a growl.

Through her anger she felt a deep connection of friendship with Jae, and her gratitude for it was undying. "She called Marita. She told her about the Septum. She betrayed us."

"No." Lucien growled. "Caia, you're mistaken." He tugged once more at her hand, trying to break her hold.

She threw him an angry, hurt look. "You believe her over me?" she whispered hoarsely, not letting go.

He glared at her. "I think you've been through a lot. Caia, for goddess' sake." He wrapped a hand around her waist and tried to pull her away from Rose.

A noise of distress drifted out of Jaeden, and Lucien was shoved away from Caia with an invisible force. Jae was using her telekinesis against the Alpha. He was glaring at Caia, though, so he thought it was her, and she wasn't about to give Jae away.

"I'm telling you the truth. Marita told me Rose told her

where to get Eliza. How else would she have found out? And she has motive. She's in love with you and wants me gone!"

"Lucien, no!" Rose shrieked from her place up on the wall. "She's lying. I didn't do that!"

Fury shot through Caia, and she gripped a magikal hand around the lykan's throat, choking her. "People died because of you!"

"Caia, stop it! That's an order!" Lucien yelled.

Seemingly out of nowhere, little Laila strolled slowly out in front of the trio and came to a stop before Rose. Tentatively, she reached up and placed a gentle hand on Rose's. The lykan watched her warily and then stopped struggling. Laila took her hand away, her shoulders wilting, and turned back toward Caia and Lucien. "I think she betrayed us to Marita, Lucien."

He shook his head in disbelief, and Rose's eyes widened. "No! It's not true."

Caia choked her harder, and she made horrible gagging sounds.

"Caia—" Magnus implored quietly.

"Caia, don't." Laila shook her head, and some of the anger dissipated, enough to bring Caia back under control.

She relaxed her grip but kept Rose suspended. "Tell him the truth."

No answer.

She envisioned a little water filling up Rose's airway; the lykan must've felt it because she began to struggle anew.

"Tell him the truth!"

She nodded frantically, so Caia made the water disappear. "Okay!" she cried, frightened tears streaming down her cheeks. "I did it! I went to Marita, but only to protect you and your pack from her!" She gestured hatefully to Caia. "She's a monster, Lucien!"

An almighty howl exploded around the room, followed

by a harsh row of snarls. When he spoke, his lykan was evident in his words. "Caia, let me go."

Caia nodded subtly at Jae, and Lucien slumped free. He straightened and clamped a hand down on Caia's shoulder. "Let her go."

Gazing up into his eyes, she saw pain and betrayal and sorrow. She wished she could take it all away from him. With a sympathetic nod, Caia retracted her magik, and Rose crumpled to the floor with a thud.

The pack all turned on her, and their Alpha approached her like a hunter going in for the kill. She scrambled against the floor until her back pressed to the wall, her lips trembling, pathetic tears spilling down her pretty cheeks.

"Please," she whimpered.

Lucien's hands curled into fists. Caia knew how difficult this was for him. "As pack Alpha, it is my prerogative to kill you for your act of betrayal against the pack and its Alpha's mate."

A terrified sob poured out of Rose.

"But I'm not going to. You don't deserve a quick death, and I'm afraid that's all I'd be capable of. No." He glanced back at Caia and his eyes begged for forgiveness. He didn't seem to be able to look anywhere else, and Caia wanted to run to him and tell him it was okay ... it was all over. She nodded to encourage him, and his gaze moved to Vil. "I'm going to leave your judgment, Rose, to the Council."

The magik instantly understood and moved toward the female. She cried and shook but didn't struggle as he pulled her to her feet, clamping a hand on her upper arm.

"Ryder, the Council knows you. Go with Vil and explain, please."

His friend nodded and strode forward to take Rose's other arm. The three of them disappeared.

Unable to resist any longer, Caia crossed the room to

Lucien and placed a comforting hand on his back. He turned into her. "I am so sorry, Caia."

"You couldn't have known."

Jae snorted. "I always disliked the bitch."

Caia winced. "Not the time."

"Sorry."

She let Lucien hold her, ignoring the pack as they mumbled to one another about everything that had happened. So much had happened. So much was still to come. Wanting nothing more than to go back to Lucien's room and lose herself in him, Caia drew back from him instead. She wouldn't be allowed that luxury for now ... perhaps ever. Her mate wanted no part in the war, but she ... she was a piece of it.

She traced the annulet on her palm she'd been trying to keep hidden from the pack and gestured for them to sit around the dining table.

"I have to tell you what's been going on," she said wearily as she perched on the chair at the table head, trying to ignore Lucien's burning gaze. She held up the palm with the annulet and they all frowned, mumbling queries.

"What is that?" Lucien demanded.

She locked gazes with him. "I told you I couldn't kill the Septum. So I asked Reuben to let me meet the Cassandrian who said all of this was going to happen because of me. The Prophet. I asked him—if I killed Marita and the coven made me Head, could I ask the gods to take the trace back? Both traces—Midnight and Daylight."

"Freeing us," Lucien said, his eyes widening. "Caia, that's brilliant."

She smiled wryly. "If only I had thought of it sooner, huh?"

Then we wouldn't be awkward with each other because I

wouldn't have lied to you and you wouldn't have kicked me out of the pack.

As usual, he seemed to understand and covered her hand with his own, giving it a quick squeeze.

"Anyway, he said the gods already knew what I wanted and he was awaiting their reply."

"You're telling me this guy has a direct link to the gods?" Aidan asked, astonished.

Caia grinned ruefully. "Yup. And the gods have a funny sense of humor. They made me wait weeks for an answer."

Jaeden's eyes sparkled with excitement. "But they said yes, right?"

"They said yes."

A whoop rushed around the pack before she quieted them, laughing at their encouragement. "That's all fine and dandy, but it means this ... this war isn't over for me." She couldn't look at Lucien. "This annulet on my palm is part of a blood oath I took with the Council. I promised them that if they made me Head of the Coven, I would complete the rite to the gods and have them take away the trace. If I don't, all my powers will be given to the Council."

"What the hell kind of risk is that to take?" Magnus grumbled.

"One I had to," she insisted. "And now I have to go back to the Center and finish this."

At their continued silence, Caia finally managed to lift her gaze from the table to look into Lucien's face. His eyes told her he loved her, but his expression told her how torn he was. He had made a promise to the pack.

And she understood that. As much as she didn't want to.

Magnus's cough broke their eye contact, and they looked over at her uncle. He pinned them both with a stern stare. "Now, look here. This stuff about protecting the pack from the war is nonsense. We've been in this war for a long time, and we're not getting out of it without every other supernatural on the planet getting out of it as well. And we will follow you, Lucien, no matter what. Marion told me after she took Eliza to the Council and explained about her being alive and all that—"

Caia almost laughed at the blasé way he said it.

"—they offered the pack a home at the Center until this is all over. So let's go with Caia. We can't leave her alone in this."

A spark of hope flared inside her, and she switched her gaze to Lucien. He was looking around at the pack, carefully reading them all. Finally, he turned back to her, and that spark burst into flame at his slow grin of agreement.

CHAPTER 27

SAVE OUR SOULS

Twenty-One Pilots played softly from the sound system in their suite at the Center. It was dreary outside in Paris, shadowing the room in a gray-blue gloom counteracted by the candles Jaeden had lit all around them. The atmosphere outside their door was tense and expectant. Inside, she lay snuggled against Ryder as they dozed on a sofa, untroubled by anything but one another. It was nice to forget about the last few months of horror, to forget about the fight that lay ahead.

"I like the name Anna," Ryder mused, stroking his fingers up and down her bare arms. Goose bumps rose where he touched, and she smiled at his turn of conversation.

"A name for what?" she teased.

"Uh, the Hummer I have a deposit on," he replied sarcastically. "A kid, Jae, a little girl."

"Whose little girl?"

"Well, I was going to say ours, but this conversation is rapidly making me rethink procreation with you."

Jae chuckled. "Sorry. I just can't believe you've thought of names. What else have you thought about?"

"I don't know. I thought we could wait a few years, have some time just the two of us. And then I was thinking maybe we could get a house next to Lucien and Caia so our kids grow up close, you know. Maybe have three or four kids …"

The warmth of his sweetness settled like a pleasant ache on her chest. "Boys or girls?"

"I don't know. What do you think?"

"Three boys and a little girl."

Amusement laced his words as he replied, "Ah, so you *have* thought about this?"

"I guess. I always thought that would be nice, you know, having three big brothers."

"I thought Christian drove you crazy?"

"Oh, he does," she whispered, thinking about her brother these last few weeks. He'd been wonderful to her mother when Jae hadn't. But now that she was acting like a sane person again, they were getting through the loss of Dimitri together. Her brother had taken on a paternal role that was annoying … and yet so welcome. "But I don't know what I'd do without him."

Ryder pressed a kiss into her hair. "Then three boys and a girl it is."

She laughed. "Just like that?" She twisted around to look at him.

His expression was serious as his eyes drank her in. "Of course. What do I gotta do to make you understand I'd do anything to make you happy?"

I love you.

Jae reached for him, pressing a soft kiss to his lips. A soft kiss that quickly grew heated. Ryder groaned underneath her and she felt a tug on her shirt as he began undoing buttons.

A gentle tapping filtered into her consciousness.

"Jae!"

Caia.

Ryder growled under her lips, and she peeled herself off him. "Her timing sucks."

Smiling ruefully, Jae buttoned her shirt again. "Coming!" she called and then threw Ryder a warning look. "I'm letting her in."

He squirmed uncomfortably, a slight flush rising on his cheekbones. "Give me a minute."

Snickering at his predicament, she thrust a cushion at him and hurried to the door. Caia stood on the other side looking a lot more put together than she had in the last few days. She looked over Jae quizzically and then blushed. "I didn't interrupt anything, did I?"

How did she know?

"Your hair ..." She gestured vaguely.

Jaeden felt her head and realized her hair was twice as big as it usually was from Ryder running his hands through it. "Oh ... I, um ... was experimenting."

She ignored Ryder's snort.

"Anyway, what's up?" She stood aside to let her pass.

"Hey, Ryder." Caia gave a little wave and threw him an apologetic look after taking in the candles and romantic setting. "I didn't mean to bother you guys."

"No bother," he assured her amiably.

Jae took a seat next to Ryder. "I thought you would be busy getting ready for the ceremony tonight." Caia was being made Head of the Coven in a matter of hours.

"Nah, I know what they want me to do. I've been hanging out in the library."

What the Hades was she in the library for? "Why?"

Caia shrugged. "Oh, just reading up on the ceremony and stuff."

"Oh, makes sense."

"Yeah."

S. YOUNG

After another pause, Ryder coughed, "Do you, uh, want me to leave?"

Caia shrugged again and threw Jae a pensive look. "It depends if Jaeden's comfortable talking about her telekinesis in front of you."

A sick feeling settled in Jae's stomach, and she felt her defenses rise. "Yes. Ryder can stay."

Her mate frowned. "What is this about?"

Caia shook her head, her hands fluttering nervously as she read their sudden tension. "No, I don't want to alarm you. It's nothing too serious. It's just … well … when we were at Eliza's home fighting … Jae, didn't you realize that your telekinesis worked on the lykans in wolf form?"

Huh?

She knew she must look stunned. Truthfully, the thought hadn't even crossed her mind. Wow. It *had* worked against the lykans. "Oh, yeeaahh."

Ryder looked confused. "What does that mean?"

"I don't know." Caia watched Jae. "I don't want you to worry about it, though … I just think that at some point, it's something we should look into."

She stiffened, panic tightening her chest. "Look into how? By experimenting?"

Caia looked aghast at the suggestion. "Gaia, no! I thought maybe a blood test. We don't know if your telekinesis is part of a transfer of magik from Ethan or if it's an emotional parting gift from what happened to you. There are theories that severe emotional trauma can cause us to tap into parts of our brain we don't normally use, thus giving us access to things like telekinesis."

This conversation was making her uncomfortable. "Does it matter?"

"Not to me." Caia smiled gently at her. "But if it's magik, then somehow you've managed to discover a new kind that penetrates the biggest defense a lykan has. That's important. And also … if it *is* magik, does that mean it's genetic?"

Ryder relaxed into the sofa. "You mean, will our kids have it?"

Caia nodded.

Wow. Jaeden hadn't even thought of that. Was this something her kids would get from her? And did that make her and any kids she had a threat, because she could hurt lykans in wolf form?

"Is this a problem, Caia?" she whispered, trying to tamp down the nervous butterflies waking up in her gut.

Caia stood, and as she did so, her power crackled around her. "No," she replied firmly. "I came here to suggest that we keep it between us. Only Lucien and I, and now you guys, know about this. I think we should keep it that way. If after all this you want to know more about it, then we'll look into it. But I think it's safer all around if this never gets out, and that you refrain from using your telekinesis against lykans in wolf form."

Relief washed through Jaeden and she gave her friend a grateful smile. "Thank you."

Caia looked shy as she turned to walk back toward the door. "Don't. I'd do anything for you, you know that."

She was the second person in the last ten minutes to say something that sweet to her. A warm revelation settled over Jae. The pain caused by her father's death would never disappear, but the loneliness was slowly melting away.

And all because she was lucky enough to have soul mates.

* * *

HER LEGS SHOOK as Caia got down on her knees in the middle of the court. Like last time, all the Daylights sat upon the rows and rows of benches, the Council seated in the row before her. Unlike last time, her pack was in the crowd, and the Council wasn't out to get her. *Well, for the most part*, she thought, ignoring Benedict De Jong's displeased expression.

The time for the ceremony had come, and she had been warned, as had the pack and everyone else, that once she inherited the title of Head of the Coven, the impact of the trace would hurt. Trace magik, when inherited as it had been for Caia, was easier to manage; it was a gradual addition to her magik. For most, however, the trace was inherited by ceremony, and it could be painful. Thus the Center had been warned not to overreact if Caia displayed signs of discomfort. Her hand twitched. Just how much discomfort were they talking about? And would the pain last long?

The rite asking the gods to take back the trace was not being performed until the Hunter's Moon, or Blood Moon as it was often called (Caia felt Blood Moon was more fitting considering she had to offer up some of her own during the rite), which was another four days away. Four days of excruciating pain didn't sound like fun.

"Caia Ribeiro." Alfred Doukas stood up. Like the rest of the Council he wore pale-blue ceremonial robes with the Fasces on their left breast. The Fasces was a bundle of rods tied together containing an ax in the middle with its blade projecting. In ancient Rome, it had been carried in front of the magistrates and symbolized authority. The Council couldn't have been clearer about how they saw themselves within the coven.

"You kneel before us today in supplication to the gods, asking them to bequeath favor upon you and grant you the gifts only bestowed upon that of this coven's leader." At that the Council all stood as one and made their way around the bench to the platform. One by one, they lowered themselves to their knees, Alfred Doukas only marginally closer to her than the others. "We, the Council, kneel with you, and ask the gods to grant this favor."

As one they pulled small daggers from their robes and slit a shallow cut across their palms before holding it up to the heavens. Caia took that as her cue and gripped tight to the dagger Marion had given her, biting her lip as she scored it across her left palm, squeezing back the sting of tears as her flesh opened and the blood ran out. She held it up to the heavens and cleared her throat.

"Mother Gaia, Potnia Theron, my lady Hemera. I beseech you, praying you find me deserving of the great gift of the trace."

A tingling eased the pain in her palm, and Caia gazed at it in amazement as it glowed with an ethereal light. Dazed, she glanced over to the Council and saw their palms also shimmered with the energy. She gasped as the tingling grew sharp, turning hard, as if a hand were gripping it tight. And then she was seized, watching helplessly as bolts of energy shot into her body, rushing through her veins as cold as ice crystallizing her very insides. The sensation of falling took over, and she blanched as her head struck something hard. The blurry view of the ceiling told her it had been the floor.

A soft buzzing started in her ears like little whispers. And then the whispers grew to voices, drowning out the buzzing.

And then voices grew into weapons.

Thousands of energies poured into her, piercing through her skin like a million fiery needles, the pain so excruciating Caia lost herself.

She was no longer Caia.

She was anguish, she was torment. She was suffering.

* * *

VANNE AND RYDER held Lucien back while Reuben held on to Jaeden and Magnus. Lucien strained against his friend and the magik's grip, sweating and spitting, desperate to get to Caia, who writhed and screamed in the middle of the floor like a madwoman.

"Get off me!" he snarled, pulling out of Vanne's grip only to be halted by Ryder's arm hooking around his neck and dragging him back.

"They told us it would be like this," Ryder tried to reassure him, but Lucien could hear the concern in his friend's voice. The Daylights all leaned forward in their seats, each wearing the same expression of horror and anxiety. Oh yes, they had been warned Caia might show signs of *discomfort*, not screaming her head off as if she were on fire! He growled again and attempted to get out of his restraints.

Caia, he thought imploringly, *I'm with you. I'm with you.*

To his astonishment, her screams died to groans and she didn't writhe as frantically. His jaw dropped and he wondered if she'd heard him through the trace. *No, surely not.* But as her screams grew again, he lurched forward.

Caia! Don't! I'm here, you're okay. You're going to be all right, just hold on.

Her screaming dimmed.

I can't get to you physically because these assholes are holding me back, but I'm here. Just take a minute, breathe. Breathe, Caia ...

* * *

AS LUCIEN'S voice fought through all the others, Caia grabbed tight to it and let its soothing comfort ease the pain. She felt her body relax as he crooned to her, and the burning ice thawed a little. Her head still pounded with all the energies, Daylight and Midnight alike, but concentrating only on

Lucien dulled it, sending it to the back of her skull rather than it being an all-encompassing pain.

"Lucien," she whispered and grew still.

After a few minutes, a face appeared above her. Alfred Doukas.

"Caia?" he queried, his eyes bright with concern. "Are you all right?"

His energy tingled in her veins, and she knew without a shadow of a doubt his concern was genuine. He was a good man, Alfred Doukas.

"I'm fine," she croaked and tried to push to a sitting position.

"Caia!" She turned to see Lucien bounding down the stairs and onto the platform. He dropped to his knees beside her, his eyes wide and bewildered.

She smiled wearily at him. "Thank you."

His silver gaze turned to smoke. "It worked? You heard?"

Her eyelids drooped. "I heard."

"I think you better get her to her bed, Lucien, before she falls asleep in the court."

"Is it done, then?" Lucien asked.

"It's done."

CHAPTER 28

IT'S BETWEEN YOU AND YOUR GODS

Getting rid of the trace for Caia was just the beginning. No one, not Reuben, Saffron, Marion, nor the Council, had approached her with explanation or understanding of what would come next once the gods had freed them all from the binding power of the trace. But as the days turned over and she fought off the painful effects of having double the trace, it niggled at Caia, taunting her and illuminating the fact she would never truly be at peace until the war as it stood was over.

"But what can you do?" Lucien asked softly as they lay together on the third morning after the ceremony. Since that night, she hadn't left his side, now fully comprehending what it meant for him to be her mate—he was the only one who could quite literally ease the pain.

At first, he still seemed anxious with her, and she guessed he was unsure of her feelings for him after kicking her out of the pack and the Rose debacle (she was now awaiting trial, sitting in prison as they spoke). She wasn't going to lie—she'd been pissed off and hurt. But so had he.

So, Caia promised him there was nothing to forgive. Life

was too damn short, and she wanted to live it with him. It had not escaped everyone's notice they hadn't left the bedroom since the ceremony, but they'd be surprised to know they'd spent much of it talking (well, mostly).

"I don't know," she replied, frowning. "I just know that even after tomorrow ... this won't be over for me."

"Are you going to stay and fight?"

Her breath hitched. "Would it be okay if the answer to that question is I don't know?"

Lucien huffed and squeezed her closer. "Of course."

"Will you wait for me?"

Chuckling, he rolled her over so he was braced above her on the bed. "No. I won't need to." He laughed again at her scowl and smoothed it away with his fingers. "I won't need to because I'll be right there with you, fighting anybody you want me to."

She raised her eyebrows, looping her hands around his neck and wriggling provocatively. "Looks like I've just been promoted to Alpha then, huh?"

Lucien made a face. "Well, the job is yours if you want it, but I should warn you that the contract is bull. I've received none of the promised perks."

"Perks?"

"Oh, you know ... a lifetime supply of beer and foot massages, a harem of women to bathe and clothe me, et cetera ..."

She snorted and pulled back from him. "A harem?"

He grinned unrepentantly. "Did I mention my sense of humor is also greatly underappreciated?"

For Caia it was a relief to know Lucien and the pack were behind her as she waded through the murky waters of Daylight politics.

When she met up with the Council the night before the rite to go through the details, she fought to ignore the strain of the trace and decided to put forth the question that had been pressing heavily upon her.

"After this, what's next?"

The Council was seated in Alfred Doukas's suite, joined by Vanne and Marion. The frosty tension between those two had caused a little awkwardness at the beginning of the meeting, but everyone seemed determined to ignore them. Caia threw a quick glance to Vanne who was resolutely snubbing Marion. She remembered how grief-stricken he'd been when he thought she'd died. Obviously, he hadn't forgiven her for not enlightening him about her plan to deceive Marita.

"Next?" Benedict sneered.

"When the trace is gone, what next? We'll be free, but the war as it stands will still exist. How do we end this?"

"*We* don't," Benedict retorted sharply. "The details of the war will be left for the Council to deal with."

"Now, Benedict—" Penelope began, but Caia wanted to speak for herself.

"You mean, you intend to use and then discard me?"

"No, Caia," Penelope rushed. "That is not at all the intention of the Council."

"I think Caia should be put forward for a place on the Council," Vanne interrupted.

A place on the Council? Caia stared at him wide-eyed. She hadn't meant *that* as such but … actually … it was an idea. If she were a member of the Council, she would have a say in how they went about ending the war. She could have an impact on the treatment of Midnights and Daylights alike.

The Council gazed at him open-mouthed for a moment, before Marion cleared her throat. "I agree with Vanne."

He glared at her. "I didn't ask you to."

"Well, I do," she snapped, muttering under her breath about idiots acting like children.

Benedict was outraged. "How dare you suggest such a thing? There are only nine places on the Council, and those have been filled."

The young magik, Derren, cleared his throat and everyone turned to face him. He was an enigmatic man and only spoke when he had something of import to say. "I agree with Vanne and Marion. Caia is too valuable a member of the Daylights to throw back out to the wolves. She should be an integral cog in our machine, as she has already proven her worth tenfold."

Shocked silence settled around the room. Finally, Alfred stood. "If it would be the will of the Council, I suggest we at least discuss the possibility of adding Caia to our noble ranks after the rite has been performed."

"Hear, hear," Penelope muttered, and a round of the same followed—from all except Benedict who was content to skewer Caia with his gaze.

* * *

THE RITE WAS NOT to be performed before the entire Center as the Acquisition of the Trace ceremony had been. It was a private ceremony between Caia and the gods, and so she was led to the deepest level of the Center where caverns had been sculpted into the building like damp, salt-smelling sea caves. The goddess Gaia, unlike Zeus who roamed the skies, preferred enclosed spaces, and so it was often thought appropriate to perform any rites to her within dwellings like a house or cave.

"Are you ready?" Penelope asked softly as they stood inside the humid space, waiting as the torches were lit around the area.

Caia nodded, shivering with nerves. Or cold ... she *was* completely naked beneath her blue robe.

"We'll be out at the elevator. Waiting."

She nodded again and watched silently as Penelope and the two magiks who lit the torches fumbled their way out of the dark caves. Taking a deep breath, she turned back to gaze at the almost-circular room. In the middle stood a *tripous*, a three-legged sacrificial altar with a large stone basin upon it. Carved into stone were the names of the living gods accompanied by a prayer for them to hear her.

With great trepidation, Caia removed the dagger from her robe, and then removed the robe itself. She stood shivering and as naked as the day she was born. Thank goddess she got to perform this one alone. She actually blushed, even though there wasn't anyone else to see her.

Except the gods, Caia, she reminded herself.

Tentatively, she approached the altar, wincing at the gritting sand and stone beneath her feet. And though she knew it wasn't possible, she swore she could hear the rush of the ocean in the distance. It was so weird.

Standing before the tripous, Caia raised her hand over the bowl. She was using her other hand this time, the one with the annulet. She took the dagger and sliced deeper than before, cutting through the silver symbol on her palm, ignoring the searing pain. Her blood trickled into the bowl. Once there was enough, she morphed her hand to wolf and back again, regenerating her skin so only a faint red line was left. Exhaling, she then placed the tips of her fingers into the blood and pushed a flow of her magik energy into it.

"Mother Gaia, hear my plea. I ask that you take back the gift of trace from your children and let us live liberated in a new world … forever your undying servants, forever loving."

Over and over she repeated the words the Council had advised her to use, and for a while, it seemed as if their endeavor was futile. But on the tenth round of the rite, Caia felt the beginnings of an inexplicable shudder jolting through her. At first she thought the ground was moving, but as she looked down, she found it still as glass. A fierce jerk knocked her back from the altar, and she shook uncontrollably. Panic suffused her as her teeth chattered and her brain jiggled in her skull. It grew fiercer and more painful, feeling as if her very organs were smacking against her bones and muscles.

And then the eye-watering pain began. If felt as if someone had grabbed hold of her insides and were pulling them out of the top of her head, the energy encased in her body shunted upward and out with supreme force. She thought she might be screaming but the chaos of her body left her ignorant to anything else. She writhed helplessly on the floor of the cavern … until a sudden stillness drew the pain to an abrupt end. Caia sucked in a deep breath, air rushing into her panicked lungs with joy and relief.

She nudged around with her energy. A giant, exhausted grin spread across her face. Caia would never have thought she would ever be this happy to be so alone inside.

The trace was gone.

* * *

JAEDEN SHOT up from her chair at the exact same time Lucien did, at the same time shocked exhalations poured from the pack gathered together in Lucien and Caia's suite, waiting for the rite to be over. An electricity had tingled through her nerve endings in one sharp, smooth maneuver, and an instant understanding thrummed in her being. It was like an instant message from the gods explaining in one concise note that Caia Ribeiro, half magik, half lykan, existed as Head of both covens and had given the trace back to the gods, unbinding them all.

"You felt that?" she gasped around at them all. Everyone nodded.

Reuben glanced between them and Laila. "There is no longer a hum in your energies to tell me who is Daylight and who is Midnight."

"Yeah, 'cause it's gone," Jaeden explained. "And it came with a message about Caia and her giving up both traces … telling us we're free."

"Which means the Midnights probably felt it too." Lucien shook his head in amazement, gazing at Laila for confirmation. She nodded her head slowly.

"They'll know about Caia?"

"Yeah, they'll know about Caia," he confirmed.

Jaeden trembled and lowered herself to her seat. What did this mean? Now the supernatural world understood with perfect clarity that there was no trace and no longer any Head for either coven. Was the war teetering on the edge of the end … or standing on the precipice of a bloody disaster?

* * *

CAIA STUMBLED out of the caverns, shaking uncontrollably. As she approached Penelope and Alfred waiting for her by the elevator with guards, she tightened the robe around her.

"What the hell is going on up there?" Alfred was yelling at the wall.

Huh?

Then Caia noticed he was pressing his ear, and she realized he was wearing one of the earpieces worn by some of the Center staff.

"Shut down the portals until we can sort it out!"

Oh goddess, what was going on?

Alfred threw up his hands in frustration. "Take those who have already gotten in into the court. But lock down those bloody portals before every Daylight on earth shows up!"

"Caia." Penelope, pale-faced, came toward her and took hold of her arm to steady her. "Are you all right?"

I was until I saw you guys. "I'm fine. What's going on?"

Alfred grimaced. "We have a problem."

"I'm getting that. What's going on? The gods took the trace back ... I thought we would be good after that."

Penelope shook her head. "The gods removed the bind from us all. We all felt it."

"You did?" Caia asked, amazed.

"Yes. But it came with a message about you being Head of the Daylights and Midnights, of what you are and how you gave the trace back to the gods. The Center has been bombarded with supernaturals demanding to know what is going on."

Holy Artemis. Oh, this was a problem.

"Do the Midnights know?"

Penelope grew even more wan. "I think we better talk to Laila."

CHAPTER 29

METHOD IN THE MADNESS

*F*rustration tickled beneath her skin as she skimmed another page. Nothing! The history section in this library sucked. Caia groaned and waved her hand above the table, a glass of water materializing in front of her. She gulped it down, hoping it would renew her energy.

The last few days had been exhausting. Along with the Council, she'd had to retell her story thrice over to large groups that visited the Center, demanding answers as to who she was and why the trace was gone. Caia wasn't shocked. A good portion of the Daylights had known of her existence, but there were those who lived quiet lives away from the war who were blissfully unaware of her.

But now they knew, and they seemed to know a lot about her ... including this miraculous power she seemed to have that no one else did. Some were hostile, but for the most part, she was a curiosity and pretty much their savior. Freeing them all from the trace had brought untold happiness to many. There were the more conservative supernaturals who believed strong leadership had been the key to winning the war, but for many, it had been an invasion of their privacy.

Once the excitement and buzz had quieted, however, the questions battered down on them. What next? Would the war go on as it was? Would the soldiers continue to train at the Center? Or was the idea to infiltrate the Midnights and find out how they were handling things?

For the Council, it was yes to all the above. Saffron had been sent in with a few other top faeries to spy on Orina Beketov and the Midnight Council. The report came with the good and the bad—the chaos of discovering Caia's existence, that Ethan and Marita were dead, that the absence of the trace had put a temporary stop to Midnight attacks, days before their assault against the Krôls. The bad news was, Orina Beketov wanted to continue her war against other supernatural races and was gradually winning over a very confused Council.

The Daylight Council took this to mean the war would go on as it had and thus recommenced classes at the Center. Caia wasn't as convinced. In fact, she had an entirely different idea. She knew from having had the trace for the past ten months that the Midnight Coven was saturated with people who would gladly welcome peace. An idea brewed in her busy brain, one she had imparted to no one, not even Lucien. But the library where she hoped to discover all she needed was proving infertile.

Ugh, she really didn't want to *have* to turn to Reuben for this one. But it was looking more and more likely.

"You look annoyed." Phoebe MacLachlan strode through the doors into the empty room. Caia found her dry tone somewhat relaxing after having been in the library by herself for hours.

She nodded and slammed the book shut. "I'm not having a good research day."

The Rogue Hunter slid into the seat opposite her. "What are you up to, Caia?"

Damn the lykan. She was nosy and perceptive and persistent to a fault. She was also trustworthy, and Caia counted herself as one of the lucky few who Phoebe trusted and respected.

"I have a plan."

"I'm listening."

When Caia was done, Phoebe threw her a look that would've been a smile if the lykan had known what one was. "You need to look in the archives."

"Huh?"

Phoebe rolled her eyes and stood, gesturing for Caia to follow her. She wound her way through the dark aisles until they came to the back wall of the room. All Caia saw was another row of bookshelves.

Phoebe approached the middle of the aisle and reached up to pull on a thick, bronzed-leather tome. A creak, followed by a rumbling shudder seconds later, and the middle of the bookshelf opened inward like double doors.

Caia's jaw dropped. "How did you know this was here and I didn't?"

Phoebe shrugged. "I assumed the archives were public knowledge."

"Uh-uh." Caia followed her into a beautiful, well-lit room with no exit. In the middle was another library desk with green bankers' lamps and bordering the entire room were shelves of books. Walking behind Phoebe, Caia's gaze fell to the mosaic floor where tales of the gods were depicted in stunning color and splendor. She winced at the sharp tap her flat pumps made against what was surely a masterpiece and should never be trod upon. Phoebe didn't seem as bothered.

"Here." She indicated a row of books. "You should find what you need."

"Phoebe, I need this to stay between us until I've done my research."

The lykan nodded, her mouth firm and her eyes guileless. "Of course. It could be a very good idea, Caia."

She smiled. "So, if they say yes, you're in?"

Phoebe snorted. "If there's a fight, then I'm in."

* * *

"You want to do *what*?" Benedict screeched, and Caia had to stop herself from laughing at his outrage.

The Council looked at her with a mixture of awe and horror. That could mean anything, right? Lucien smiled up at her encouragingly along with Marion and Reuben. Vanne seemed to be chuckling as if he couldn't quite believe her gall.

"I think it's the only way to end this," she insisted.

"It's completely insane and out of the question!" Benedict bawled.

Caia narrowed her eyes on him. Okay, he wasn't so amusing anymore. He was just plain annoying. "Last time I checked, there were eight other people on this Council with a vote."

He growled at her, "By all means, let us see you humiliated by the rest of my colleagues for your depravity."

She gasped. "Depravity? I'm not depraved just because I have the courage to actually do something about ending this war!"

"Benedict," Vanne warned quietly, "insult her again and you will have me to answer to."

Caia flushed under Vanne's protectiveness but was glad for it because the warlock immediately blanched and sat down. Despite his place outside the Council, no one had forgotten how powerful Vanne was. Caia noticed Marion throwing him a mournful look. Caia sighed. After this was all over, she was going to have to do something about those two.

"Yes, let's be civil," Penelope agreed, before looking up at Caia with worried eyes. "This is quite a proposal, Caia."

It was. It really, really was. After the trace had gone, Caia had contemplated a measure that would help sort the wheat from the chaff. No matter what happened, there was going to be bloodshed, but Caia reckoned it would be better if the bloodshed happened in one fell swoop and gave them the closure they needed to build a new world for supernaturals.

She thought about the battles that must have been fought many years ago, when honor had been settled on the battlefield. The history books in the library had been of no real use until Phoebe took her into the archives. It was there she learned of the spells cast to summon both covens to a battleground that had been cast in protective magik, shielding it from human eyes. There, those brave enough to fight would convene, and a great bloody battle would be fought until one side had destroyed the other. It was a mighty style of warfare in which even the faeries—who were used only for spying now—shifted into their animal of choice and took part in the combat.

Caia believed they should cast the old spell calling to those Midnights who had no intention of ever making peace with the Daylights to fight them on the battlefield.

"Caia, most, if not all, of the Midnights will show up because their pride and superiority will expect no less of them," one of the older Council members insisted. "We'll be completely outnumbered."

"No." She shook her head. "You have to trust me. When I had the trace, I felt them all. I felt such a need for accord in them, for unity and harmony, it broke my heart. There are thousands who will meet us on that battlefield, who will never see us as anything but lesser beings, but there are thousands more who will stay home and wait for us to come to them with an offer of peace. Let us destroy those who stand in the way of that."

She saw the glimmer of hope in their eyes, their indrawn breaths, the way they leaned forward into her words. They wanted to believe but were afraid to do so.

Trying to contain her excitement, her desperation, Caia lowered herself into a seat before them, her eyes wide and honest. "Have I not proven myself to you time and again? Do you not trust me to protect our people?"

Penelope nodded, her eyes shining bright.

One down.

"We can meet them in battle and win because all they have is hate. And believe me, our weapons are a lot stronger than hate."

Alfred looked determined. "The Council has a very big decision to make. Perhaps you should retire to your room, Caia, and we will call for you when we have come to it."

* * *

As soon as the bedroom door closed, Lucien drew Caia into his arms and lifted her into a searing kiss, wishing he could stay locked like that forever. She gasped when he finally let her go but hung on to him, wrapping her legs around his waist.

"What was that for?" she asked as she nuzzled his jaw and neck.

For a lot of things, he thought. But mostly for being the most extraordinary person he'd ever had the honor of knowing. He kissed her again. "For making me prouder than I have ever known."

She smiled sweetly, blushing. "Yeah?"

Lucien nodded, chuckling at her modesty. "That was some speech."

"Do you think they'll say yes?"

Gods, he hoped so.

Instead of answering, he made love to her, knowing if they did say yes, he would follow Caia to that battleground. He would fight for her because he loved her; he would fight for his pack and the hope of a future in which their children could grow up untroubled by war. It was a cause he believed in. And one he was willing to die for.

CHAPTER 30

BATTLE FEVER

* * *

The answer was a resounding yes. Not just from the Council who had voted in Caia's favor—except for Benedict and the elderly magik who had raised his own concerns—but from the Daylights themselves. First the Council spoke with those at the Center, and Caia was blown away by their eagerness to march into battle. When their plan to bring the war to an end was put forth, the walls shook and the floor thudded with the stamping and animalistic cries of the supernaturals. They were ready for it. This was what they'd been waiting for. Their enthusiasm eased some of the Council's apprehension, and preparations for the spell commenced.

Not too many days after that, Caia was invited to take part in casting the spell that would request willing Daylights to fight for their cause as well as those Midnights, who would never see themselves working side by side with other supernatural races, to meet them in battle. It was a powerful moment for Caia as she joined hands with the Council and added her energy to the summons, connected to these nine people in the exhausting spell that required the combined strength of these incredibly gifted magiks.

The spell took a great amount of control and precision; their message was sent out mentally to all supernaturals and had to be called in pace with one another. A pendulum swung in the middle of the circle with a slow click to keep the time of each sentence in their minds to ensure they spoke out as one.

When at last they could be sure the message had been delivered, they broke apart, their limbs trembling with weariness.

* * *

THE DOOR to Alfred's suite blew open, and Reuben marched inside with Lucien and Marion at his back. "We have visitors." He grinned.

Caia shook her head, still dazed from the spell. "Visitors?" To steady herself, she grabbed hold of Lucien's arm as soon as he reached her.

Marion smiled triumphantly. "Daylights who want to fight."

Alfred scowled. "Why are they here now? We gave them the battle date, which isn't for another two weeks."

Reuben was grinning from cheek to cheek, rubbing his hands excitely. "Some of them want to train with the best."

Caia couldn't help but smile back at him. The vampyre had been waiting an especially long time for this moment. Last night he had presented her with a gift.

"What is it?" She'd eyed the black box suspiciously.

Reuben shrugged. "A token of my gratitude."

Tentatively, she took the box and opened it to reveal a tiny, ancient coin. "Reuben?"

"It belonged to my mother. It was one of the two coins

that should've been placed upon her eyes when she died to pay for her passage into the Underworld. When Hades made her a vampyre, she took revenge upon her father who had thought so little of her to leave her unprotected in the afterlife. She became a monster because of him. She took these coins from him after she drained him, and she carried them with her always as a reminder of who she was. I think it offered her forgiveness when no one and nothing else could. When I was ten, she gave me this one and told me to always remember who I was and to never be ashamed of it."

Caia shook her head slowly. "Reuben, I can't take this."

"Please, Caia," he insisted. "They say that hope dies last, and I think that is true. I thought I had given up hope a long time ago, but I hadn't. And because of you, that hope was not in vain. When we fight the Midnights, when we meet them on that battlefield, it will be because you have reminded us of who we are and why we shouldn't be so unsure of ourselves that we would let a race of people keep us down for centuries under the decree that we *should* be ashamed. Take the coin, Caia. I hope it will always remind you of what you have done for an old creature like me—and for all the young creatures who deserve a chance to live without persecution."

Caia placed the coin under her pillow, keeping it safe until she left the Center and could find a more secure place for it.

"There is one visitor I'd like you all to meet," Reuben spoke to the Council, and everyone turned toward the door. Caia gasped as the tall, elegant warlock strode into the room, dressed as dapper as ever in an expensive three-piece suit and greatcoat.

"Nikolai." She hurried to shake his hand. He smiled kindly at her and then gazed warily over her shoulder. Uh-oh. The Council.

As she feared, when she spun around, the Council had all lined up, prepared to defend or attack, Caia wasn't sure.

"He's not an enemy," Reuben snapped. "I've already explained Nikolai's position."

"Forgive us for being a little unsure," Alfred snapped back. "You've just allowed the Regent of the Midnight Coven into our midst."

"Ex-Regent," Nikolai corrected and spread his hands in a surrender gesture. "I'm not here to harm anyone. I'm here to fight *with* you."

The Council seemed to sneer collectively, and Caia felt a rush of annoyance. She understood they were nervous about having a Midnight among them, but they didn't treat Laila and Eliza with suspicion.

"I can vouch for him," she said, suffusing authority into her words. "He's on our side. The Petrovskys have been on our side for three centuries."

"We have only Reuben's word on that," Benedict huffed.

Caia exhaled in exasperation. They needed someone to soothe the situation. She looked around and met Marion's gaze. *Laila,* she mouthed.

Marion nodded and hurried away.

"There's someone I want you to meet, Nikolai." Caia smiled brightly at him, trying to show the Council she wasn't afraid of the man. "She's a Midnight as well."

Nikolai raised his eyebrows. "Little Eliza? Reuben told me her tragic story."

At the thought of the poor girl, Caia's smile dimmed. Eliza wasn't having such a good time of it. She wouldn't speak to anyone, and she refused to join them in any social sense. The only person she was unafraid of was Penelope who appeared to have grown quite attached to the little girl. The Council had thought to place Eliza in a home where she would be safe and free from abuse because of her blood, but

Penelope had requested she be allowed to care for the girl, and no one could think of a better situation for her. Penelope was trying her hardest to see Eliza through her grief.

"No, not Eliza." She shook her head. "Another special young lady."

Laila drew forward and shook Nikolai's hand as they were introduced. Caia could see Nikolai was intrigued by her, not only because of her unusual energy but because such a tiny person of Midnight blood had managed to gain the trust of the most important people in the Daylight Coven.

"It's a pleasure to meet you, Laila," he said gravely.

Laila smiled sweetly at him, her eyes shining with honesty. "You, too, sir. I much admire what you have done for Reuben and Caia."

As Caia had hoped, the tension eased out of the Council like a deflating balloon. Laila's calming presence melted their distrust as they watched her with the Midnight. In her short time at the Center, people had grown to like Laila as much as Caia did and to trust that, for some reason, she had a greater sense of intuition than others. If she approved of Nikolai, could he really be that bad?

Glad her plan worked, Caia turned to Penelope. "Perhaps the Council would like to sit with Mr. Petrovsky to discuss his time with the Midnights." She glanced at Nikolai. "Would that be all right? You do know who the major players are, and we don't know much about Orina Beketov."

"Of course." He nodded.

Penelope shrugged away from the Council, taking charge. "Mr. Petrovsky." She took hold of his hand tentatively. "I am Penelope Argyros."

"A pleasure to meet you, Ms. Argyros."

"Please, call me Penelope."

"Then you must call me Nikolai." He grinned at her, his eyes twinkling.

Caia almost laughed when Penelope blushed under his regard, a girlish giggle escaping her. "Would you care to sit down, Nikolai? Some refreshments, perhaps?"

"Please." He followed her to the table as she gestured for the rest of the Council to take their seats, Benedict scowling all the way. "Coffee would be wonderful."

Caia grinned, satisfied, and squeezed Laila's shoulder. "I don't know what we would do without you."

Laila smiled back.

CHAPTER 31

CITY OF LIGHT

*P*aris smelled wonderful. It was a perfect day, crisp and clear. Caia perused cool postcards and trinkets displayed on the shelves of the stalls that lined the sidewalk of the Seine, snuggled warm in her duffel coat and the purple scarf Lucien had bought for her that morning.

"Caia, what do you think?" Jae grinned, holding up a postcard with four haggard old women in black witches' hats and robes, sitting around a table drinking tea. "It's you, Marion, Laila, and Penelope in a hundred and fifty years."

Caia snorted and reached for it. It was pretty cool. "If we buy four postcards, we get them for two euros."

Her friend's eyes lit up, and she immediately turned back to hunt for three more funny cards. A sparkle caught Caia's eye and she looked at the cluster of Eiffel Tower souvenirs. There were little ones, big ones, medium ones, tiny ones on key rings. Some were made of plastic, others metal, but the one that caught her eye was a very kitschy one on a key ring, the entire thing sparkling with diamanté to resemble how the Tower appeared during the light show. Apparently a lot of Parisians hated the light show, but Caia loved it. She and Lucien had taken to sitting on the window seat in their room at the Center every night to watch the Tower flash in and out of existence, a million brilliant diamond lights bringing it to life in the dark.

"Do you want it?" Lucien whispered in her ear, heating up skin that had grown cold without a hat. She leaned back into him.

"Yeah, but I'll get it."

"No need." He reached past her before she could do anything, lifting the key ring from the display. He turned to pay the market seller for it.

At the sound of a giggle, Caia glanced over to see Jaeden had abandoned the postcards and was wrapped around Ryder in a passionate kiss. Caia immediately knew the tourists from the French. The tourists were the only ones who paid attention to the couple as they passed them.

"Hmm, that looks nice," Lucien murmured as he came around in front of her to hand her the key ring.

Caia smiled and took it from him, putting the gift deep into her pocket for safekeeping. "Thank you."

Lucien frowned. "That's all?"

She made a face and reached for him, pressing a sweet kiss to his lips. She wasn't really into the kind of PDA that Jae and Ryder were. Lucien threw her an amused look and then put an arm around her, drawing her into his side. "Where to next?"

Tomorrow was the battle, and Caia had wanted to escape from it all for just one day, just one glorious day of normality and fun. She was only nineteen, after all. And she was in love and in Paris, no less. It hadn't taken much to convince Lucien, Ryder, and Jae to join her for a day out in the city where they could just be young and have fun.

That morning they had a sweet breakfast of cakes and

pastries from an amazing *chocolaterie* and patisserie on the Avenue de Friedland. Afterward, they strolled up to gaze at the Arc de Triomphe and then wandered down the Champs-Élysées, where Jae ogled the clothing stores and Ryder marveled over the McDonald's restaurant that sported the only white *M* in the world.

"It's not that cool, Ryder." Jae pulled him away as Lucien and Caia walked on.

"It is unique. The golden arches can be found anywhere on earth … here it's white. It's one of a kind. You know how I feel about one of a kinds."

"I do?" she asked dubiously as they caught up with Caia and Lucien.

Ryder grinned at her. "I'm with you, aren't I?"

"Dude." Lucien smirked. "Smooth."

Caia laughed. It may have been cheesy but Jaeden loved it, pulling Ryder down for an amused kiss.

They made their way to the Seine and perused the markets and the city's architecture. At present they were at Pont Neuf, not far from where they'd come out of the Center at Notre-Dame. The Louvre sat across the river.

"Louvre, then?" Lucien asked, following her gaze.

"Actually"—Jae appeared beside them, entangled in her mate—"I heard Musée d'Orsay is better."

"It's certainly smaller." Ryder raised his eyebrows pointedly. "Got my vote."

"Caia?" Lucien asked, and she chuckled as Jae and Ryder frowned at being ignored.

"Musée d'Orsay sounds good."

"And then lunch," Ryder begged.

Caia huffed, "We just ate a little while ago and *you* had the most to eat."

"Hey, that chocolate cupcake thing was tiny."

"The three *pain au chocolat* and two croissants that followed it were not."

He puffed up his chest. "Me man, me need more food than tiny waif female."

THE MUSÉE D'ORSAY was wonderful, but Caia decided it was time to leave when a bored Ryder thought it a great idea to clamber up on a priceless sculpture of the Archangel Gabriel to get his photograph taken. She masked the incident with magik and hurried them out of there with one last look at the stunning clock that graced the high wall above the exit.

"Now the Louvre?" Jaeden queried as the cold air nipped at their skin.

"No." Caia blanched, thinking of the damage Ryder could still do. "I don't think we should take the risk."

"I wanted to see the pyramid from *The Da Vinci Code*." Ryder took hold of Jaeden's hand and led them toward the museum.

"OK," Lucien gave in. "But we're not going inside the actual museum."

"OK, *Dad*."

The rest of the afternoon fell away in laughter and ease. They tucked into a great lunch at a café on the corner of Rue d'Arcole beside Notre-Dame Cathedral. Despite the weather, Caia insisted on sitting outside at the wicker tables. During lunch her eyes continually went to the cathedral.

"It's something else, isn't it?" Lucien mused, following her gaze.

She nodded. "I wish we could go in."

"Why don't we?" Jae asked, munching on her crêpes with gusto.

Caia laughed humorlessly. "We have a battle tomorrow … I don't think we should piss off the gods the night before a fight by entering the home of the god who stole their fan base."

"Ah, true."

After lunch, they jumped on the Métro to Montmartre, where they got lost before eventually finding the steps that led up to the Sacré-Cœur. Ryder raced past them like a big kid, using his lykan grace to bound up the stairs past tourists without knocking them over.

Caia grinned as he bounced at the top, punching the air before raising his hands in triumph.

"What the Hades is he doing?" Lucien muttered in amusement.

Caia laughed. "Rocky!"

He raised an eyebrow.

"Sylvester Stallone!"

He shrugged. "Some actor, right?"

Caia raised an eyebrow. "I have no idea how you and Ryder became best friends."

The *Basilique* was beautiful, but as the light started to fade, they shuffled back down the steps to find the nearest Métro station. The pack was having a special dinner tonight and had invited Marion, Vanne, Reuben, Nikolai, and Saffron to join them. Of course, Laila and Vil would be there, but they were part of the pack now; they weren't guests.

There were only two seats available on the train and, like the gentlemen they were, Lucien and Ryder made sure Caia and Jae got them before wandering a little away to stand in the middle of the aisle. Everyone else held on to the poles and handrails. With their balance, Lucien and Ryder didn't need to.

"I hope Alexa likes her gift." Jae bit her lip, worry creasing her brow.

"Let me see it again." Caia held out her hand.

Jae pulled out the jewelry box and Caia took it from her,

opening it to look over the necklace nestled on velvet. They'd been passing the window of one of the many antique stores in the city when a silver necklace had caught Jae's eyes. The pendant was stunning. Lounging on the silver crest of a half moon was a sleeping wolf carved in jet.

"She'll love it," Caia whispered.

These last days had not been easy for Alexa. Not only was she still mad she hadn't been able to take revenge against Marita personally but she'd felt betrayed by Jaeden who she thought had become a good friend. Jae was trying her best to make it up to her. Last night, when Lucien gave Alexa permission to fight in the battle, her mood improved somewhat. Jae was hoping the necklace would finish the job.

When they reached Notre-Dame Cathedral, Caia cloaked them with magik and took hold of them all as they entered the portal that Penelope had promised to leave open and guarded for the day. They stepped back into the Center, now old pros at using the portals.

It was a bit of a hurry to get back to their rooms and wash up in time for dinner, but they got to Ella and Magnus's suite where the dinner was being set up with time to spare.

When they arrived, however, everyone was already there. The anxiety and fear over the next day had brought them together early. Even the kids knew something was up, sticking close to one another and eyeing the adults perceptively. It made Caia feel guilty for not telling them what was going to happen in the morning.

Isaac, Imogen, Christian, Lucia, Julia, Mal, and Cera would not take part in the fight tomorrow. They had children and siblings who needed them. As for Draven and Kade, they wanted to fight, feeling they had nothing else to lose but each other. That meant Vil, Laila, Lucien, Ryder, Jaeden, Irini, Alexa, Aidan, Ella, Magnus, Draven, Kade, and Caia were the members of the pack who would be on the battlefield in the morning. They would be joined by Marion, Vanne, Reuben, Saffron, the Council, Phoebe MacLachlan, her Alpha, and fifteen members of their pack. That was only the beginning. The entire Center would be there, along with thousands of Daylights. It was going to be the most awe-inspiring thing Caia had ever witnessed.

Laila and Vil fluttered from person to person, trying to ease the tension and fear. It worked somewhat, but Caia thought perhaps there was just too much emotion among them all to be soothed. Lucien tried to keep it light as everyone took their seats. Caia watched carefully as Vanne and Marion sat next to one another, their shoulders brushing, their eyes meeting often. Caia smiled, hoping they were friends again … and maybe more someday, she mused.

"This looks amazing." Lucien gazed over the myriad dishes decorating the table.

Vanne shrugged. "I had the kitchens put in a little extra time. Thank you for inviting me."

"And me."

"And me."

The grateful murmurs of Marion, Saffron, Nikolai, and Reuben filtered down the table.

"I'm glad you all came." Lucien smiled back and squeezed Caia's hand. "For tonight, why don't we forget about tomorrow and just enjoy each other's company."

And that's what they did. Friendly teasing and banter accompanied the meal. Reuben was battered with questions about how old he was and was he there when Marie Antoinette lost her head and did he meet William Wallace and was Julius Caesar really such a dick?

He laughed it all off, answering the questions gamely, looking to Saffron for help when he could. As for the pack, they looked happier than they had in a long time. They laughed and were able to speak of those they had lost with a sad humor and sweet remembrance. Alexa laughed at something Jaeden had said, twiddling the wolf pendant that hung around her neck.

For a moment, Caia was debilitated by a sharp feeling of utter terror. Would all this be gone tomorrow? Would the pack be destroyed once more, just as they were regaining themselves? And would it be her fault?

Caia, don't, she pleaded with herself.

Fear was for everyone else. They needed her to be confident and assured of what they were doing, of what she was taking them into. This had been her idea. She had no right to fear or doubt.

"You okay?" Lucien whispered, leaning into her.

She sipped her wine and threw him a smile. "Of course."

"I don't believe you."

Sometimes Caia wished her mate didn't understand her so well. "Really, I'm fine."

He didn't say anything more, but as they lay together that night, trying to catch their breath after having lost themselves in each other, Lucien propped himself up on his side and gazed down at her, his eyes narrowed and serious. "You're allowed to be afraid, Caia."

Warmth sprung to life in her chest at the knowledge he understood her so perfectly, but she shook her head with a sharp jerk. "No, I'm not."

He scowled. "Of course you are."

"Lucien, I started this. This was all my idea. I can't be afraid when everyone else is or they'll think I'm not sure we're going to win this thing."

"Caia, they know there is a risk we won't win. They're not stupid. They're not blindly following you into battle because they think you've given them a 100 percent guarantee of survival. They're following you into battle because they *believe* in this … not because they think your lack of fear is a promise of victory."

Her laugh caught on a sob. "Then I guess I should tell you I'm terrified."

Snuggling her close, Lucien kissed her softly on the cheek and rested his head next to hers. "Me too."

CHAPTER 32

PISTOLS AT DAWN

*U*nlike human battlegrounds where terrain and weather could determine the outcome, the supernatural battlefield was perfect. The chosen spot was a massive beach with towering sand dunes to Caia's left. To the right, the tide remained out and would do so for the entire length of the fight due to a spell that had been cast on it by the Daylights. The sand beneath her feet only looked like sand; she didn't feel the familiar sinking of her feet into the grains. Instead, the ground was compact and smooth, as was the entire beach.

A dome-like barrier had been suspended over the area to shield the supernaturals from human view. To prevent humans from wandering onto the beach and banging up against the barrier, another spell clouded the atmosphere, one to muddle the human brain temporarily so that any thought of approaching the beach was quashed and replaced with one to go elsewhere. The weather was still and perfect. Not too hot, not too cold. And although the water could be heard lapping in the distance, its spray didn't come anywhere near them.

Caia's stomach was in knots. She was sickly white with fear and anxiety, just as the rest of the pack was. Her heart was pounding so hard and fast, she was constantly fighting the need to be sick or pass out. The buildup to battle had been excruciating. It had taken hours for the Daylights and Midnights to arrive, and now finally, the Council had announced it was time.

Across the beach—some three thousand yards in the distance—stood the assembled Midnights. Their battle lines were a fair mirror image of the Daylights' own. In a crescent-shaped line stood five different divisions of Midnights. From left to right, the first two consisted of daemons, the third and fourth of faeries in the shape of big cats and large vultures, and in the fifth stood magiks. Behind that line was another crescent made up of four more divisions. Behind the daemons stood more faeries (all big cats), and guarding Orina Beketov and the Council, who led from the very back, were two blocks of magiks. The fourth block of magiks guarded at the back of the faeries and magiks in front.

The Daylights stood in the same crescent formation. Up front from the left in the first two divisions stood faeries in the shape of big cats (when Caia had asked about the choice, Saffron said that faeries had an affinity for them and felt stronger as felines)—panthers, leopards, tigers, you name it—purring and growling and bussing up against one another with affection and encouragement. Vampyres made up the third division center in line, and the last two were all lykans. Guarding the lykans from behind were magiks.

The second division of the second line was made up of more vampyres who, along with the third branch of magiks, stood to defend the Council, leading from the back. The fourth on the far left was comprised of magiks who waited behind the faeries in front.

Yeah, they were ready to go, all right. Caia exhaled slowly.

"Caia." Alfred's voice echoed through the lines by the use of a spell. "It's time."

Everyone had attempted to talk her out of speaking with the Midnights, warning that it would make her a target. But the Midnights would recognize her as soon as she got close enough, thanks to the earlier message from the gods. As such, Caia decided to go ahead.

Trying to ignore her trembling nerves, she looked to Lucien. Even in wolf form, he managed to throw her a bolstering look. She stepped forward from the front line among the lykans. Caia strode with determination, her shoulders back, head held high, her face devoid of expression.

Standing at the halfway point between the two covens, using the speaker spell Penelope had taught her, Caia addressed the Midnights, surprising herself with the maturity and authority in her words. "I am Caia Ribeiro. The gods have seen fit to tell you who I am and what I have done. I have given the trace magik back to the gods, freeing us all from Galen's revenge. Without the trace, I believe we can build a road to peace."

She heard the snickers and roars of outrage and denial among the Midnights. She hadn't expected anything else. They hated her and her kind.

"You don't believe me but it's already begun. I am half Midnight and yet I stand and fight with Daylights. I stand and fight with two other Midnights who are willing to die for us."

"And they will!" someone screamed in the distance.

Ignoring the sickness that roar encouraged, Caia forced herself on. "You don't believe our world can exist in peace, but the trace that bound us to the war is gone. And after today … so will the war itself be!"

Cries of support and growls of anticipation battled

against roars of hate and disdain. Caia turned her back on the Midnights, showing them she was unafraid, and walked calmly back to her spot on the front line. Her insides felt as if they'd snapped apart.

Lucien nudged her leg, and she ran her hands through his pelt in thanks.

A rumbling sounded in the distance as a first wave of daemons moved as one toward the Daylights.

"Faeries!" Alfred cried from the back. "Take out those daemons!"

A thundering exploded in Caia's ears as the faeries leapt forward as one. Their large paws pounded into the ground, propelling them forward at awesome speed, their muzzles drawn back, their eyes focused on their enemy. Caia's heart raced knowing Saffron was among them.

"Magiks on the left flank, move forward!"

The beauty of the faeries' race across the beach, the blur of colors, momentarily made Caia forget what their goal was. And then, as she had known they would, three hundred yards from their target, the leading faeries, many of whom were leopards, shifted as smoothly and wondrously as a waterfall. The ground shook under their feet and what sounded like trumpeters deafened Caia as they turned from graceful feline into oversized elephants and massive rhinoceroses with lethal tusks.

A cry rose among the Midnights, but they weren't quick enough to defend the daemons crushed beneath the faeries' massive feet. Some managed to scamper out of the way and attempted to clamber onto the shapeshifters to pierce them with their weapons. They were merely shaken off and trampled underfoot. Behind those faeries leapt those still in cat form. They launched around the mass of bodies and huge mammals to attack the Midnight faeries behind the daemons.

An order rose from the Midnight Council and faeries in the front line moved in to help while the magiks that had stood to the far right closed ranks, covering the gap in the line.

Caia watched on in horror as screams and whines rent the air as cats fought cats, and vultures swooped onto the elephants and rhinos, pecking at their eyes to blind them. Even from her position, she could see blood flowing in the sand.

"Vampyres!" Alfred bellowed. "Front and second line! Move forward!"

Led by Reuben, the vampyres sped off in a blur of movement. Caia felt the earth behind her tremble as the magiks who'd guarded at the back of her closed in, in front of the Council. The vampyres were in among the battle in no time, and the urge to throw up grew greater as she watched the mass of struggling bodies. Most of the elephants and rhinos had disappeared in the crowds. Caia assumed they were either wounded or they found fighting as a cat more efficient.

When the magiks guarding the Midnights' front line moved in on the battle, sparks of fire and cascades of water crashed through the air onto the scene. Caia felt the change in the atmosphere as air magiks began to fight; she watched as huge rocks came out of nowhere and crushed the Daylights underneath them as earth magiks triumphed.

It all seemed like moments, but Caia knew she'd been standing shivering with terror for a long time.

"Lykans!" Alfred screamed. "Take out those magiks!"

As the wolves rushed across the sand, Caia morphed instantly into her own wolf self and ran with them. The sand didn't kick up around them as they sprinted, and the ground acted as a wonderful springboard for their flight. The air rushed by in fragile lightness, and Caia realized just how perfect the spellcasters had made this terrain for them.

The lykans collided into the fold, tearing magiks who screamed in outrage. Gore and body parts flew; jaws clamped on necks, sending spurts of blood everywhere. Caia changed and instantly put up a shield as rocks and earth shattered against it. She caught the eye of the magik who'd targeted her and narrowed her eyes, flooding his lungs with water. He gasped and fell to the ground.

She then turned, pulling witches and warlocks off lykans and faeries with her magik, dousing vampyres who'd been set on fire, rescuing faeries by sending up shields. She was battered and targeted, exhausted by her need to defend not only herself but others while also being on the offensive.

Magik came out of nowhere, and Caia felt her lungs squeeze as they filled with water. She fell to her knees, grasping at her throat as a woman approached with victory in her eyes. There was a blur of movement and the water dissipated and she could breathe again. Reuben stood before her with the woman's head in his hands, her body already decomposing on the sand.

"You're welcome." He grinned and then was off into the fight at warp speed.

Caia's eyes took in a sight she would never forget. The ground swam with blood and pieces of supernaturals. Insides spilled onto the sand, limp hands trailing into the gore. Blank eyes of Daylights and Midnights alike looked up at her as she stumbled over their bodies. The noise of the battle grew muffled as she dove in front of a tiger, a bolt of fire heading toward it. Her water hit the fire, and the magik canceled out.

The tiger growled and sprang at the attacking warlock, its claws slicing Caia's arm as it swiped at the enemy. Caia hissed back a growl at the stinging agony and looked down at the bleeding claw marks on her arms. She turned as the warlock's muffled screams reached her ears. She couldn't imagine how painful his death was if a "scratch" like this hurt so badly. Dazed, Caia morphed her hand into wolf and back and then spun around. Immediately her heart exploded in her chest.

No!

Her eyes darted from witch to warlock as one by one, they pulled out vials of golden liquid and threw it into the air, controlling it with their magik as it descended on the nearest lykan. A girl shuddered back into human form, followed by an older female, followed by Alistair MacLachlan. Stunned, she stood unable to comprehend that the fluid discovered by Pierre du Bois had found its way into Midnight hands again and she hadn't known about it.

A young lykan girl went up in flames. Caia roared in disbelief and threw up her hands, a tidal wave appearing among the battle. Like last time, she tried to avoid Daylights but was afraid some were soaked despite it. The wave crashed down on two of the offending Midnights, and Caia rushed the water into their mouths. She saved Alistair, and the Alpha began changing back into wolf—Caia put up a shield around him to let him do so.

Once he had transformed, Caia focused on finding magiks with the fluid. A blasting of fire and magik exploded above her head, and she looked around to see Daylight magiks approaching the battle. Thank goddess. One by one, she took out the witches and warlocks with the liquid, her body bruised and bleeding from the hits they'd managed to land. Her throat was dry from oxygen deprivation from having encountered air and water magiks.

Satisfied, she made to take on another warlock when her neck prickled in warning. A dark feeling crept over her. A sense of unreality descended, and Caia turned slowly.

A flash of black hair on the ground in the distance caught

her eye.

No.

Blasting the man in front of her back absentmindedly, Caia stumbled through the fight, her view of the body growing sharper.

No.

Being trampled by fighting magiks and lykans, a naked Lucien lay in the sand, bloody and empty, a hole through his chest where his heart should be, his silver eyes blank as they stared straight into the heavens.

No.

Caia fell upon him, her hand knocking away a vial with a tiny drop of golden liquid. Her hands fluttered over the gaping wound uselessly.

"No." She shook her head and then grasped his cold face in her hands. "No."

Caia pressed on his shoulders. "Lucien, wake up," she whispered and then hissed as rocks smacked against her back, and she sprawled over him. Sobbing, she lifted her face, now bloody from Lucien's fatal wound, and moved up his body to look into his eyes. He wasn't in there.

He was gone.

An unbearable pain ripped across her chest.

Something inside her died.

Replacing it was an unforgiving fury.

SHE SCREAMED with agony as a fire incinerated her insides, traveling from her toes like a snake slithering up her body. It wound its way around her heart and squeezed and seemed to burst the organ into gory pulp. White light blinded her, and the sensation of falling accompanied her scream of death, her soul begging for the destruction of those who had dared to fight them for their right to peace.

CHAPTER 33

LAILA

*I*t was the whispering that brought her out of unconsciousness. Followed by the pain. The pain was like a harsh, pounding wake-up call. Her eyes flew open with a gasp, and Caia shrunk back from the white of the room.

"It's okay, it's okay," a gentle voice soothed, and she felt a cool hand on her forehead.

Caia groaned. This kind of exhausted, "been run over by a truck" feeling was familiar and yet so intense, it was alien too. One by one, faces popped up in front of her. She blinked. Jaeden. Ryder. Laila. Magnus. Marion.

"Come on, now, get back, let her rest," Ella's familiar voice called from the bottom of the bed and her pack shuffled backward.

Her pack.

Lucien.

"No, no, no." She struggled violently with her bedcovers and then with Jaeden as her friend paled and tried to press her back onto the bed.

"Ryder, help," Jae screeched, and Caia thrashed against them both, too weak to do any serious damage.

"No!" she cried, tears gushing down her cheeks as the image of Lucien lying murdered in the sand flashed through her mind. She didn't want to be alive if he wasn't with her. Panic made her hyperventilate, and she struggled to draw breath.

"Someone help her," Jae pleaded.

"Caia, breathe. Caia … *Caia.*"

Her heart stopped at the voice, and she drew in a ragged breath, her chest opening. Jaeden smiled at her and moved aside so Caia could see past her into the next hospital bed.

Sitting upright, tucked under his own set of covers, was the most beautiful man she'd ever seen. He wasn't real. How could he be? Could everyone else see him? Looking through blurry eyes, Caia watched the expressions on the pack's faces as they glanced from her to Lucien.

"Is he real?" she croaked.

A tear slipped down Jaeden's cheek and she gave her a wobbly smile. "He's real."

There was no stopping her as Caia ripped back the covers and bounded out of the bed and onto Lucien. She collapsed in his arms as her body seemed to lack any real energy. But she was strong enough to return his mammoth hug as they smothered one another with kisses.

"How, how, how?" she mumbled against him, breathing in his wonderful scent.

Lucien's arms tightened around her, his chest rising and falling rapidly. "Laila."

Caia stiffened and managed to turn in his arms to find Laila by her bed, Vil standing behind her, protective as always.

"How?"

Laila smiled shyly.

"She's an Asclepian." Marion squeezed the magik's slight shoulder.

Through the haze and confusion, Caia's jaw dropped. "An Asclepian? I thought they were extinct?" Little Laila had the power to heal and bring people's souls back from the Underworld? Caia shook the moss out of her brain. "I mean … I thought there were none of you left?"

Laila shrugged. "My family kept our gifts hidden because we knew we would become targets. Not only is it against the law to bring someone back from the dead but it is a much-coveted gift. My family are gone. I'm the only one left."

"She risked a lot healing me in front of the Daylights," Lucien said, his voice rumbling against Caia's chest.

"I couldn't let you die," Laila retorted, but her eyes were on Caia. And Caia understood. She meant she couldn't let him die for Caia. Tears bubbled up again.

"Thank you so much," she whispered, more grateful than the little magik would ever understand.

"Laila must be protected from now on," Marion insisted.

Caia bit her lip, trying not to show fear. "No one will harm her for breaking the law?"

"Everything is a mess right now, Caia. There is very little hold for the law."

"So that's a no, right?"

"That's a no. But there will be a lot of people interested in acquiring her."

Caia felt a primitive growl shudder in her chest. "They'll have to go through me first."

Laila beamed, and Marion grinned appreciatively. "Then I think she'll be fine. Outside the hospital walls there is a world of very shocked, awed, and frightened supernaturals."

"Frightened of what?"

Lucien huffed, "You."

Caia's eyes widened and she gripped Lucien tighter. "Me?"

Jaeden rushed at her. "Caia … you've been unconscious for five days."

"W-w-what?" She shook. Five days? What had happened? Who won? Was the pack all alive?

The questions rocketed through her and as she tried to ask them, they tumbled out in a jumble of nonsense. Lucien stroked her back and Marion spoke again, "When you found Lucien …" The witch shook her head in wonder. "I don't know what happened. I saw you fall across him and then this white light exploded out of you, along with this inhuman screaming."

The others nodded, seeming to remember. "I was blasted off my feet. I couldn't hear or see a thing. And then after a few minutes, the light faded and I could see again. And when I got up … there were no Midnights left. Ash blew into the breeze, whispering by me with Midnight energy. Caia … you killed them all."

CHAPTER 34

A week passed during which Caia and Lucien tried to rebuild their energy. Caia often wondered how Lucien was feeling. Did he feel different now? Could he remember the Underworld?

"No." He'd seemed amused by the question. "I don't think I was gone long enough."

After Caia killed the Midnights, a feat she still couldn't come to grips with, she collapsed, unconscious. The pack scrambled over to them, grieving at the sight of Lucien's body, when little Laila pushed through them all, dropped to her knees, placed her hands upon Lucien's chest, and sang.

Marion told her it was the sweetest, saddest song she'd ever heard, and as it filled the air, magik—the likes of which Marion had never felt before—lit up Lucien's body, giving off an ethereal warmth that eased everyone's pain. Marion watched in awe as Lucien's flesh regenerated, his heart reforming, his gaping wound closing, the color returning to his body. And then he gasped for breath before his eyelids slammed closed and he fell into unconsciousness.

Caia found a reason every day to see Laila, somehow

needing to be near her, to reassure her she was real and that she was alright. In one act of kindness, she had become one of the most important people in Caia's life.

As for the pack, they'd been incredibly lucky.

"Luck had nothing to do with it," Lucien huffed. "We are an exceptionally wily bunch. I knew we could take 'em."

Caia laughed. It was amazing. Despite some wounds, they'd all returned in one piece, along with Saffron, Reuben, and Vanne.

Alistair MacLachlan and his pack hadn't been so lucky. Three of them had been killed, some wounded, but when Phoebe came to visit Caia, she reassured her that to them, it had been a great death, and a victory. She hugged Caia, and Caia knew as the Rogue Hunter left her suite that in Phoebe, she had a friend for life.

But the loss Caia felt most keenly was that of Nikolai who had fought his way through the crowd to attack Orina Beketov. Caia was unsure of what damage he may have inflicted on Orina, for like the other Midnights fighting against them, she was gone in the wind.

Nikolai, despite being a powerful earth magik, had perished from Orina's fire attack. Caia was saddened by his sacrifice, as was Reuben, the magik's truest friend.

As for the Council and the Center, it was all a little chaotic. After what she'd done on the battlefield, even Benedict was politer to her, although the fear in his eyes made her uncomfortable. She didn't want anyone to be afraid of her. As for the rest of the Council, they were awed and gratified; Vanne had bet her she would be on the Council in no time. It worried her a little, thinking perhaps Lucien would be upset by the notion—not just Lucien but the entire pack.

She couldn't have been more wrong.

"Caia, great things are about to happen, and you need to be at the center of that," Jae predicted.

To Caia's surprise, her words were greeted with nods of agreement as the pack lounged in the dining hall of the Center. "Really?" She looked to Lucien.

He grinned at her, looking healthier these days. "We need to stick around, sweetheart."

"So you guys don't mind staying here for a while?"

"Are you kidding?" Alexa snorted. "We're in Paris. I'm going shopping first chance I get. Oh, that reminds me." She smiled sweetly at Lucien. "Can I borrow four hundred euros?"

"Where are you going shopping?" Jae asked dryly. "Chanel?"

"Duh, of course not ... you'd be lucky to get a scarf for four hundred euros from Chanel."

They were all surprised when Lucien agreed to part with the money. All except Caia. Alexa had been through a lot, and she'd fought like a wildcat in the battle. She deserved to feel young again for a day. But only one day. Otherwise, she'd bankrupt the pack.

* * *

CAIA STROLLED into Alfred's suite with more ease than she'd felt in the last year. The war was almost over, but there was much to do ... yet she couldn't help the pure happiness that thrummed in her veins every morning she woke up.

She greeted the Council who all shot to their feet in deference, all wearing wide smiles. She tried to cover her laugh at their expressions. Caia wished she'd seen what they had seen her do on the battlefield. People at the Center were acting a little crazy. It had somehow convinced them that Caia was the purest child of Gaia in their existence. They actually believed Caia herself was godlike.

Some blanched when they saw her coming down the

ASCENDED

corridor and pressed themselves against the wall to let her pass. She tried to smile softly to ease their anxiety, but it never worked. Others were different ... they bounded up to her with enthusiasm and hero-worship, which was equally exhausting. The Council were over-the-top polite, and Caia unhappily noticed the twinge of fear in some of their eyes. She didn't want to frighten people, for Gaia's sake!

Caia was glad to see Marion and Vanne in the room with Reuben and Saffron. The four of them treated her as they always had.

Caia grinned at Marion. A few days before, she'd had a few quiet moments with her mentor for the first in a long time. She asked how Marion was coping with the loss of her sister and her position at the Center. It was difficult, she'd said, but not impossible. And Vanne was helping, she'd admitted with a blush. Caia had laughed. Marion was usually so cool and together but Vanne had reduced her to a swooning teenager.

She told Caia how she'd been crushed at first when Vanne stopped courting her to court her sister, how, over the years, she felt their connection hadn't died, how she'd felt guilty for feeling that way. Marion didn't know Vanne was still in love with her, however, or the real reason he'd left her for Marita. So, they were trying out a relationship ... a very tentative attempt. It was strange for them both with Marita between them. But Caia thought they should turn that into a positive. No one else could understand the helplessness that comes from a betrayal by someone so close.

Reuben grinned wickedly at Caia, making a face at the way the Council deferred to her. Caia rolled her eyes. For an old guy, he could be quite petty and immature. She threw a quick smile at Saffron. As for those two ... Caia didn't know what was going on. Maybe they were both too old to have any kind of meaningful relationship. But there were feelings there, and Caia couldn't wait to watch that particular show unfold.

Not that she didn't have anything better to do.

Laughing at herself, Caia took a seat before them all. "You wished to see me?" she asked politely.

Alfred cleared his throat and nodded. "We wanted you to be the first to know that peace negotiations with a community of Midnight magiks in Paris are going well."

Exuberant elation shot through her. "Really?" She gasped.

Penelope smiled sweetly at her excitement. "Really."

"What next, then?"

The Council shared wary glances. "The negotiations are complex. As you might understand, the Midnights are not happy to exist peacefully with us if we have a controlling council in power."

She frowned. "You mean you guys?"

"Exactly."

Fair enough, she nodded thoughtfully. They would just have to come up with a solution.

"We should begin negotiations with other Midnights and see if that's going to be a recurring theme," Caia suggested.

The Council nodded, but Reuben sighed. "It's not that easy, Caia. This could take awhile."

A slow smile spread across her face. "I can be patient."

EPILOGUE

SOMETHING NEW

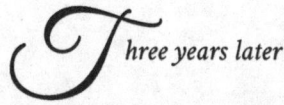 *hree years later*

CAIA SHOOK HER HANDS OUT, wishing her palms weren't so sweaty. She exhaled and then did the breathing exercises Marion had taught her.

"Caia." Lucien soothed, putting a hand on her shoulder. He stood behind her with Jaeden as they stared at the massive double doors to the courtroom at the Center. Despite all the other changes, the Center was still called the Center, but now by those who'd once been Daylights and Midnights alike. Those terms were one of the first laws she was going to insist upon—no use of Daylight or Midnight. It would be considered a racial slur. They were all the same now. She trembled.

"You can do this, Caia," Jae encouraged.

Magnus's words from this morning came back to her in a rush of comforting warmth.

"Your father would've been so proud of you, Caia." He'd

hugged her close, and she'd choked back the tears at the thought of Rafe, of the picture she had of the two of them she kept tucked under her pillow. Magnus pulled back, his eyes glittering suspiciously. "I know because I'm so proud, I can barely contain it sometimes."

The people who loved her believed in her. *I can do this.* Caia pushed back her shoulders and threw open the doors. The high wall before them was covered with plaques with lists of names of the supernaturals who'd fought and died during the Great Battle for Concord, as it was now called. In the center was the largest plaque with Nikolai's name scrawled across it in beautiful calligraphy. Below it, Caia had the inscription from Oscar Wilde's tomb carved into the stone for Nikolai. It read:

> *And alien tears will fill for him*
> *Pity's long broken urn*
> *For his mourners will be outcast men*
> *And outcasts always mourn.*

CAIA SMILED AS SHE PASSED, knowing Nikolai would've loved it, an opinion shared by Reuben. She strode up the stairs and into the court, Lucien and Jae at her back, acting as her second and third in command. The benches of the court were empty but set up in the middle of the room was a huge round table. Seated in beautifully carved chairs that Lucien and his apprentice had worked on for months (each chair depicted a moment in the Great Battle for Concord) were ten supernaturals of influence and power: four magiks, two faeries, two vampyres, two lykans, and of course, Caia, their Chairwoman.

She strode to the largest chair at the northernmost point of the circle and Lucien pulled it out for her. She stepped between it and the table and lowered herself upon the comfortable cushion. Reuben, Saffron, and Alfred stared back at her among less familiar faces. Faces of people she knew she would come to know very well over the years as she led them in the new world.

It had been a grueling and exhaustive endeavor to bring them all together, among them three magiks and a faerie who'd once been Midnight. But after the battle, and months of hard work, Caia's wishes had come true. The war had ended and in its place sprung something new. These people before her, their actions and decisions were only the beginning ... for there was much work to be done.

She smiled in joy that this moment was finally here. "Ladies and gentlemen, welcome to the first meeting of the United Council of Supernaturals."

ABOUT THE AUTHOR

S. Young is the pen name for Samantha Young, a *New York Times*, *USA Today* and *Wall Street Journal* bestselling author from Scotland. She's been nominated for the Goodreads Choice Award for Best Author and Best Romance for her international bestseller *On Dublin Street*. *On Dublin Street* was Samantha's first adult contemporary romance series and has sold in thirty-one countries.

Visit Samantha Young online at
www.authorsamanthayoung.com
Instagram @AuthorSamanthaYoung
Facebook @AuthorSamanthaYoung
https://bingebooks.com/author/samantha-young